HOW TO MURDER A MARRIAGE

HOW TO MURDER A MARRIAGE

THE EX-WHISPERER FILES #1

GABRIELLE ST. GEORGE

LEVEL
BEST BOOKS

First published by Level Best Books 2021

This novel is entirely a work of fiction. The names, characters and incidents portrayed in it are the work of the author's imagination. Any resemblance to actual persons, living or dead, events or localities is entirely coincidental.

Gabrielle St. George asserts the moral right to be identified as the author of this work.

AUTHOR PHOTO CREDIT: Hooman Mesri Photography

First edition

ISBN: 978-1-953789-50-1

Cover art by Level Best Designs

This book was professionally typeset on Reedsy.
Find out more at reedsy.com

This book is dedicated to my soul sister, my partner in crime, a great, generous, and hilarious woman, an amazing mother and cook, a brilliantly talented writer, a world traveler, an underdog ally, a fierce fighter, and a loyal lover, my Best Friend Forever, Delia Gaskill. She departed this world tragically early, leaving massive swathes of grief in the hearts of many but also gifting immeasurable riches, and unending joy to those same hearts. I miss you every minute of every day, Dee. Call me in five.

Praise for How to Murder a Marriage

"Fun, clever, and suspenseful, *How to Murder a Marriage* is a feel-good mystery featuring a protagonist I instantly wanted to be friends with. Gina Malone has experienced her share of drama and is looking to unwind at her lakefront cottage. When she finds herself the target of not one but two potential stalkers, plus a possible missing woman, Gina and her loving, hilarious crew of family and friends set out to protect her and catch the criminals. With a touch of romance, delicious food, adorable dogs, and a superbly fluid voice fizzing with perfectly timed wit, this novel will make you laugh out loud and give you the ideal escape."—Samantha M. Bailey, *USA Today* and #1 national bestselling author of *Woman on the Edge*

"*How to Murder a Marriage* is written from the heart. Gabrielle St. George draws from her own considerable experience to create a fun and intricate story with terrific characters and a surprising twist at the end."—Authorlink.com

"Gabrielle St. George mixes razor-sharp wit with a healthy dose of edge-of-your-seat suspense to give us a page-turner thrill ride. Who knew being an advice columnist could be so deadly...or so wickedly funny?"—Annette Dashofy, *USA Today* bestselling author of the Zoe Chambers Mysteries

"Gabrielle St. George brings a fresh voice to Canadian crime writing which is simultaneously chipper yet chilling, and she introduces us to characters who are simultaneously engaging yet alarming – a perfect combination for a writer of psychologically suspenseful stories which are also fun to read."—Best Selling and Award Winning Author, Cathy Ace

Chapter One

TOP 6 MOST STRESSFUL LIFE EVENTS

Divorce: Check (After six years, my crazy ex-husband is still dragging me through the courts.)

Death of a Loved One: Check (My best girlfriend/soul sister died in my arms four months ago. Fuck cancer.)

Moving House: Check (I built my dream house and intended to be carried out of it in a box. Instead, I'm carrying boxes out of it, packed with the belongings I didn't garage sale when I had to hawk my house at a fire-sale price.)

Becoming the Victim of a Crime: Check (My sociopathic, obsessed ex is stalking me.)

Dismissal from Work: Check (My four wonderful children have fired me. Apparently, my services are no longer required. They have all run away from home to attend universities in Europe. I make my living as a writer and artist, but those are just jobs. Being a mom was my vocation.)

Imprisonment: No Check. Yet. (If I act on any of the fantasies I'm currently entertaining regarding my ex or my real estate agent, I'll be able to cross this one off the list in short order.)

Yes, I'm feeling sorry for myself. Somebody has to. This is one sad fricking state of affairs. In the past two months, I've dyed my blonde hair black, lost ten pounds, pierced my nose, sold nearly everything I own—including my home of twenty years—and made the decision to leave the largest city in Canada and move one hundred miles north to a small town on a big lake where most of my extended family waits in smug anticipation. Really nothing too extreme by my standards. Moderation is not my middle name.

As the Ex-Whisperer, a best-selling relationship book author of the Gal Guides, and advice columnist on Slate, I'm able to take my work with me wherever I travel. And I travel everywhere, often.

I need a mini escape, and I've arranged one.

My amazing daughter Ella and I are flying to London. I've successfully convinced her she needs me to get her settled into the new city of her new uni. My three sons are traveling from their respective European nations to join us for a weekend of family fun in The Old Smoke. Can't wait.

We've got three hours to kill in the airport before boarding. Ella is sampling perfumes in the duty-free shop. I've set up a portable office at a café table. I've been pressed for time the last few days and have fallen behind in answering letters on my advice column. I'm hoping to catch up before we depart. I read an email sent two days earlier.

Dear Ex-Whisperer,

I moved to this country to marry my husband ten years ago. I have no family here, no friends to speak of. I had a receptionist job for a few years, but I came home late from work sometimes, and my husband had an argument with my boss over it, and I got fired. I don't leave the house much except to shop, run errands, walk my little poodle, Snowflake, or go to the library. When I'm out, I constantly get the feeling I'm being watched, and then sometimes I run into my husband unexpectedly. I think he follows me. My husband doesn't like me going anywhere without him. He insists on having all my passwords and checks through my computer and phone regularly. I don't do anything wrong, but he doesn't trust me. He's always angry and says I should be happy that he cares so much, but I don't like being spied on.

He says a husband has the right to know where his wife is and what she's doing at all times. Do you think that's true? If not, does that mean that my husband is stalking me? Can your husband be your stalker?

Lillian

My reply:

Dear Lillian,

Your husband's behavior is neither normal nor acceptable, and I am seriously concerned for your safety. Stalking is stalking even when it's your partner. It's illegal and unbalanced. There is nothing remotely flattering about being told you can't be trusted. It's an insult no matter how much sugar it's coated with.

Following someone around without their knowledge has nothing to do with protecting them unless the person being followed is under four years old. When someone is watching us secretly, it's because they're hoping or expecting to catch us doing something we wouldn't do if we knew they were there. When women are being stalked, they're often in physical danger and almost always in psychological and emotional danger.

There is nothing healthy or sexy about possessiveness or obsession. I speak from experience. My ex-husband stalked me while we were married and continues to do so six years later. I got myself out of a very bad situation, and I am afraid you may need to do the same. You might have to take your pup Snowflake and get to a shelter. I'm posting some links for you to some great organizations where professional counselors will be happy to help you free of charge. Please reach out to them.

Affectionately yours,
    The Ex-Whisperer

I hit Post.

In my line of work, I hear from all kinds of people on all sorts of topics. If they're writing to me, they're usually in the midst of a relationship crisis and don't know where else to turn. Many times, they already know the answers to the questions they're asking, they just need reassurance and confirmation. They also need to be reminded to trust that little voice inside. It never lies. Deep down most of us understand the dos and don'ts of intimate relationships. I strive to be the voice of reason and also the boot that will kick ass when required. Lillian's letter has me genuinely worried for her. I hope she follows through with getting herself help.

My brilliant baby girl, Ella, pulls up a chair at my "desk" and sips a chocolate peanut butter smoothie with dates and chia seeds while she checks her phone. "Oh my God, Mom, the aunts are spamming all our walls. Why did you give them your old laptop? They don't understand how to use social media. They're so embarrassing."

Cringe. "I thought it would be fun for them to dabble on the internet. I didn't know they were going to sign up for seniors' center computer classes and wind up with Pinterest addictions."

Ella is deleting her great aunts' posts from her Facebook wall. "I guess they skipped the class on how to send PMs. Zia Angela wants to know the exact date you're moving back to town, and Zia Rosa is asking if you want ravioli or manicotti on your first night there."

"Cripes, I already told them September fifteenth and risotto."

Ella rolls her eyes, carries on deleting.

I check my own Facebook wall—with dread. And there they are. Eight, ten, twelve posts from my zany twin Italian aunts all pretty much saying the same thing, *"Gina? Gina? Are you there? Where you are? Hello? When you moving here? Che cavolo!"* The feisty old gals swear like sailors but always in Italian, thinking no one knows what they're saying. Potty mouth is in the DNA. It's not my fault. They always sign their online comments with their names, *bacio Zia Angela* and *bacio Zia Rosa*, even though Facebook tags their posts. The aunts' messages are like virtual cheek pinching: painful but done with love.

Ella's cell dings. A text from Air Canada. "Damn. The flight's delayed two hours." My girl is a chip off the old block in the bad language department.

Now I'm the one with the eye rolls. "Time to switch to wine." I dump my empty paper coffee cup in a bin, line up for a nice dry white.

* * *

Three hours and a couple of chardonnays later, I have posted replies to a few more letters on my column and have also responded to the aunts. Again. I'm pretty confident my writing is exceptionally witty, my advice transformative tonight, although to be honest, it read better with each glass of wine, which is slightly troubling. Note to self—It worked for Hemingway. Onward.

Ella has been texting back and forth to her brothers while listening to *My Favorite Murder* podcasts. A regular little Murderino.

A second letter comes in from Lillian.

Dear Ex-Whisperer,

My husband checked my phone and found the letter I sent you. He went bananas and took my laptop away. I'm using a computer at the library now. Hopefully, he doesn't find out I'm writing to you again. He said he'll give my dog, Snowflake, away if I send anyone another message. I talked to the police, but they can't help. They told me I have no evidence to prove my husband is stalking me and that his having a bad temper is not a crime even if it scares me. There's nothing they can do unless a judge orders my husband to stay away from me. He'd go crazy if I took him to court. There's no point in me going to a shelter because I can't stay there forever, and my husband swears if I ever try to leave him, he'll find me and "make me go away for real." He said there's nowhere in the world I can hide from him. What should I do? Can you help me, Ex-Whisperer?

Lillian

My reply:

Dear Lillian,

I am so sorry the police refused to help you. That is not uncommon, and it does not mean you are wrong or overreacting to your husband's behavior. You have to trust your instincts. If you feel you are in danger, you must take your pets and leave. Please reach out to the good counselors in the links I sent you. They will be able to guide you and help protect you. Be strong, Lillian, and please be careful.

Affectionately yours,
    The Ex-Whisperer

I hit Post.

Poor Lillian. Unfortunately, her horrendous situation is frighteningly common.

I close my laptop with a heavy heart, look up, and exhale loudly. Despite the half hour to go until boarding, throngs of passengers hefting carry-on bags way too big to be carry-on bags crowd the gate agents in their desperate mission to board the plane first and hog all the overhead storage space. Ella and I make our way to the gate.

Thirty minutes later, our row is called for boarding, but I always wait until the last possible moment before entering the tin can of stale air in which I will hurtle through space. I check my messages one last time. Big mistake.

Dear Ex-Whisperer,

Stay the hell away from my wife, Lillian. She doesn't need your crackpot "advice" messing with her head. As her husband, it's my duty to protect her from phonies like you. You'll keep your nose out of our business if you know what's good for you.

I've got my eyes on you.

Chapter Two

I often say I don't care for confrontation, and yet I find myself putting up my dukes and jumping into the ring at the drop of a hat. Unfortunately, I usually swing way above my weight class.

My reply:

Dear Eyes On Me,

How dare you spy on your wife, and how dare you troll me. In my experience, men like you who threaten and berate women are desperately trying to compensate for serious deficiencies in the dick department. Obviously, you also have serious deficiencies in the brain department. I'd say you've got a terminal case of dickhead syndrome. I hope your wife and her little dog get the hell outta Dodge before you can say "controlling jerk." Also, the next time you threaten me, I'll cut your tiny balls off.

Affectionately yours,
    The Ex-Whisperer

I hit Delete.

Arrggghhh, I so want to post this. Of course, I would never do anything as reckless as to endanger anyone. An aggressive response from me could trigger this creep to take his anger out on his poor wife.

My daughter is on her feet and tapping her toe impatiently. "Mom, it's time to board. We've gotta go."

My fingers are flying across the keyboard. "Okay, I know. One more minute."

Last call for boarding is announced. Ella is exasperated with me. "I'm getting in line." And she does.

Dear Eyes On Me,

Your wife sounds like a good woman who has never given you any reason to distrust her. She deserves to have a loving husband who appreciates her. Marriage is hard work, and all couples go through rough patches from time to time. There are many good counselors who can help provide you with tools to make your relationship the best it can be. I am providing links for you here that I hope you will follow up on. I wish both of you well.

Affectionately yours,
    The Ex-Whisperer

I hit Post. Maybe a little harder than necessary.

Painful to write, but caution is required.

I throw my laptop in my bag, gallop toward the gate agents. My daughter disappears down the jet bridge. The airline employee scans my boarding pass without a smile. They hate the eager beavers but also detest the stragglers. I book it onto the aircraft.

No room left in the overhead bins, as expected. I squeeze my bag under my seat and settle in next to Ella. "Let's have some fun."

I smile. Ella smirks, clearly still a little ticked with me.

The flight captain introduces himself. We will arrive in London in under eight hours and take off in less than ten minutes. The desperation among my fellow passengers is palpable. This aircraft hasn't been updated with satellite Wi-Fi. In a short while, we'll all be disconnected from the World Wide Web for the length of an entire workday. Will we survive the withdrawal? I quickly download the most recent emails, letters, and comments from my column so I can work on the replies while in the air.

Four hours late, we finally have takeoff.

Ella is staring at me loudly, a skill she honed as a toddler. I'm helpless when I look into those velvety eyes that render me incapable of ignoring her. My little girl requests that I not work on the flight but goof off with her, instead. I happily oblige. We share a few cups of tea and simultaneously marathon an entire season of *Veep* together on our seatback video screens, laughing out loud at all the same parts. Five hours and two mushy vegetarian meals later, we are in and out of the uncomfortable, quasi-sleep one gets on a red-eye.

I'm strangely fascinated by the semi-circle neck pillows that many passengers unabashedly wear like Coachella chokers. I can't envision any outfit I might wear tromping through an airport that I'd willingly accessorize with a whiplash-like collar. Some of the pillows cover the entire head with only a tiny slit to breathe through. The sight of these suffocating restraints triggers my claustrophobia. I take a moment for a few slow, deep breaths.

I must admit, it's difficult to argue with the facts—everyone in the cabin wearing one of these neck braces is fast asleep. The rest of us, while we may look far cooler, endlessly shift in a futile quest for slumber in our torturously uncomfortable seats. I cringe at the ragged, wheezy breathing of an older gentleman across the aisle. I'm worried he may put himself into cardiac arrest as he labors to blow up a larger such pillow that, when fully inflated, his whole head, chest, and arms disappear into, straightjacket style. I look over at him later and wonder if he may be dead inside there. Who would know?

Sleep and I have a precarious relationship at the best of times. My circadian rhythm is averse to time clocks. I resign myself to the fact that I'm not going to be catching any *z*'s on this flight. My daughter drifts off, her head resting against my shoulder, a position I find blissful.

I boot up my offline MacBook, see a response from Lillian's husband. Wish I hadn't.

Dear Ex-Whisperer,
No counselors. No divorce. No dating gurus. Watch your back.

Eyes on you

Point taken. And no more replies from me.

* * *

Twelve hours later, my daughter and I have enjoyed a delicious dinner of chana masala with fresh baked naan and a spicy aloo gobi at a neighborhood Indian restaurant in the East End. We've picked up groceries to feed her perpetually starving brothers and unpacked our bags in our charming Airbnb. My three little boys will arrive shortly, and then the festivities and the chaos shall ensue. So exciting. Ella showers and I pour a coffee and squeeze in one last bit of work time before I unplug completely and focus on family time.

Dear Ex-Whisperer,

My BF cheated on me three years ago. I forgave him, but he said he couldn't deal with the guilt, so he broke off with me. I've been in therapy ever since, but I just can't move on. His Insta and Facebook blow up with pics of all the bitches he's messing with. It makes me killer angry, and I comment on all his posts to let him know how I feel. Like you always say, open communication is super important in a committed love relationship. My therapist says I shouldn't be on his social media at all, and I swear I was going to unfollow him anyway, even before he took out the restraining order.

My question to you is, how long should you wait for the love of your life to realize that you are the love of his life? I think I would wait forever but forever is a long time. I need some of your Ex-Whispering expertise.

Btw you're awesome, Ex-Whisperer! I have all your Gal Guides books. You've been through so much. How do you keep it together and stay so strong? What's your secret? :)

Sincerely,

Prisoner of My Past

Either my books suck, or Prisoner hasn't gotten around to actually reading them yet. I'll choose to believe the latter. My mandate is to always tell the truth. I succeed in varying degrees. I adore my readers, but the batty ones can be a challenge How do I gently tell Prisoner that her ex-boyfriend is a loser, and she is a nut-bar in a delusional one-sided relationship without risking pushing her over some possibly dangerous edge? How do I let her know that in the present moment, at least, I am not the pillar of strength she imagines me to be? A bare-it-all level of honesty is my usual MO. My audience seems to appreciate my candor. It can be too much for some, but those followers disappear quickly.

I open the large casement window in the living room of our rented flat and lean out of it. It's dark now, and a patchy fog conceals slick cobblestones on the ancient street below.

Dear Prisoner,

True story. This is how I am currently coping with my present circumstances...

I am standing on a window ledge, ten floors up. I can hear the sounds of the traffic below but can't bring myself to look down. The Pilates has paid off. My butt and thighs actually fit on the sill, which is probably only twelve inches deep. My fingertips are sore from digging them into the rough lines of mortar between the bricks. It's all I can find to hold on to. The biting wind is pinning me against the cold blocks, and for now, it's the only thing keeping curvy me from becoming flattened me.

My polished toenails curl over the stone ledge. I chose Don't Ya Wanna Kiss Me pink at my pedicure last week but am now realizing it was a bad call. I almost chose Pretty Prussian Princess blue. I'm thinking that when I jump perhaps this wind is going to propel me through open French doors in the building across the street and blow me into the arms of a Pretty Prussian Prince. The nail polish color would have been an icebreaker, but still, he

11

will whisk me away, and we will live happily ever after.

Or maybe when the wind dies down and I float off this window ledge, I will land on a trampoline that well-muscled, heroic firefighters have fashioned from freshly pressed bedsheets, and I will bounce off it into the arms of a bare-chested Mr. January, and he will whisk me away, and we will live happily ever after.

I give my head a shake to rid it of these mindless myths. Charmless princes and non-superheroes have contributed to my landing here on the edge of my world and could land me head over heels on the unforgiving pavers below.

All at once, a thought that has never before occurred to me in my nearly fifty years comes crashing in on my frazzled mind, and suddenly I get it. Eureka. It's not about falling in love with the love of my life. It's about falling in love with my life. I have to fall in love with me. Truly, madly, deeply. I have had an epiphany. I don't want to die. I look down at the street. There is no trampoline to catch my fall, just worn cobblestones that have seen their share of spilled blood and guts and won't have a care about the likes of my remains trickling over them and dripping into their putrid sewers. Damn it, how the hell do I get myself off this ledge?

Affectionately yours,
   The Ex-Whisperer

I hit Delete.

Alright, somewhat true, a little embellished. What good story isn't? Perhaps a bit TMI. Will rewrite.

Ella yells out, "Mom what are you doing hanging out the window? It's freezing in here. Can you close it, please? Tea's ready and *The Great British Bake Off* is starting." My impatient daughter has set us up with Scottish shortbread and rosemary, sea salt, and olive oil popcorn, on the couch in front of the TV for the evening while we wait for the boys to arrive.

Okay, so I wasn't exactly standing on the ledge ten stories up, but I was leaning pretty far out of our third-floor window, and I was also up on my toes. Technically my entire upper body was outside of the building, and that can be very dangerous. The point is I could have climbed out onto the narrow ledge, and my butt and thighs may have fit on it. I could have chosen to end it all. But I chose life instead. And *The Great British Bake Off*—I chose that too. It is a strangely calming hour of television. Highly recommend.

I am inspired. I am determined. I am born again. I know what I need to do now; I need to fall in love with me and create a new life for myself—the life of my dreams. I shall eat chocolate and shortbread to celebrate. The hell with disappointing partners. And to hell with thin thighs.

I close and lock the window. I hate heights.

Dear Prisoner,

The secret to keeping things together is not keeping things together when they (situations and people) are clearly beyond repair. We have to know when to give up the ghost.

You need to accept the fact that your ex is not the love of your life. How can you know for sure? Because he doesn't love you. Not because he doesn't yet know you exist, but because he has been in a relationship with you and cheated on you and ended it and moved on with other partners. He's also enlisted the legal authorities to make sure you stay out of his life.

You're right. Forever is a long time, and that is exactly how long you could spend in jail if you don't stop futilely trying to keep this long-dead (as in flesh-eating-zombies-stage) relationship going. Forever is also the length of time your current therapist is hoping you will require treatment for. I'd advise that you also dump your therapist and find a new one since, after three years, you're still hung up on this jerk ex who used your heart for batting practice.

I don't care if your ex-boyfriend has redeeming sexual qualities or cute dimples. Remember that he cheated on you? Remember that he made you crazy while you were together and continues to make you crazy while you are apart? Remember that you are a beautiful goddess who deserves a life of love and happiness, and that this wanker is not capable of providing you with either? He's certainly not worth doing jail time for. Three years is enough of a sentence served. You're released on parole. Go make yourself happy so that a good man can find you.

Affectionately yours,
The Ex-Whisperer

I hit Post.

* * *

My three fabulous sons, Heath, my eldest, and Leon and Miles, my twins, finally arrive to join my daughter and me for a great weekend of food and fun, museums and pubs. In the four-bedroom apartment I have rented, the kids choose to all bunk in one room, dragging mattresses onto the floor and sharing beds. I dearly love that some things never change.

The five of us speak most days and FaceTime often, but I needed a real live fix right now. I needed to have all my offspring under one roof where I could see and smell and touch them. I am very grateful for this time, and I love these rare chances I get to spoil them.

In the kitchen on the lower floor of our flat, I prepare vegetarian antipasto, with plates of tomato bruschetta splashed with a balsamic glaze creamy burrata with peach and heirloom tomatoes, sliced melons and mozzarella drizzled with strawberry fig vinaigrette, and set out bowls of spicy marinated olives, huge hunks of salty parmesan and pecorino and a large loaf of crusty bread. As fast as I lay the long trays of food on the long dining table, eight not-so-little hands swipe and devour the offerings. Have to admit, I still derive enormous joy from feeding my babes. Everyone is speaking at once, overtop of everyone else. There is just too much catching up to do. There always is. Regardless of how often we talk on the phone, sharing in person is different. Raucous bursts of laughter drown out the delta blues my eldest has belting from an iPad. I love the sights and sounds and smells of love.

My computer has been turned off for hours, and I intend to keep it off for the entire weekend. Unfortunately, my phone is not on silent, and I can hear the relentless pings of my ever-growing, overflowing inbox. I open two bottles of Merlot and empty one of them into five goblets. Then, before I take a seat at the table, I make the momentous mistake of discreetly peeking at my emails just in case there is some emergency. You know how it is, the road to hell is paved with checking your emails.

I see one from Lillian's husband, and I can't help myself. I start down that road. Hello, Hell.

Dear Ex-Whisperer,

Where the hell is my wife? She didn't come home last night. She's gone because you put evil ideas in her head. I know you know where Lillian is, and you're gonna tell me. Be seeing you soon. Promise.

Eyes on you

Chapter Three

Why did I open the door to this shit show? I'd kick my own ass if I were flexible enough. Does Lillian's disturbed husband actually think I could or would tell him his wife's whereabouts? I hope she's fled to one of the shelters I recommended. I hope to God she doesn't cave and return home to this menace. Unfortunately, this psychopath is now apparently looking to track me down, too. Another one. I suppose he'll have to take a number and get in line.

I've ruined for myself this precious evening with my children. I paste on a smile and try to focus on the ten conversations happening at once, which is challenging at the best of times, but at this moment, it's proving impossible to distract my amygdala. That tiny almond-shaped mass of nuclei has broken the in-case-of-emergency glass and pressed the panic button in my brain. My defenses are down, to begin with. I've gone twenty-four hours without sleep, and I'm pretty sure I'm experiencing the onset of full-fledged delirium. I down my glass of Merlot, pour another, and attempt to rationalize, forgetting that alcohol is not exactly known for its rationalizing powers. The kids notice I'm off as they always do.

Heath is on it. "What's wrong, Mom?"

All four of them stop talking over one another. The eating comes to an abrupt halt mid-mouthful. They turn to stare at me and through me. Inspecting me for signs of distress. The matriarch is not allowed to falter. Ever.

"Nothing." I take another gulp of wine.

There's no unringing the alarm bells now. The kids won't have it.

"No, really. I'm great." Forced smile.

Miles, my scientist, is matter-of-fact as always. "That's your fake smile, Mom."

The accusatory looks fly from all four detectives.

I lift my wine glass to hide my mouth behind it. "It's definitely not." I suck at fake, but I try again for the children's sake. The fake smile of all fake smiles stretches across my lips. Damn my crummy acting skills.

The kids laugh, albeit somewhat nervously, at my feeble attempt to fool them. Eight perfect eyebrows are knitted with unease.

Leon always masks worry with anger. "What the hell Mom? Why are you trying to hide you're upset? We know you're not okay."

Ella's eyes are saucers of concern. "What happened, Mom? Just tell us."

Heath jumps to the conclusion we all leap to when one of us is out of sorts. "Did you get some weird junk from Dick?"

Years ago, shortly after our separation, when the children stopped communicating with their father, they began calling him by his first name, but they spit the word *Dick* out as an insult. Sadly, very little healing has taken place in this fractured family. Dick isn't interested in repairing relationships—he's too busy exacting retribution. He's the superstar of sore losers. Dick had always been a workaholic, but if I had taken even the smallest spoonful of the same medicine I prescribe to my readers; I would've known that nobody spends that much time at the office. After I packed him up and put him out, the receipts I found for massage parlors and dinners for two at romantic restaurants, to which I wasn't invited, were the damning evidence that dismantled my denial. Adding insult to injury, my son's friend sent him copies of explicit emails she found on her mother's computer, sent by—my son's father. The verdict was unanimous—guilty on all counts.

I had been conned by a master manipulator, but I was a member of an elite club. Hundreds of North American investors had put up millions to fund the Italian film company Dick was forming. He was able to convince savvy businesspeople that he was bringing back the spaghetti western, and he had signed co-production contracts from producers in Palermo to prove it. It worked for him for a while until it didn't anymore. Like all Ponzi schemes, his house of cards collapsed eventually. My world came tumbling down around me when Dick's shady business endeavors exploded in my face. I learned about it in the headlines along with the rest of the country. I tortured myself trying to figure out how I could be that stupid—how anyone could be that stupid—but I came to the conclusion it wasn't that I was not smart, it's that Dick was smarter—than everyone. Or at least more cunning, I suppose there's a difference. The investors accused Dick of stealing millions for himself although I never found the money trail and it wasn't for a lack of looking. He's not in jail—he blamed the failure on the suspect Sicilian cinema. Both policing and bookkeeping are basically nonexistent in Sicily—it's as easy to bury a few bodies and get away with it as it is to bury a few million.

The kicker that almost did me in for good came long after Dick was gone. After four years of battling it out in divorce court, the judge awarded me the matrimonial home and a million dollars in lump-sum support. By the time the house was transferred into my name, Dick had declared bankruptcy and booked it back to Italy. It was then that the many liens against my home were brought to my attention by the wake of vultures who circled above waiting to feed on my carcass since Dick's delinquent ass was nowhere to be found. Eight hundred and seventy-two thousand dollars of liens were filed before Dick was protected by insolvency, leaving me holding the bag. The executions were made by Dick's investors and their law firms for unpaid costs, by the Canadian Government for ten years of his unpaid income tax, and even by some of his own brothers for personal loans he'd skipped out on. For crying out loud there were even claims by two of Dick's ten divorce lawyers he stiffed for fifty thousand bucks. The whole thing stank, but my having to pay Dick's divorce lawyers for him stunk the most.

I was determined to hold on to my house—I wasn't going to let Dick rob me of that dream, too. Through Herculean effort, I made it work for a while. I was Sally Field in *Places in the Heart* near killing myself trying to bring the cotton in on time to save the farm. Unfortunately, my story didn't have a Hollywood ending. I make good money from my books, but the weight of having to pay off my ex's crushing debts while carrying the expenses of a big house on my own eventually took its toll. If I wanted to have the disposable income I needed to visit the kids overseas, help them with their student loans, and do all the things I love to do—like eat, I had to let go of my home. For a time, it felt as if Dick had won, but after a while, I understood there aren't any winners in divorce. There are only those who move on in life and those who stay mired in the muck. Fuck muck. One thing I pride myself on is never making the same mistake twice. The mistakes I do make are usually monumental and often extremely costly, but I definitely learn from them. I'd never again give up my home or lose anything else because of a man.

I bring my wandering attention back to my four grown children who are waiting patiently to call me out if I attempt to present them with anything less than complete honesty. "No, I did not get any weird junk from Dick. Really. It's just a work thing. I read something that kind of threw me, but I'm fine."

Ella is stern. "You're not supposed to be working this weekend. You promised."

"You're right. Technically, I didn't work, but I did check my email, and I shouldn't have even done that. I'm sorry. Anyway, it's all good. I'll deal with it when I'm back in Canada." I dig into the hummus. "C'mon. Let's eat."

Heath wraps his long arm around my shoulder. "Love you, Mom."

The others chime in, "Love you, Mom."

"Love you guys, too." I can't help but smile, and it is definitely a genuine one now.

The conversation picks back up, and the noise level rises once again. After the party gets rolling afresh, I'm free to secretly turn my thoughts back to the creepiness of the message from Lillian's husband. Not that I want to, but it's skulking in a dark corner of my skull. How can I help it?

I'm worried about Lillian. She managed to get out. She escaped her controlling husband, a monumental feat, but that bully is already hunting her down like a baying hound in pursuit of a frightened little fox. I hope she's safely tucked away in a women's shelter. With her wee dog. Lillian said her husband promised he'd find her. I hope she's wrong about that. Truth be told, I'm a little worried about myself, too. I don't need another maniac tracking me down. Not that anyone ever needs any maniacs coming after them. But really, one stalker is quite enough, thank you. For now, I'm glad my kids live in Europe, an ocean away from the shit hitting the fan back in our homeland.

I'm on my third glass of wine now, and the more I consume, the more I'm convinced the nectar of the gods is helping me rationalize the situation. Lillian's husband is threatening to pay me a visit, but the fact is, he doesn't know where to find me. I never post my address online, of course. Does anyone? If he tried hard enough, maybe he could track me down through the Internet, but I'm moving the day after I return to Canada, so I'm probably safe. I'll be disappearing into the wilds of the Great White North. Flipside, disappearing into the wilds of the Great White North sounds more scary than protective.

The ping-pong match between my left brain and right brain is exhausting. *Gavel smash, gavel smash*, the jury has returned a verdict—the wine is actually not helping me sort out the situation. I need to make a decision here. Stop drinking or stop thinking. Tough one. I open another bottle, top up everyone's glass. It's a no-work weekend. *Cin cin!*

The rest of the evening is a blast, and we end up partaking in one of my very favorite pastimes, kitchen dancing. Who can resist when the playlist loops Drake and Rihanna?

* * *

There are two bathrooms upstairs in our flat, so the lineups for bedtime won't be long. I turn out the lights in the kitchen and living room, double-check that the exterior doors are securely locked. I pick up my phone. See the number thirty-two in a tiny red bubble next to my email icon. I'm tempted to click on it. Working, or thinking about working when I shouldn't, is as close as I get to masochism. I'm not a fan of pain. Didn't make it past the first twenty pages of *Fifty Shades of Grey*—and that wasn't only because of the BDSM theme. But no, I won't check my inbox. Not tonight. Not this weekend. Turning my phone off, I stumble up the stairs in the dark.

There is way too much laughing, screaming, and roughhousing thumping coming from the kids' shared sleeping quarters. I crash their party with multiple bags of salt-and-malt chips, or crisps, as the Brits ineptly call them. I squeeze my wine-logged body into a narrow, vacant space on one of the mattresses between two extremely silly boys and pass the snacks around. The bottomless pits that are my sons welcome more sustenance.

Even when drunk, my mothering instincts prevail. "Now you guys will have to brush your teeth again."

Leon, "There's always tomorrow, Mom."

Me, "I have failed as a mother."

Sleepiness is settling into our sacred space at last. Ella turns the lights down, and we've got some smooth Ella Fitzgerald (her namesake) playing softly to carry us into dreamtime. We're all finally mellowing out. It would have been story time not so many years ago. It was hard then to keep my eyes open at the end of a fun-filled day of child wrangling, but it seems even harder now.

The weight of my lids is too much to bear, and my heavy eyes slowly drop to shutter my blurry vision. Relief. But only for a fleeting moment.

Miles drops what, for our family, is considered a bomb. "I got some weird stuff from Dick yesterday."

My shuttered eyes fly open. My mind is way too tired for this, but my body doesn't care. It's instantly alert and back in fight-or-flight mode. My children need protecting—hormones are at the helm. "What did you get?"

Leon chimes in, "I did too. Super weird."

I'm sitting up now or perhaps levitating. "Was it the same old weird or a new kind of weird?" Making this distinction is imperative.

Leon doesn't attempt to spare me. "A next-level weird. Like a reeking-of-desperation weird."

This is scary stuff, and we all know it. Dick is constantly on the verge of being on the verge. His nervous strain could unsettle a meditating monk. Desperate Dick is the worst kind of Dick.

"I think he's freaking out because you sold the house." Miles was imbued with logical thinking long before his science education honed it to perfection.

Leon's voice is drenched in disdain. "Yeah, it was like five hundred words on how the courts stole everything he owned and how you made out like a bandit."

I pointlessly make a point I've made a thousand times before a hundred judges. "That might be one way to look at it if he ever coughed up the million in child support the courts ordered him to pay." I am an old vinyl record that skips mercilessly over the same lyric. Six years later, still pointless.

Leon continues, "He was asking a lot of questions about where you're moving to and if you're moving in with anyone."

"It'll make him crazy not knowing where I'm living. Correction, crazier." Anger is flooding my muscles with adrenaline. If I hadn't had so much wine, I could probably lift a car off a small child. The equivalent in my current exhausted/inebriated state is, I'm able to walk. I pace back and forth in the couple of square feet of floor that is not covered with mattresses. I am aware this basically means that I look as if I'm gesticulating hysterically.

Heath deduces, "He probably thinks you're moving in with a boyfriend."

Ella's eyes are huge again. "I'm scared, Mom. He's such a jealous jerk. If he thinks you're moving in with someone, he might really go off the deep end. Your selling the house could set him off."

I try to placate her, tone down my nervous twitches. "Anything could set him off. We can't live in constant fear of that. Anyway, he doesn't know where I'm going. I'll be fine."

I haven't succeeded. Ella pulls the blankets over her face.

She talks through the sheet. "Why would he care if you had a boyfriend? He's been with the cockroach for four years already."

The cockroach is what the kids call Dick's girlfriend, Rochelle. I also refer to the nasty beatch as *the cockroach* although I do restrain myself in front of the children. In my defense and theirs, the cockroach has been truly horrible to us and has caused us much unnecessary anguish. At this point, knowing she's still breathing causes me anguish.

Heath has been my great protector since he was a toddler. "It's probably not safe for you to go back to the house alone. You never know how far Dick might go. Why do you have to stay there another night? Isn't all the furniture gone already?"

I have to do whatever I can to lighten the load of stress my children constantly carry on their shoulders because of their deadbeat dad. "The movers took most of the stuff I didn't sell, but there are still a few things I have to grab. Anyway, I won't be alone. I'm picking up the dog and cat from the boarding kennel on my way home from the airport, so we'll be three Power Rangers watching each other's backs. And to be perfectly honest, I need to say a proper goodbye to my dream home where I raised my dream children." I reach out to ruffle a few dreamy heads. "I'll miss that beautiful farm so much."

Miles sounds sad, "I miss the pets."

Heath reaches for my hand. "We're going to miss the house too, but there are lots of new adventures in store for us. So many great times yet to come. As long as we have each other, we're good." He leads the cheer, as usual.

"You're going to fix up the cottage, and we're going to have a blast visiting you there. I'm stoked." Leon's voice is genuinely excited.

I squeeze Heath's hand tightly. "You're right, my sweethearts. It's just a new chapter in this wild ride called life." I hate rides.

Ella joins in the rah rah-ing like a good sport although a little weakly. "An exciting new chapter."

"Agreed. Time to sleep now." I kiss my four once-little munchkins on their foreheads, flip the light switch off, and head to a bedroom down the hall where I crawl beneath a white cotton duvet that feels like a cloud.

First thought when my head hits the downy pillow: *How did I end up with a colossal asshole like Dick?* My great kids deserved so much better. Second thought, in my deceased best friend Sinead's voice: *Come on, you must have known what you were getting into. You married a guy named Dick.*

My left brain tells me to think good thoughts, and before my right brain can come up with an argument in favor of worrying, I'm out, more unconscious than asleep, I think, but it hardly matters. I sleep the sleep of the dead.

* * *

I wake to one of my favorite smells in the world. Strong coffee. I follow my nose down the stairs into the kitchen, and a broadly smiling Heath hands me a huge mug. Heaven.

Once my caffeine levels are sufficiently elevated, the breakfast brigade begins, and I go through an entire loaf of organic sourdough making avocado toast with feta, drizzled olive oil, and crushed chilli peppers for five ravenous vegetarians.

By noon, we're off to Hackney City Farm, my favorite place in London. I'll always be a country girl at heart, and few things make me happier than a massive muddy pink pig and a coop full of chicks. Late in the day, we hit up my second-favorite place in London, Tate Modern. Swoon. Double swoon. I'm on inspiration overload. Excited by the prospect of finally getting settled after my move and starting to paint again. Yay.

A hearty dinner of grilled portobello mushroom burgers dripping with provolone, roasted red pepper, and caramelized onion, at a cozy pub, is followed by shenanigans at the flat, followed by two more days that should be blissful. But I can't get my hackles down. *Do I now have* two *stalkers?* I think I might. My gut tells me Lillian's husband is the real deal.

Heartbreakingly for me, all too soon, my boys are back on trains and planes returning to their studies. Ella now has bedding and teacups and a fully stocked miniature kitchen in her tiny new flat in a somewhat sketchy area of East London. She melts into my arms the way she has done since the moment she was born. A puddle of tears forms at our feet on the sidewalk next to my Uber.

I've raised four intelligent, ambitious, resourceful adventurers who have all struck out into the wide world to manifest their dreams, but at this moment, I wish I'd failed at parenting. I wish my kids were unemployed dropouts, playing Dungeons & Dragons in my basement and smoking weed well into their thirties.

At least I wouldn't be jamming my shattered heart into a carry-on bag and flying home alone to face an unasked for, entirely new chapter in my life, the details of which are still unknown. I might as well draw those details out of a hat and make that my game plan. In this dreaded new life, I'm no longer permitted to identify as a primary caretaker of dependent children, which conveniently happens to be a very effective method of avoiding focusing on oneself, shielded as one is by the martyrdom of motherhood.

Who am I, if not Super Mom to my four super kids? The new me, who must surely be lurking just around the corner, feels like a strange visitor from another planet. Hopefully, she can change the course of mighty rivers and bend steel in her bare hands. That would be cool.

I suppose I'm meant to leap tall buildings in a single bound to rescue myself, rather than others, for the first time in twenty-five years. It would appear that I have no option other than to create a wildly successful, fabulous new life in which I play the heroic, starring role, Super Me, whether I like it or not.

Change, you are a cruel master.

Chapter Four

Another entire season of *Veep* and another sleepless night, sans fugly neck pillow, and I am home not-so-sweet home.

A full moon lights the way as, for the very last time, I drive up the long laneway of my hundred-acre farm toward the beautiful house that I built for my beautiful family. Twenty years later, I'm still struck by the dreamy design of this Nantucket charmer. Salty shingles and sea-kissed shutters are surrounded by an ocean of wavy wheat instead of water, but it's just as gorgeous. I love this place, but it would have been ridiculous for me to live here on my own. Running costs aside, it's far too big for one person. It was more space than anyone needed when there were six of us living here. Go left brain, go. Logic is what I need to get me through the next twelve hours. Don't want the new owners to call the authorities and have me bodily dragged from the premises.

The moonlight floods the cornfields in the valley and illuminates two deer sauntering toward the forest. I slow my Jeep, and they stop and turn to stare, their goodbye to me, I'm certain of it. The deer hold me in their gaze for a lingering moment before slowly moving along. Their wild beauty hurts my heart. Emotion is my frenemy and has decided to plonk itself in the middle of my throat and swell like a mother. Bye-bye logic.

The dog and cat, Zoe and Spook, wild from a ten-day stint in their boarding kennel confines, whine and meow incessantly in the back seat. They know they're finally home. I haven't told them it's only for a night.

I park in the garage and carry out my ritual as I've done for the past six years since my marriage ended. Before I exit my vehicle, I check my

26

surroundings for any signs that my ex-husband may have been lurking around the premises. Then I cautiously open the door between the garage and the breezeway, peeking through the widening crack, hoping I don't find Dick's body swinging from the rafter outside the door.

It sounds paranoid and dramatic, I know, but I've held that frightening picture in my mind since the day we separated. I'm an early riser, and every morning for six years, I've tiptoed downstairs and flinchingly checked my front door to make sure my ex isn't hanging there all bright blue and bulgy-eyed.

In our excruciatingly drawn-out divorce proceedings (embarrassingly, we've actually set records for numbers of hearings held in one case), Dick has filed thousands of pages of material, including hundreds of pages of medical reports that he hopes will get him off the hook for the ridiculous crap he's pulled and also to offer excuses for his never paying the child support he owes. The judges don't buy any of it, but still, he persists, and our overburdened, broken judicial system allows him to do so.

The eerie thing is that, about two years ago, I read one psychiatric report where the doctor stated that my ex has "suicidal ideation" and described the details of his suicide fantasy, which entailed his wanting his death to have as great an impact on me as possible. Dick's plan was to hang himself outside the door of my home so I would find his body.

Yup, intuition is a powerful thing. In truth, I don't think Dick has the balls to do himself in. Rather, he weaponizes suicide threats and attempts to use them against me. I wouldn't want him to know this, but it's quite an effective strategy. He's a textbook narcissist.

No noose. The coast is clear. Thrilled to be free from the boarding kennel, Zoe bounds out of my truck, and before I can stop the mammoth oaf, she's halfway across a field of alfalfa, chasing a petrified rabbit. I yell after her, but she doesn't listen. Nothing new there with my dumb as a stump Giant Schnauzer. My indoor cat, Spook, incarcerated in a large animal crate, is terrified at being this close to the great outdoors. I place him on the grass, he yowls, and hisses as befits his black-cat name, and I pursue the damn dog, screaming at the top of my lungs.

After two minutes of jogging, I throw in the towel, head back toward the house. It's humid for mid-September—the night air hot and still. My T-shirt is already damp and clinging to my chest. The cat is traumatized and growling at having been left in contact with the elements. The dog never goes too far away, she'll be back soon enough. As I cross over the front lawn, I notice a whole lot of footprints in the soft ground below my windows. Large men's boots. Naturally, my mind goes immediately to my ex, and my heart begins to pound, but I calm myself quickly. There was a house inspection while I was away, and the new owners were probably here as well, excitedly snooping around their future home.

I carry the cat crate indoors, and before I can turn around, the dog is also at my feet, nervous herself now. I lock the door but can't switch the security system on—the service was canceled along with the landline and internet for the house closing tomorrow. Forgot about that slight detail.

I said I'd never leave here, but I'm leaving here. The stalking didn't drive me out. The specter of a hanging man didn't drive me out. For a long time, even Dick's debts didn't drive me out—they made me work harder, made me more determined to stay. But after six years of scrapping, it's time for some ease. I repeat my mantra, *I am deserving of peace.*

An uncharacteristic strangeness is starting to creep into the space around me. For the most part, I've never felt frightened in my home, even though the nearest neighbor is a good quarter mile away and out of earshot of even the shrillest of screams, which by the way, I am more than capable of producing. But a house never feels the same when it's empty.

Suddenly, my romanticized idea of a solitary fond farewell to my farm doesn't sound like such a great idea after all.

The pet's nails and my bare feet echo through the hollow spaces. The house looks sad and lonely with all the furnishings gone but the architectural details shine in its nakedness—the weathered, wide plank floors, the beadboard walls, and sunny yellow linoleum in the pantry, the open kitchen shelves that once displayed a cheery rainbow of depression glass. The house was empty when it was under construction, but it wasn't bereft then—it was brimming with possibility and promise. The six of us used to have rollicking pizza dinners on the unfinished floor, excitedly planning where the TV and toy shelves would go. Our family had years of happiness here. The bad times can't erase those good memories. I won't let them.

My truck is loaded with my personal belongings, but I'm traveling light for now until I finish the reno on the old family cottage and figure out whether I can handle living in Mayberry again. I love my eccentric old aunts and my multitude of cousins who never ventured farther from the tiny town they grew up than the closest college, and then it seems, returned to the familiarity of Sunset Beach as quickly as they could. I've put my treasures that I'm not bringing with me, the kids' artwork, family photos, some inherited antiques, and other favorite possessions into storage for the time being.

I spread out a sleeping bag and pillow on the family room floor. Zoe and Spook are weirded out by their empty home, and as soon as I settle on my makeshift bed, they're both fully pressed against the length of my body. I pull my dinner out of my purse, a soggy egg salad sandwich I picked up at a gas station that tastes as bad as it sounds, and I share it with the dog.

I smile when I read the multitude of texts that my four extremely worried children have been sending me all day. They know I'll be a sentimental wreck on this last night in the home I love so much. They tell me that I'll be fine, that it's just a house, and that change is good. They remind me that we have each other, that that's all that matters. And of course, my head knows they're right. My heart, however, is not in agreement.

Now that I'm safely tucked inside, I'm glad to have this last night in my house. I keep the lights off and stretch out on the floor to look at the bright stars and big moon that look back at me through the soaring living room windows. The dog and cat keep me warm. I wait for the tears to come, and they do. I'm surprised at how long they hang around.

At some point, I fall asleep. I only know this because, sometime in the middle of the blackness, I awake to pain and a deafening break in the silent night.

The cat leaps across my chest, scraping off a pound of my flesh with his claws as he flees. He frantically searches for a piece of furniture to hide under. No such luck. He scrambles into the basement. The dog pulls a full-on Cujo, snarling and snapping, attacking the front door, throwing herself against the glass panes.

I jump unsteadily to my feet, still caught in the stupor of half-sleep. Like the cat, I also groggily search for a place to hide and am also shit out of luck in my empty house.

An incapacitating concoction of confusion and fear leaves me dumbstruck and vulnerable, standing in the center of the room, illuminated by the moonlight, like the deer caught in my headlights earlier. I can't even decide which direction I should move in, and it feels as if I'm moving in all of them at once. I know my limbs are in motion—I'm just not getting anywhere.

My senses begin to sharpen at last, and I shoot across the living room, press my body against a wall in the foyer. Unfortunately, I've left my phone on the floor next to my pillow.

Slowly, I inch toward the dog and the front door, trying to slow my ragged breathing, and peek out through the window without being seen. I can make out the long shadow of someone standing on the porch, but I can't see the body. The shape darts to the left, and the silhouette disappears in blackness. The light of the full moon makes it hard to hide, but this person manages to stay shrouded in a wedge of darkness. I keep to the shadows between the windows, avoiding the wide shards of bright white that slash across the floor, hoping this visitor doesn't see me, either.

Why isn't he retreating at the threatening, relentless barking of the dog? Why isn't he afraid of Zoe's menacing snarling? Does he know her and know that she's all bark and no bite? Or is he actually incapable of leaving? Perhaps because he is now hanging over, rather than standing on my front porch? Is it my ex or just some random serial killer? Strangely, I'm struggling to figure out which of the two I'd prefer to encounter.

Zoe's bared teeth shine in the moonlight. She's not barking anymore, but the low, steady growl gurgling from the base of her throat is the most frightening sound I've ever heard her make. She's no longer throwing herself against the door. Her eyes are fixed on the door handle. It turns slightly. Her growl deepens.

I scan the hollow house for something to defend myself with. Every shelf, every drawer is empty, every sharp or weighty object has been packed away. My only potential weapons are the pillow and blanket on the floor. Maybe I can smother myself before my assailant spends hours torturing me.

There's a loud ring, and I jump out of my skin, let out a half scream before I can stop myself. It's my cell phone. I sprint toward it, grab it. No Caller ID. I answer, wait. Nothing. I hang up and dial emergency, start down the stairs into the darker basement.

The phone call drops. We've never gotten reception in the basement. Damn it. Calling for the dog in a loud whisper, I rush toward the French doors of the walk-out basement and throw them open. Zoe is at my heels in a flash.

I run through the doors out onto the expanse of lawn in the backyard. Illuminated with the flood of full moonlight, it's as bright as a Friday night football field. I try to stick to the long shadows that the tall pines throw, make my way toward the woods a couple of cornfields away. The soft soles of my bare feet are assaulted by sharp twigs and ragged pinecones. Zoe is right beside me. The mugginess has only intensified with the hour—the wet heat claws at my throat. Sweat pouring down my face stings my eyes and runs between my lips, and I swallow salt—along with at least a pound of mosquitoes.

A flash of light streaks across our bodies. Car headlights. I drop down on all fours in the grass, crawl into the cover of darkness behind a bush. My knees sting as the skin opens up against thistles and broken branches. A vehicle heads down my curving driveway. The dog resumes her alarm barking. This guy is certainly going to know exactly where to find us now if he wants to carry out his murderous plan. In truth, I don't know if Zoe's barking is any louder than my hyperventilating. I could just as easily be the one to give us up.

I dial the emergency number on my phone again. No service in the cornfields, either. All we can do is make a break for it. I know these woods. He probably doesn't. Unless it's my ex, of course, in which case all I can do is try to outrun him.

I yell for the dog to follow me, and we take off toward the forest, but a few seconds later, I look back over my shoulder and realize that the car has slowed but hasn't stopped. It's continuing down my laneway. It's leaving the property. I reverse directions and run toward the driveway up to the top of the hill to catch a glimpse of the vehicle in case I can identify it. It's a dark color, maybe black or navy, and small. That's all I can gather.

Red taillights flicker, creep down the road until they disappear around the bend. I take a moment to slow my breathing, feel safe for a few seconds until the thought crosses my mind that perhaps he wasn't alone. Perhaps only his driver has left. Perhaps the criminal mastermind is still standing on my front porch.

Or waiting inside my house.

I don't have a lot of options. I'm in bare feet and underwear, and I have a cell phone without reception and no car keys. I've got to hedge my bets.

The dog and I run back inside the house, lock the basement doors behind us. We head upstairs slowly, silently taking one step at a time. It already seems as if I've made the wrong decision. The dog stays pressed against my calves. She doesn't know what's happening, but she's picked up on my energy, and she's as terrified as I am now. I feel like one of those dumbass coeds in a slasher flick. Why is she going back inside the house where we know the killer is waiting to slice and dice her? Because it seems the least shitty of all the shitty options before me, that's why. And because it's too late to turn around now.

Chapter Five

My guard dog has turned in her badge, but she'll definitely let me know if there is an intruder in the house if only to protect herself. She's sniffing around but doesn't bark or growl.

It looks as if there's no one here.

I cross the foyer to check the front door. It's still locked. I flip the outside lights on, look out the window. No dead guys suspended from the porch roof. No live ones hanging around, either. I know for sure there's no stranger danger now because my scaredy-cat Spook has emerged from the basement and is rubbing against my ankles, purring.

I contemplate calling the police, but what do I tell them? Someone stood at my front door in the middle of the night and touched my doorknob but didn't break-in, didn't steal anything, and after a while, they drove off, but I didn't get a good look at the person or his vehicle? I can guess how it would go.

Cop, "Perhaps it was a friendly neighbor who popped by to say so long and wish you well in your move."

Me, "It was the middle of the night, Officer."

Cop, "Perhaps he didn't know you were there and was checking up on the empty house for you. Or maybe he'd had a few too many and didn't realize the hour."

The cops will do what they've always done whenever I've called them about my ex's stalking. They'll downplay the event, explain away the circumstances, and then when I insist that they take some action, they'll walk around my property shining their flashlights under bushes and inspect my garage. I always felt as if they were humoring me, but still, when they told me that they'd keep their eyes on my house, it made me feel a little safer, even though I wouldn't sleep well for weeks after.

Dick has poked around my property ever since we separated, peering through windows, often with a camera. Sometimes he sends me copies of the pictures to make sure I know that I can't make him stay away, that I can't make him do anything, or stop him from doing anything. Dick is a control freak who seeks to control others because he has zero self-control.

The police called me a couple of months ago to tell me that after a multitude of dealings they had with Dick, they had concluded that he's obsessive, that he's escalating, and that he's made fighting me in court his life's work. These things I already knew. They urged me to get a restraining order against him, but the cops don't realize that judge's rulings don't mean a thing to a guy like Dick. Obtaining a restraining order would only force me to spend more time in court with him which is what he wants, so I didn't do it. To be honest I have no idea what Dick is capable of. I do know that he's a loose cannon, unpredictable—especially when he's off his meds. A judge said once that Dick was the perfect example of the lengths to which a spouse will go to avoid his responsibilities. That said it all for me, and I've always wondered what lengths he will go to. I hope I never find out. I think his ultimate goal is to stop me from living happily ever after, and he does that by keeping me constantly on edge. So far, he's been wildly successful.

So, was it Dick who came calling? It sure as heck wasn't someone selling Girl Guide cookies at three a.m. It could have been any opportunistic thief or even a trouble-seeking teenager. It's a big, beautiful house, the For-Sale sign says Sold, and it's plainly been unoccupied for a couple of weeks. But why didn't the person take off as soon as the dog started barking? Why did he persist and try turning the doorknob knowing a large, aggressive dog was going berserk on the other side of the door, jonesing to sink its teeth into a meaty thigh?

The intruder was also likely aware that there was a dog owner inside, too, albeit armed with only a pillow, but regardless, he didn't know that, and still, he didn't flee. Was it because he wasn't here to steal appliances, he was here to steal my peace? Was it because he only came to scare me? On my last night in my dream house, was this trespasser's mission to deliver me a nightmare? That's what it's beginning to look like to me. And if so, I believe my late-night, unwelcome visitor was indeed my ex. My night-stalker.

* * *

A brilliant morning sun and reverberating dog barks rouse me from some sort of rest although I wouldn't call it sleep. My eyes are swollen, and my head hurts. We made it through the night with no more unexpected guests, thank Christ. Just to be sure, as per my routine of the past six years, I tentatively check for any dead men who might be hanging around my front door. Negative.

I let the dog out, feed the pets, and curse when I remember the coffee maker is packed away.

Before I leave a life and twenty years of memories behind, I take the time to step into each room to say farewell to the beautiful spaces and look through every window, taking mental snapshots of the lovely views of the fields and forests beyond.

In my children's bedrooms, I stand still, close my eyes, and breathe deeply. I remember how the rooms looked and felt when they were filled with my angels' treasures—posters and books, favorite toys and love-worn stuffed animals, skateboards, and prized collections of rocks and shells. The most cherished memories I hold are those of my four sweet babies tucked into their snuggly beds, sleeping soundly under my roof. Those times I will forever miss.

I say goodbye to my gorgeous kitchen and play back all the fun times and good food we shared around our pine harvest table. Candles burning, laughter, music, and the smell of baking cupcakes filling the air. And in the family room, I remember all the chaotic Christmas mornings and the cold winter nights spent cozily curled up in front of the roaring fire, munching popcorn and watching old black and white movies.

Everyone has their challenges to deal with, but I can't complain. Life has been wonderful to me. I choose to only remember the blissful times in this house, and that's easy to do because truly there were too many to count.

Knowing that perhaps the best times are past is a difficult pill to swallow. I remind myself that even if the next chapter in my life is only half as good as the last, that means it's still going to be epically great. That greatness will be up to me to create. I'm going to give it one hell of a college try.

One final walk through my bountiful, thriving gardens. A last look at my fantastical forest. The weight of these goodbyes is pressing down on me with so much pressure that I feel like my chest could crack open. There's no way for me to leave this place other than by my performing a complete amputation. With no anesthetic. I rip a piece of my heart out and bury it at the foot of a favorite oak tree. I water it with tears. I will love this land forever. It will always be a part of me and I of it.

* * *

The surgery is a success. Although excruciatingly painful, the prognosis is the patient will survive the amputation. I am out of the woods. Literally. My old home and the forest shrink in my rear-view mirror as I drive away and my heart aches, tears and snot flying profusely. I have loved this place dearly, and I will miss it terribly.

Change, I make peace with you.

I hit up the drive-thru to grab a couple of lattes, then head across town.

The temperature has dropped sharply, and there's a much welcomed, cool breeze blowing now. Dark clouds are gathering in the sky above—my increasingly frizzy hair indicates that I probably don't have a whole lot of time before they open up. The dog and cat are happy to curl up and sleep on the back seat of my truck—they're as exhausted from last night as I am. I leave the windows open a few inches for them and lock the doors.

I weave between the headstones in the cemetery, balancing the hot paper cups, following the worn path to Sinead's final resting place. I hate the word *final*. I sit down on the grass in front of her and lean my back against her tomb so my BFF and I can share our millionth coffee together.

"So, gal, tell me. How am I supposed to handle all this change without you here to kick my ass and tell me to pull on my big girl panties? How the hell am I supposed to say goodbye to everyone I love in this world, and my farm, and start some stupid new life without you or the kids by my side?"

I wait for her responses, and I hear them. I'll never stop conversing with my best friend. Predictably, she tells me to get on with things. To suck it up and be brave. To not confuse excitement with fear—to choose to be excited by the change instead of afraid of it. And after a long while, an hour or more, she tells me that it's time for me to be on my way. And she tells me to be fabulous. And I promise my friend that I will be.

Drips of water splash down my cheeks—A mixture of rain and tears. I down the rest of my coffee, pour Sinead's onto the grass at the foot of her tomb. I run my fingers over the raised letters of her name on the bronze plaque. It's still impossible to comprehend that this vibrant, vivacious bad-ass-boss-babe is gone at fifty. This unexpected and unfair turn in the road has definitely been one of the greatest shocks of my shock-filled life. I miss my number one gal pal every day.

It's time. My duties are done. I'm being drizzled on, and I've run out of excuses for delaying pushing the eject button and parachuting into my future. There's no choice for me other than to move forward and having no choice has me feeling as if I have no options. But deep down, I know that's bull.

At this moment, the world is my oyster. I'm free to do whatever I want wherever I want, and how flipping amazing is that? I'm one of the fortunate few on the planet to even reach that pinnacle in life. No more boohooing for me. Time to find that bright side and focus on it, my signature fallback survival mechanism. I point my jeep north, crank up the volume on a Spotify Road Trip playlist, and venture out on my new feckin' life.

Change, I will master you.

The constant, even swish of the windshield wipers lulls me into meditation. My mind turns over, pulls apart, reconstructs everything I'm leaving behind, and heading toward for the first two hours of the drive. Wavering between feeling lost and feeling found is exhausting.

Halfway along the journey, the rain lets up. I pull over to let the dog out, consume caffeine, and check my email. I immediately regret doing the latter. There's one from some disposable temporary email generator, which is never a good thing. It's one of those email addresses that self-destructs after ten minutes. I wouldn't even open it except the subject line reads "Last Night's Visit."

Dear Ex-Whisperer,

Sorry I missed you last night. Will catch up to you soon.

Chapter Six

I dump out the rest of my coffee and hurry to load the dog into the truck, get back on the road. I feel as if I'm being watched even though I know that's impossible. My imagination regularly runs the gamut between serving me brilliantly and sabotaging me brutally. This is one of those times when those fantastical thoughts of mine are not helpful. It could be pure paranoia, but at the moment, I feel safer locked in my truck and quickly putting distance between me and whoever "missed" me last night.

Maybe it was Lillian's husband who came calling unannounced in the dark. Logically, of course, I realize that's not possible. There's no way he knows where I live. Can't let the irrational thoughts creep in. Can't let the creeps creep in, either, although they do seem to be making a valiant effort between Lillian's unhinged ex and my unstable ex. Maybe the timing of my move is perfect after all.

The good news is nobody knows where I'm heading. Except for my kids. And my old neighbors. And all of my friends in my old town. And the multitude of my extended family who all live up north and love to post everything they do on social media. I mean literally every meal, shopping trip, alcoholic beverage, wedding, funeral, flu, pox, good date, and bad breakup. I'd consider asking them to respect my privacy and not post about my personal business. I could also consider growing two heads—my chances of success would probably be greater.

My family has let me know that the prodigal daughter returning to the sleepy town of Sunset Beach is the biggest news of the year. My aunts Zia Angela and Zia Rosa are seventy-two-year-old identical twins. Angela Rosa and Rosa Angela share a business and a flat in their old age, finish each other's sentences in both English and Italian, and I'm pretty sure, finished off each other's husbands. The aunts are enjoying gloating with their version of, "I Told You So. *Te l'avevo detto*" They knew I'd move back home. Their little town was infinitely better than any big city. No matter that I left over thirty years ago and lived a full and happy life in the big city. My returning now means I've realized the error of my ways, and they've won out in the end. Patience may be my aunts' only virtue. Also cooking, cooking is their virtue.

Ah well, if it's true that there is safety in numbers, then I'll be well protected in Sunset Beach—the upside of a whole ton of relations. I don't remember what it's like to feel safe. I'm hungry for safety. I'm searching for security. I want the warm blanket of family wrapped around me. Also, would not be too shabby to be enveloped in the strong arms of a handsome prizefighter who retired concussion-free. Bodyguards are good, too.

My little chicks have flown the nest. In fact, the nest has been knocked right out of the tree. My overwhelming need for family is probably the answer to the question I keep asking myself about why I'm going backward in life, but at this moment, it feels right. Even if it turns out to be a short stint, I believe returning to my roots will be good medicine.

The rest of the drive north is even blurrier than the past few days have been. There are so many moving parts right now I'm punch-drunk with confusion. I should probably pull off the road to protect my fellow motorists, but the dog and the cat have nearly reached their limit for confinement, and in truth, so have I. This day needs to end. This week, this month, this year needs to end. I need some fresh air to clear my head. I need the lake waves to wash the noise away. I need to ground my feet in the sand of the beach. I need to get drunk. And to have sex. And to sleep like the dead.

Autumn settles over the land earlier up here in cottage country. The maple leaves are burning bright orange and crimson and the birch flaming yellow. It seems every golden farm field is dotted with a tractor, the farmers working round the clock to bring in the crops before the weather turns cold. Carpets of rolling hills are decorated with endless rows of the haybale harvest. The sun is dropping quickly. It'll be dark by the time I reach the lake.

It's been two years since I've stayed overnight in the little cottage, I inherited at the age of twelve when my parents left this earth on a rocket ship blasting off into outer space. Their cherry-red convertible actually flew off a cliff, and my dad always told me that he had rocket engines under the hood of that car, so I'm pretty sure that's exactly what happened.

I regret my timing, wishing I'd gotten my act together sooner and been on the road earlier to arrive at my cottage in daylight. The cupboards will be bare, the fridge unplugged, the heater off, the beds not made up. I need to stop for provisions, aka coffee, but unfortunately, unless things have really changed in Sunset Beach, the grocery store shuts at six o'clock sharp.

The cottage will be encased in an inches-thick quilt of dust, sewn together with cobwebs, and decorated with the shrapnel of hundreds of cracked walnut shells from the family of squirrels that will have taken up residence. Hopefully, the raccoons have squatted elsewhere.

My stomach growls, which is a good sign since I've hardly been able to eat a thing for days. I pull into a McDonald's and order a couple of grilled cheese and a coffee. The menu at the yellow arches is limited for us vegetarians. I'll swing by my cousin Florrie's bakery in the morning and gorge on her fabulous lemon cranberry scones and a frothy cappuccino. My mouth is already watering. The cat is restless in his crate, and the dog is starting to whimper, or maybe that's me doing the whimpering. I can't be sure.

* * *

At the edge of the town of Sunset Beach, I leave the farm fields behind when I turn off the empty stretch of highway. I wind my way past historic clapboard homes, painted pastel shades of blue and green and yellow, that all housed fishermen's families once upon a time in this 1800s harbor. Between the highway and Lake Huron are half a dozen parallel, frequently bisected roads. The closest to the lake and most coveted is Coastline Trail. That's where I'm headed. I take Island Street until I hit it and drive a final quarter mile. Coastline Trail is pitch black, as are most of the cottages at this time of year.

Snippets of the moonlit lake flash between the trees. Even in the dark, and even after all this time, the lay of this land is imprinted indelibly on my brain. Perhaps it's even stamped on my DNA. Four generations of my family lived their lives in this tiny sailing port. I know exactly where I am, and I remember the position of every tree, the shape of each rock. This place smells like home even if it doesn't quite feel like it anymore. Maybe it will in time. Or maybe as Thomas Wolfe wrote, you can't go home again.

I pull onto the scrubby lawn of my yard that serves as a driveway and park. The unlit, uncared-for cabin looks lonely. We'll be a perfect match.

It's a quiet night except for the rhythmic breaking of the rolling waves and the whip-poor-wills chirping on the forest floor. I leash the dog to a tree and leave the yowling cat in the truck until I can get the lights on inside and ensure that my two will be the only animals in residence.

I use the flashlight on my phone to illuminate the lock as I fumble with the keys. Finally, it turns, and my muscle memory kicks in as my hand automatically performs the correct twist, pull, and jar combination that magically unsticks the old door. The hinges complain with their familiar loud creak as they swing inward. I expect to smell damp and dust, but instead, I smell…coffee?

Then, "Surprise!" I'm accosted by the shrillest scream I've ever heard.

Then, "Aahhh!" No, that was the shrillest scream I've ever heard. Or ever made. That one's coming from me. I'm dead.

All the lights blaze on at once, and I'm momentarily blinded. "What the fuck?"

My assailant's laughter is uncontrollable. I think I see the shapes of bodies actually rolling on the floor in the periphery of my vision, which is all the sight I have outside of the white balls of light blocking my pupils. I've been shocked into silence, my lips moving but no sound coming out.

The dog has lost her marbles tied to the tree outside, her frantic barks to protect me reverberating off the lake.

A couple of women wrap their arms around me and do that crying-laughing thing. I still stand, frozen in place, dumbstruck. The white spots in the center of my vision shrink. I'm beginning to make out the faces of my assailants now.

"Oh my God. We are so sorry, but that was the funniest moment of my entire life." My cousin Florrie is weeping with laughter. She dries her happy tears on my T-shirt.

"Your reaction. Your face was priceless. I videoed it. Here, watch.Omg, my stomach hurts." My childhood friend Cordelia holds her stomach. She plays the video, shoves her iPhone in front of my face.

My vision still hasn't recovered enough to see the tiny picture, but the replay of the high-pitched screams is crazy loud and sets the dog off again. I'm quite sure there will be nothing left to find of the cat.

The room comes into focus now, and everything is shiny. My cousin and my old friend have thoroughly cleaned my rickety and neglected little cottage. They've turned the heat on. They've laden the table with plates of homemade sourdough pizzas with fresh pesto, mozzarella, and arugula, plates of salads and breads and sweets. They've covered the kitchen counter with bottles of wine and sparkling crystal glasses and fresh-cut flowers. They've hung balloons from the wooden rafters in the ceiling and strung up a glittery banner across the large lakeside window that says, Welcome Home Gina. They've made up my bed with fresh sheets, and they've even set out bowls of dog and cat food and fresh water on the floor for my pets. They've thought of absolutely everything, and clearly, they've spent hours executing their clandestine plan.

How could anyone be pissed off? I finally allow myself to laugh, too. "You assholes!"

They are family. That makes this home, and I am blessed.

I hug the girls back now. They pour me wine and coffee all at once, and we clink glasses and mugs. I run outside to grab the nerve-wracked dog and carry the traumatized cat in from the car. Both pets are thrilled to be free in the little house they both seem to remember, and after the dog finishes sniffing about and the cat finally emerges from under the bed, they eat and then happily settle down for the night, lulled to sleep by the comfort of the silly giggling and non-stop gibberish of chatting humans.

Florrie, Cordelia, and I ensconce ourselves on the couches and talk. And talk. And talk. Hours pass, and still we haven't even scratched the surface of all there is to share, and that's a beautiful thing. We eat and we drink. And drink. And drink. That actually, is not such a beautiful thing. At least not come morning.

* * *

The sun is up when the girls depart, and I use the walls as support to make my way to the bed. The sheets smell so lovely and fresh that it seems a travesty for me to crawl between them unshowered. However, the idea of actually taking a shower is not something I can wrap my thundering head around at this juncture. I lie down on top of the quilt. Perhaps I'll manage a shower after days of sleep and gallons of coffee and a few bottles of Advil. Then again, this is the hangover of all hangovers. It's possible I may never fully recover. SOS.

* * *

My laptop and cell phone ping away, accosting my senses, offensively announcing the arrival of emails and website comments. Throngs of inconsiderate people are asking me to do things. Like work. These abusive alerts sound like that obnoxious carnival game where bros show off their strength by pounding a sledgehammer to drive a weight up a pole and ring a bell at the top of a tower. I will never drink alcohol again. I swear.

There is a pounding inside of my head and outside of it, too. I mean there is actual pounding. I know this because the pounding outside is causing the dog to bark frantically. This next level of noise in my fragile state is seriously hazardous to my health. I may be in danger of ending up with a fractured skull.

I shamble to the door against my will. How is this happening? And who pounds on people's homes like that? I'm going to open the door to make the noise stop, and I promise I'm going to hate whoever I see standing there more than anyone in the world for the rest of my life.

I do. I open the door, and that stops the pounding, and I do hate the man standing before me. I hate him even more because I think he may be exceptionally good-looking, but it's hard to tell because my eyes are swollen nearly shut, impairing my vision.

Again, I ask what kind of monster shows up at this hour pounding on people's houses, looking this good when the people inside are incapacitated and look like utter poop warmed up and have moved house and road tripped and so haven't showered in two days so that their hair is basically a Brillo pad, one that's been used to scrub a greasy pan? And to top it off, said Brillo-girl has just realized that they are braless in a T-shirt and panties, which circumstance they forgot when they recklessly leaped out of bed and swung their front door open in an effort to prevent the fracturing of their own skull.

Chapter Seven

I don't have the strength to hold the dog back. I'm going to have to let her eat this person. The offensive man kneels down to pet the dog, and she's all over him like a sloppy puppy. Some guard dog. Oh my God, he's a damn dog whisperer, too. Somebody, please shoot me.

I speak, and it pains everywhere. "I hate you, whoever you are." A promise is a promise.

"Good night, bad morning?" His voice is exceptionally deep, like excess testosterone deep. It's the first sound that hasn't hurt my ears this morning. Damn him.

On the off chance that there may be some shred of decency, despite my near nakedness, that I might be able to recover for myself, I offer an explanation, "You know how sometimes your eyes feel gummy as if there's Vaseline smeared over your eyeballs so everything you look at is blurry?" How attractive am I?

The Adonis nods. "I've read about that phenomenon."

Damn it, he reads, too. What are the chances? A good-looking dog lover who reads. This actually makes me hate him more. "Whatever it is you're selling, I don't want any. If there's something else you want, can you please come back when you're not so blurry?"

"Can't do that. I'd feel like I was taking advantage of you."

My brain is a massive cotton ball that has spread into my dry mouth. "I'm so confused."

"Are you Gina Malone?"

"Who wants to know?"

"Hugh McTavish. You're paying me a lot of money to reno your cottage, and the clock started ticking half an hour ago. It's eight-thirty already."

A good-looking, dog lover who reads and is handy. Oprah's Ideal Mate Wish List Quiz that I filled out a decade ago just bound its quarks and leptons together and walked off the page as fully formed matter. Help.

I subtly cross my arms over my chest on the off chance he hasn't yet noticed the flimsy fact that I'm braless. "I'll pay you double if you leave. And oh my God, I didn't think we were starting right away. I just got here last night. Also, I'm not sure that you are really who you say you are because even with blurry vision, I can tell that you don't look like the picture on your website. At all." The photo online was a jolly old Santa type. Everything about this man standing before me is square, broad, upright and lean. His thick dark hair contrasts his silvery beard. He's familiar—I scan my foggy brain trying to place him—the memory of a People magazine cover surfaces. I'm certain Jeffrey Dean Morgan hasn't left Hollywood to reno cottages in the wilds of Canada, so it's safe to say I'm eye to eye with his doppelganger, which is very concerning. Who could resist a Jeffrey Dean Morgan character? When he showed up in *The Good Wife* we all knew Julianna Margulies was going to sleep with him—because she's alive. In *The Walking Dead*, the guy has too many hot wives to count, and alive or dead they all surrender to him. Remember terminally ill, irresistible Denny, in *Grey's Anatomy*? I'm doomed. Hopefully, this clone is happily married.

"That's a photo of my dad on the website. He started our construction company, but I run the business now. He's retired."

I rack my brain to come up with a covert way to conceal my nearly naked bottom half. No solutions forthcoming as of yet. The dog steps in front of me, unfortunately still six inches too short for crotch cover. Will have to attempt to distract with my razor-sharp intellect. "Well, it's kind of false advertising. I didn't know I was hiring a blurry person." Missed that target by a wide mile.

"I'll tell you what. I'll come back after lunch, and we'll go over the plans. That'll give you time to get your eyes cleared up, get some hot coffee in you, and have a cold shower."

If I can pull off sounding indignant, perhaps that will imply that I have some dignity left to offend, after all, they have the same root word. "Seriously? You think you put women in need of a cold shower?"

"No. I think hangovers do, though. See you at one o'clock, Gina Malone." Hugh McTavish disappears.

I close the door as softly as possible, but the hinges still assault me with their screeching creak. If one could truly die from embarrassment, I'd be dead as a freaking doornail by now. I'm the personification of embarrassment, *bare ass* being the root of that word. So far, the opening chapter of my fabulous new life is a complete and utter shit show.

I go back to bed for a couple more hours, then take a shower but not a cold one. I love myself more than that. I wash down a handful of Advil with steamy mugs of coffee at the old dining table, nibble on some dry crackers left over from my surprise party, and watch the waves roll in across the lake, and that, more than anything else, cures my ills. My hangover is slowly ebbing away. I may make a full recovery after all.

The Great Lake shimmers in the sunlight, vaunting its magnificence as if it knows it's the largest body of fresh water in the world. The view through the mullioned kitchen window to the shore, a mere fifty feet away, hasn't changed in as long as I can remember. Tall, crooked cedars forged sideways by wicked winter winds stretch away from the harshness of the water and reach toward the refuge of the cozy cabin. Their broad evergreen branches shade the cottage year-round, and only dapples of sunlight seep through. Near the bunkie stand three sisters of silver birch and a towering, gnarly walnut that spits its huge spiny seeds at the dog whenever she passes beneath it. Lanky beach grasses, that hold the vast and tenacious dunes in place along the coastline, dance sensually in the constant breeze—but rogue rollers of pale gold sand manage to slip away to drift across my scrub-brush yard and creep inside my door at every opportunity. In the offing, flotillas of white sailboats glide into an infinite horizon, and colonies of cawing gulls ride the whitecaps. There'd be no way to know this wasn't the ocean except for the air—instead of salt, it smells of pine and woody pencil shavings, campfires, and wet leaves.

I open my laptop to find way too many ignored emails and notifications. I decide to tackle the letters sent into my column first. Wrong choice. I'm seeing a pattern here with that. I may have to switch careers, which would be a real drag since it's the only thing in my life that hasn't changed in the past few months.

Dear Ex-Whisperer,

I've read all your books. You're definitely anti-cheating and it seems like family is important to you, but maybe it's only your own family you care about. Flirting with other people's husbands is pretty low. Busting up a family is a capital crime in my book—that would be The Book. The only Book. His Book. The Bible. BTW your relationship advice books have some fierce competition. They can't hold a candle to God's advice on love and marriage, so maybe you should just admit defeat. Also, you need to turn in that Ex-Whisperer card of yours. You're not a good friend to other women. You're a husband thief.

P.S. You should wear more than underwear when you open your door to strange men.

Faithfully yours,
  Bible Babe

My confusion with this letter is laced with extreme creepiness which is slowly fingering its way up my spine. I'm not in the habit of answering my door in my underwear. In fact, I'm pretty certain this morning was a first for me. If this letter writer was watching my cottage this morning, why was she there, and how did she know that I am me? How would she connect the nearly naked lady at my door with The Ex-Whisperer website? And fire me off a letter this quickly? Maybe her God told her? She sounds like the type who could be hearing voices. Who the hell is Bible Babe? All this might be too much for my brain even on a good day, but today it's a Code Blue. Somebody, call for a crash cart.

One thing's for certain, there was only one man at my door who saw me in my underwear, so Hugh McTavish must be the hubby this jezebel is accused of attempting to pilfer.

I knew I was moving back to a small town, but the scene here is virtually microscopic. Except for the drama. The drama is monolithic. Drama is what I'm looking to escape from, so my new situation in this locale may not work out for me after all. Drama is what will drive me out of this place faster than anything else. Also, religious fanatics. We've got a double whammy going on here. I don't think it's wise for me to unpack my suitcase just yet.

Dear Bible Babe,

You've got the wrong girlfriend, girlfriend. I don't advocate or condone cheating for anyone, including myself, but nor do I judge. You're slinging a lot of arrows here, and maybe even casting the first stone? Sounds like you and your hubby need to sit down and talk some stuff out, preferably with a counselor, or maybe in your case a pastor at least? Either way, you need to deal with your own garbage and refrain from dumping it on other people's doorsteps. Speaking of doorsteps, why were you spying at mine this morning? That's super creepy and possibly even illegal. Also, I'm staying at the beach. How do you know I wasn't wearing a bikini? BTW, I'm not competing with the Big Man's Book on bestseller lists. We're in different categories. I'm in Self-Help and He's in Fantasy.

Affectionately yours,
    The Ex-Whisperer

I hit Post.

* * *

At 1:01 there's rapping at my door. Still so loud. Is this guy Bamm-Bamm or what? Also, note to self: annoyingly punctual. Also, note to world: married.

I open the door, cringe at the creak of the hinges that still scratch against the inside of my skull like nails on a chalkboard. "First job on the list, can you please make the creaking sound in this door go away?"

"Sure, no problem." Bamm-Bamm is already at the table, spreading blueprints across it. He looks up at me and smiles, also too loud. "You didn't have to dress for our meeting, really."

"I'm sure I'll come up with some snappy retort by tomorrow. Come back then to hear my brilliant reply." I move gingerly to the coffee pot, pour two cups.

"I look forward to it, Gina." He's up for the challenge, takes a seat.

"You're enjoying this a little too much. Not very neighborly of you."

"Perversely, I may be, yes."

"I'm too fragile today to care. Cream?"

"Black, thanks."

I join him at the table.

The coffee is extremely hot, and I marvel at how Hugh McTavish swallows it without flinching. Today I shall only notice small and quiet things that do not tax the brain. I'm also noticing his ropey forearms and admiring them. Swinging a hammer all day long for decades is surely far more effective at building muscle than any pec deck machine at the gym.

Hugh must have noticed my fixation with his forearms. He shifts uncomfortably, pulls his rolled-up sweatshirt sleeves down.

My head is still in too much pain to make room for shame. Conveniently, I seem to be building up an immunity to humiliation. My personal standards have plummeted. I simply shift my gaze to his thick thighs.

"How are the eyes?" I can't tell from his tone whether the question is rooted in concern or pure sarcasm, but based on his one-sided smile, I'm betting on sarcastic.

"All cleared up, thanks. Just suffering from a blurry brain now."

Hugh looks out the window at the rolling waves. "The breeze off the lake will take care of that for you. Best hangover cure there is. Only one I use."

I rally a little sarcasm back over the net toward him. "Local travel tips are always useful. You should post that one on TripAdvisor."

Hugh laughs good-naturedly. It's a nice laugh, warm and deep. Damn it.

He has already drained his cup. I pour him another one. He continues to sip the scalding brew without wincing. Tough guy. "I'm excited to get going on this project. This place is already gorgeous, and I don't want it to lose any of its original charm." He waves his arm at the airy cottage, its hand-hewn timber roof, wide plank floors, and rustic cedar-paneled walls. The kitchen and living area share one space lined by lake-view windows. Two bedrooms and a bathroom run along the back. "We're going to update it to suit your needs but not sacrifice any of the character. I checked out the archives at the library. Your grandfather built this cottage in 1932. He replaced an old log cabin that his grandfather had built on the site in 1856."

"Really? How did I not know that?"

Hugh shrugs and passes me a couple of sepia photos of the original cabin that he's printed off. There is a stern but proud-looking young couple standing in front of their tiny new log home by the lake, holding a baby in a long linen gown and a lace bonnet. "Those are my great grandparents?"

"On your father's side. And the wee one is your Grandad."

I marvel at my roots. Such sturdy folk. "People never smiled in those old photos."

Hugh nods. "Life was hard. But I hate to think there wasn't a lot to smile about."

I run my fingers over the vaguely familiar faces of my ancestors. "Sometimes there's not a lot to smile about in our generation, but we've mastered the art of faking it. Anything for a good selfie."

Now Hugh is shaking his head in disdain, a healthy dose of cynicism is always good. "You never know what anyone's thinking these days. Almost everyone's full of bullshit."

I look into Hugh's eyes, try to get a read. "You too?"

He meets my gaze boldly, confidently. "I said almost everyone. No, not me. I'm bullshit averse. And unbullshitable."

I quickly realize I'm not up for this level of eye contact and break it off immediately. "Good, I'd be worried about the building contract I signed with you."

Hugh laughs, turns to the blueprints. "I'm planning to start with the bunkie that you want to use as your art studio. There's no sink drawn in the plans, but I assume a sink would come in handy for washing up your paintbrushes and whatnot?"

"That's actually a great idea. I thought it would be too complicated to install plumbing in there."

"Not really. I can have the plumber run a line and hook into the one in the cottage. I also figured a toilet would be a good idea in case you ever convert it back to sleeping quarters, and we have to put in a new septic system anyway, so it's not that big a deal. Once the construction on the bunkie is complete, you can sleep in there while we work on the cottage."

"That actually sounds brilliant." I like his ideas. Practical and well thought out.

Hugh stands. "Well, we're good to go then for now. Don't worry. We won't be making too much noise today. Mostly picking up and dropping off materials. The real ripping and banging starts tomorrow, so no partying tonight." Hugh winks. He gathers up his plans and is at the door. "Those photos are for you to keep."

"Thanks a lot, I appreciate that." I'm not sure how to broach the subject, so I fall back on my usual communication style and just blurt it out. "I wanted to mention, your wife . . ."

"I'm not married. Do you mean my ex-wife?"

"Oh maybe. I guess." I'm thrown. "Is your ex-wife aware that the two of you are no longer married?"

Hugh breaks out in a loud laugh. "She's aware but unaccepting."

"As in delusional?"

"Definitely."

"Charming. Did it just happen recently, the divorce, I mean?"

"Nope. Ten years ago."

"Wow, that is one long learning curve. It would seem that this morning, your exish-wife was watching me, well watching you I suppose, and happened to see me half naked at my door in the process. And in my defense, what I was wearing covered more than a lot of bathing suits do these days."

Hugh smiles, shakes his head. "Still, something different about a woman in a bathing suit compared to a woman in her underwear."

I refuse to go down that conversational path. "Anyway, Bible Babe, as she calls herself, wrote a letter to me today and, on the universal stage of the Internet, accused me of trying to steal her husband, which would be you, I assume. She threw the Book at me. The Good Book and basically carried out a public stoning for my inappropriate attire this morning."

Hugh is laughing loudly now. "I am so sorry."

I can find nothing amusing about any of this. "How would your ex-wife even know who I was? She wrote to me right away."

Hugh looks at me surprised. "Everyone in these parts knows who you are, Gina Malone. You're the small-town girl who made it big. The Ex-Whisperer is famous in Sunset Beach."

I roll my eyes. "Thanks to the aunts—fan girls extraordinaire."

Hugh chuckles. "Iris, Bible Babe, is certifiable and pathetic, but I'm pretty sure she's harmless."

I'm not convinced. "Not to one's reputation, I'd venture. My public persona is my business. A person like your ex-wife can cause a lot of damage to careers and to peoples' lives in general."

Hugh stops laughing and distaste registers on his face. "You're actually right about that. I'll go out and talk to her now." Hugh steps out the door and starts toward the road.

I call after him, "You mean she's out there right now?"

"She's never too far away. Don't worry. You'll get used to it and learn to ignore her. I have."

"I'm actually not so great at ignoring deranged people."

Hugh takes long, purposeful strides toward a small silver Nissan parked across the street from my place. I can see a pale and puffy figure at the wheel, bleached blonde hair and oversized, dark sunglasses, sporting that middle-aged, faded and failed wannabe Sunset Strip Starlet sort of look. Before he reaches it, the car speeds off, kicking up a cloud of dust on the dirt road. Hugh throws his arm up after the vehicle, middle finger raised, waves his offending appendage fiercely, and fires off a few curse words in his ex-wife's wake.

I think I've seen this episode of *Desperate Housewives* before. I'm beginning to suspect I may be a meshugener magnet. I can hear my girlfriend Sinead's voice in the back of my head. *"No shit, Sherlock."*

Any way I look at it, I'm pretty certain a serious detox is in order for me, physically, mentally, and perhaps psychically if not a complete freaking exorcism. I know just the place to start. The aunts. Their eggplant parmesan and tarot card lunch combo is what I need to order up for my ailment. I let the dog out for a piddle, then grab my bag and a sweatshirt, and drive into town.

Chapter Eight

At first glance, it doesn't look as if the main drag, High Street, has changed a stitch since I was a kid. It's the classic Ontario small town shopping street with a mix of stately and petite houses tucked into avenues and boulevards behind. But these two-story yellow-brick Victorian buildings selling everything from gourmet breads to spray tans, and freshly caught fish to camping gear, are nestled between a stoplight at the top end of the street, and a hundred- and sixty-year-old lighthouse keeping watch over magical, mystical Lake Huron at its foot. High Street is also not so affectionately referred to as Widow's Walk for the many sailor's wives who wore down trails of dirt and tears, pacing back and forth from their homes to the water's edge. They waited and wailed for their missing husbands, some of them refusing to ever stop searching for signs of life from the thousands of shipwrecks that ran aground on the treacherous granite shoals and disappeared in the blackness of deadly storms. Lethal violence lurks beneath an often gentle and inviting surface—lakes and people can be like that. I love all the vintage store signs and the vintage people behind the counters inside the shops. Even the old movie theatre is still operating with its 1940s marquis advertising a movie that closed in the city six months ago. No blockbusters or big box stores to be found in Sunset Beach. Shop local, y'all. Further along, there are a few new additions which are pleasantly surprising, a yoga studio and juice bar, an organic coffee shop, and a cannabis dispensary with gourmet edibles. Nice. Will hit all of those up in short order. First, I have family obligations to fulfill. Also, a stomach that needs filling.

I park on the street in front of Happily Napoli, the aunts' Italian eatery.

Before I can climb out of my truck, both of my cheerful, zaftig zias have scurried out of their restaurant and descended upon me, pinching my cheeks and rubbing my head as if I were still a cute little eight-year-old. Their pinches sting just as much now as they did then.

"Oh, my Godda. You're for real!" Zia Angela.

"Look at you, still like a baby!" Zia Rosa.

"Just like your mama. Bella, bella."

The twins still dress alike every day—both in mourning black for the husbands they buried decades ago. I can only tell them apart from the crucifixes around their necks, Ange wears yellow gold, Rosa, rose gold. These gals are my mom's older sisters, and they seemed more crushed by the death of their baby sister than by the passing of their life partners. They never quite forgave my mom for marrying an Irishman and have always pitied that "inferior" Irish half of me. Whenever that side of the family comes up in conversation, they click their tongues and share long sideways glances with each other. Never mind that loads of my and my father's Irish kin operate businesses on the same street as the aunts' restaurant and love the aunts dearly.

"No time for your zias anymore. Whatsa matter for you?" Now I get a gentle slap upside the head, kinda playful, kinda not.

"I've been busy, Zia, but I'm here now."

They herd me inside their little restaurant, pull off my jacket, and corral me to sit at a table next to the kitchen. Nothing much has changed in Happily Napoli over the past forty years either except for the wait staff. Still the same red-and-white checkered tablecloths on the tables and faded photos of the Calabrian countryside decorating the dark wood paneling. The other diners hardly notice the fuss. Everyone in town knows how the aunts are, big and loud. No one ever questions them, and for God's sake, no one ever dares tell them no.

Zia Angela leans across the table. "We told you you'd come back home to live. See? The cards never lie." She taps a pocket in her apron where she always keeps a deck of tarot cards stashed just in case someone needs an emergency answer on the spot.

"I've been gone for thirty years, Zia."

Zia Ange wags a finger in my face. "Thirty years is nothing. Joey's been dead for nearly thirty years, and I've barely had time to miss him."

Rosa throws her arms up dramatically, disagreeing with her sister. "Don't listen to Zia Ange. She misses Joey every day." Rosa points an accusatory finger in her twin's face now. "I hear you sniffling in the bathroom at night, Ange. Don't you deny." Loud.

Zia Ange is angry and embarrassed. "It's the sinuses!" Louder.

"*Cazzate!* You're crying over Joey!" Louder still.

Cazzate is Italian for *bullshit*. I think when it comes to the Italian language, my memory has only retained swear words. Did I mention that the aunts love to argue? Loudly? Especially when there's an audience? Is there another way for Italians to speak to each other? Loud is their normal volume level and arguing their normal manner of conversing.

I'd love to change the subject and also maybe get some food. "So how about a menu?"

The aunts both stop in their tracks and stare at me as if I've got horns. There are some hand signs flung around in the air, and two pairs of twisted lips, following which the aunts disappear through the swinging door into the kitchen. I don't get a menu. I get fed. I should have known better than to ask.

The parade of dishes begins. First up, a steaming plate of sausage and peppers. It smells wonderful but...

"Zia, vegetarian. Twenty-five years now. Remember?" I shrug only half apologetically.

"Mama Mia! You didn't grow up out of that phase yet?"

Zia Rosa bustles back into the kitchen, the plate of sausage still in her hand, a trail of Italian curse words in her wake.

Next out, a steaming bowl of linguine with broccolini and mushrooms in a rose sauce. Yummm.

It's followed by crusty bread with olive oil and balsamic dip, salad, and tiramisu with a cappuccino. All of it amazingly delicious.

The aunts tend to their lunch customers and swing back round to my table at every opportunity. They inform every single diner in the place that my real name is Gina Malone, not The Ex-Whisperer. They tell each customer that I am famous, I am their niece; I am divorced; my ex-husband is the devil; they tried to warn me of this before I threw my life away on him; and that my four children are the most brilliant and beautiful bambinos on the planet. They also whisper that I'm a celebrity sex therapist on the internet and that I've moved back home just like they always predicted I would. They slip their fortune-telling business cards in with the bill for each customer.

Tiramisu means *cheer me up* in Italian, and it has—the good food has helped my headache, but I know I'll run out of steam at some point soon. As I shovel my last forkful of ladyfingers, there's a momentary lull in the lunchtime rush, and my Zia's take advantage of the break, pull up chairs at my table. It's no secret, they are dying to know if I'll marry again. Agreeing to have my privacy invaded is the only way I'll ever manage to get out of here. Zia Angela whips out the deck of tarot cards from her apron pocket—Her shuffling skills would put a Vegas Blackjack dealer to shame. She hands the deck to me—my turn to shuffle. I drop half the cards. *"Dio mio!"* Zia Rosa shakes her head in exasperation and snatches up the wayward pentacles and wands.

Zia Angela deftly lays out a Celtic Cross face down on the table. She flips over the Two of Swords. Rosa gasps. Next is the Tower, followed by the Death card.

"Dio ci salvi!" Under her breath, which can basically be heard all the way down the block, Angela asks God to save us.

"Ah cielo!" Rosa is repeatedly crossing herself and kissing the rose gold Jesus dangling from her necklace.

I can't read the cards, but even I know this can't be good. The pictures in the tarot are pretty much self-explanatory. Since the aunts aren't forthcoming in English, I take a flyer on my interpretation of the spread. "Okay, so the next guy I'm going to end up with is going to stab me in the heart, then send lightening to burn down my house, and then kill me? I guess I should've stuck with Dick."

My reading is abruptly halted. Both zias leap into action at once, gathering up all the tarot cards and stuffing them back inside the safety of Angela's apron—all while praying feverishly to Saint Benedict, imploring him to ward off the evil spirits that have obviously followed me into their establishment.

To be honest, I'm a little crushed, I could have used some good news. Also maybe, I'm a little spooked. I mistakenly look to the aunts for support. "It's not all bad, right? The rest of the cards in the spread could have been happy ones."

Niente from the aunts. They look at each other for too long, eyes flashing, then back at me, expressionless. Their stony faces say it all. I'm done for.

Actually, I'm more than worried—I'm weirded out. I don't mean to, and really I should know better, but I can't help but plead, "Come on, give me something here to cheer me up."

"You had the tiramisu." Zia Rosa shrugs. *Whatta ya gonna do?*

Zia Angela looks around the restaurant. Most of the diners are watching us now—they all look extremely nervous for me, too. Angela pulls my chair out. "You're bad for business. Come back tomorrow, and we try again with the cards upstairs in the apartment where no one can see."

Zia Rosa tries to placate me as she gently pushes me toward the door, "Don't worry too much. We say some Novenas for you tonight. Nobody's gonna die. Yet." She tucks a container of leftover spaghetti under my arm. "*Mangia* eat. You're gonna need your strength."

One bum's rush later and I'm standing on a sunny sidewalk feeling anxious and vulnerable. The aunts can have that effect whether they're trying to or not.

My eyes scan the townscape—where can I find a little comfort before I head back to my cottage all alone and hope that nobody's gonna die tonight? And then I spot it—The Bakehouse, my cousin Florrie's fabulous bakery and café. Florrie is from the Irish side of the family. Our fathers were brothers. I scoot across the road to pick up something for tomorrow's breakfast and some shamefully sugary treat to use as a salve for my heebie-jeebies.

The Bakehouse has a gorgeous décor of pink and mint punctuated with white stoneware and black graphics. Hot loaves of sourdough bread are pulled out of a massive brick oven on long wooden boards by seasoned bakers. My eyes scroll down the chalkboard menu and if I wasn't so stuffed with the aunt's pasta, it would be impossible to pass up the thyme, caramelized onion, and white bean pot pie, the wheatberry, and kale lentil soup, and the butternut squash and black bean chili. My mouth waters at the list of delectable offerings and I am acutely aware that my brain has never made the connection between food and hunger. Ginger molasses cookies and perfectly iced brown butter chai cupcakes stare me down but alas, I prevail. I scoop up a loaf of parmesan herb bread and a couple of still warm blueberry scones with zesty lemon glaze off a pine rack and hand them to a young girl behind the counter.

"Is Florrie around?"

The young girl wraps up my goods. "She's sick today."

"Is she upstairs?" Like the aunts and many of the shopkeepers downtown, Florrie lives in the flat above her bakery.

The girl crinkles her nose. "I'm not allowed to say."

I laugh out loud. "Tell her Gina was here and that I'm doing a lot better than she is."

"Oh, are you The Ex-Whisperer?" The salesgirl actually squeals.

I nod my head, mostly apologetically.

The salesgirl is star-struck. "Florrie told me all about you. I have all your Gal Guide books, and I read your Ex-Whisperer column religiously. You're the reason I figured out my boyfriend was cheating on me." She seems thrilled.

"I'm sorry?" I really do ask it as a question.

"No, I was happy I found out. You taught me not to ignore my bullshit detector. Your book *The Ex-Whisperer's Guide to Cheaters and Liars* is a classic and chapter 4, "Top 17 Body Language Signs That He's a Big Fat Liar" was a game-changer for me."

I do my best to smile but am pretty much just dying of discomfort. "Glad I could help." I wish I were in better spirits. I'll make it up to her next time I'm in.

The fangirl/salesgirl watches me excitedly with her wide eyes while she uses long tongs to gather up the goodies I point to on the shelves behind her. When she packs my purchases neatly into a delicate cardboard box, I close my eyes and breathe in the heavenly scents. How is it that baking pastry can smell heartwarming and caramelized sugar can be so reassuring? Unfortunately, for me, it doesn't last. On the heels of soothing childhood aromas, I sniff a whiff of fear. Unease creeps back into my senses, and the cheeriness of my hometown bakery is ruined by the sour odor of dread.

I pass the girl a twenty, and she hands me my baked goods in a pretty pink-and-mint paper bag. I peek inside it to make sure my date square and butter tart are safely packed. I'm hoping a sugar stupor will induce some serious brain fog to take the edge off my thoughts. Depressingly, I may have to mainline fructose syrup to get this creepy crap out of my head.

The drive back to the cottage is healing. I keep the windows down to let the balmy breeze in. It's warm today, more like August than September. The scent of the freshly cut hay from the surrounding farm fields has drifted downwind to the lakeshore. I inhale deeply to fill my lungs with the sweet air.

When I reach my road, my hackles go up, and I'm on the lookout for:

1. My crazy ex
2. My reader/follower, Lillian's crazy ex
3. My contractor's crazy ex

I'm not called The Ex-Whisperer for nothing. I've definitely got a CV heavy in hands-on experience. Being a Whisperer implies that one has the ability to tame the thing one whispers to. Not all exes can be tamed, but they can be handled correctly. Personally, I'm most partial to the tried-and-true method of You Are Dead to Me. That one never fails. Everyone knows where they stand. You know what they say: we teach best what we most need to learn. And in that regard, I've gotta have a flaming PhD in exes by now.

I pull onto the scrubby front lawn of my neglected little cottage, soon to have a serious facelift. Thankfully, there is no sign of anyone's ex in the immediate vicinity. Also, no sign of my contractor although he has left neat piles of fresh lumber next to the hurting old bunkie. Off to the side and closer to the road than the cottage, the small structure was built to house a constant overflow of overnight guests. The weathered clapboard cabin has seen better days—all it needs is a little love and care—join the club.

Zoe is whining inside the cottage, so I hurry to unlock the door for her.

I step inside and realize that the whining is actually coming from outside the cottage and around the back. I step out again and walk around to the lake side of the house to see who's crying.

Wtf? A little white dog is tied to one of my birch trees. He's yapping and jumping up now, clearly distressed. I bend down to pet him, then walk toward the water to check in case his human is at the beach. If so, they really should not be trespassing on my property and leaving their dog tied up in my yard while they go for a dip. The uneven cedar steps dug into the path that lead to the beach are slippery with moss, and wayward roots and vines purposely try to trip me up. Everything here is crying out for care and attention including the tiny dog. And me.

The long and broad sandy beach runs for miles. It's empty in both directions. Tourist season is over, and aside from the next few weekends in October, and only then if the days are extra warm and sunny, it's just townies around here now. Townies don't come down to the beach on cold weekdays.

Hopefully, there's a phone number on the pup's collar. I cross back to the dog to check. He's looking frantic now. Zoe is barking like mad inside the cottage. Through the kitchen window, she can see the tiny canine jumping all over me. When I kneel next to the scared little dog, he can't sit still for trying to leap into my arms. I don't see a phone number, but the dog has a name engraved on a metal medallion hanging from his rhinestone-studded collar.

Snowflake.

Chapter Nine

Snowflake. The name of Lillian's dog. I don't know Lillian's last name, so I can't search for her on Facebook or anywhere else online, but I remember that the profile picture on her emails was of a dog.

I'm pulling that up on my laptop now. And there it is. Lillian's Snowflake looks identical to the Snowflake curled up on my lap in my kitchen, the little white dog that was left tied to a tree in my yard. What the hell? Shivers slither up my spine. This is no coincidence. Lillian's husband has found me. The most unsettling part—I have no idea what he looks like. Was he the man-bun slurping minestrone at the table across from me in Happily Napoli today? Was he the shaved head, tattooed punk ordering petit fours next to me in the bakery? Did he walk along behind me on the sidewalk in town after tying Snowflake to the tree in my yard? Is he still in town? Is he still in my yard?

I snatch up my phone and call Hugh, who picks up on the first ring. "What's up, Gina?"

"You were at my place this afternoon, right?"

"Sure. We've been coming and going all day."

"Did you happen to notice a little white dog tied to a tree in my yard?"

"No. Is it alive?"

"Of course, it's alive. I'm sure I would sound a lot more upset if it wasn't."

"Point taken."

"Did you happen to notice anyone other than your freaky ex-wife skulking around the premises today?"

"Nah. It wouldn't be her, though. Bible Babe is afraid of dogs."

"Figures. I don't like people who don't like dogs. Anyway, I think I know who owns the dog. I was just wondering whether you saw the person who left it here."

"Sorry I can't help. If you know who the owner is, can't you return the dog to them? Or call them up and give them crap at least?"

"I wish. I don't know their last name or where they live. I just sort of know them online. Thanks anyway." I hang up.

Zoe is acting out a little, getting jealous of tiny Snowflake. She's not great with other dogs at the best of times and moving house coming on the heels of being boarded for two weeks is a lot of change for my big fur baby to process. Hell, it's too much for me to deal with. I don't entirely trust Zoe with nervous little Snowflake, a fraction of her size. And I definitely don't trust the cat, even on a good day. We don't call Spook the Prince of Darkness for nothing. I put Snowflake in my bedroom and close the door because I need to think, and I won't be able to do it if there's a pet explosion. Right away, I hear the old mattress springs squeak as the little guy jumps up onto my bed. Zoe curls up at my feet under the kitchen table and gets some extra belly rubs.

I need to find Snowflake a place to stay while I sort out this situation. I can't ask the aunts. They have matching twin Chihuahuas, Peppita and Peppeto. Those dogs are like having two little budgies that never stop screeching. I mean never. The aunts dress the Chihuahuas alike the same way they dress themselves. I'm a dog person, and in truth, Peppita and Peppeto are cute, but they're also the real reason I don't spend much time at the aunts' place. I'm pretty sure Merriam-Webster has photos of these dogs under the word *annoying*.

I dial Florrie. "Hey, gal. If you're not up, please get up. And get over here ASAP after you're finished work. Weirdly, a dog has been abandoned in my yard. You interested in fostering for a bit? Or know someone who can? Call me when you get this. Thanks."

I can always count on Florrie. I know she'll show up as soon as she can. Truth be told, I wouldn't mind some company. I don't want to freak myself out, but I don't relish the thought of being alone tonight. I don't know if

Lillian's husband plans on popping back over for a chitchat.

I stare out the window at the lake to see whether it holds any answers for me.

First question, how does Lillian's creepy husband know where I've moved to? I suppose I'm not untraceable online. I suppose if someone figured out where I last lived, and they knocked on some of my old neighbors' doors, they might find out that I moved up to Sunset Beach. But the person who dropped the dog off in my yard figured out exactly where I live on the first day I arrived here. That's some efficient detective work. Unless the guy found his way to my aunt's Italian restaurant, of course, in which case he would know every intimate detail of my personal life before he even finished his ravioli. I shudder again at the thought that this man could have been there, watching me.

Next question, why would a person who doesn't even know me leave their dog with me? It couldn't have been Lillian. This dog was her main concern when she was considering going to a shelter. I don't think she would abandon her pet just anywhere. Maybe the shelter wouldn't let her keep Snowflake there? But wouldn't Lillian leave a note or get some sort of message to me asking me to take care of her dog until she gets herself sorted? Lillian said she didn't have any friends or family in the country. She could have chosen me because she didn't have anyone else who she could trust with her fur baby, but I think that's a stretch.

Makes more sense that it was her demented hubby. He did promise to track me down after all. It looks as if he succeeded. I sure hope I'm wrong. It's not dark out yet, but I get up to turn the lights on. I'm not doing so great in the not-freaking-myself-out department. I pour myself a glass of water to hydrate my gray matter. I'm perplexed—perhaps pacing will help.

I walk back and forth across the slanted kitchen floor, sipping my H20. Why would Lillian's husband leave me his wife's dog? And how would he get his hands on Snowflake in the first place? I doubt Lillian left the pup behind when she bolted, but of course, anything is possible. If Lillian returned home, her hubby might be punishing her for having left him by giving her dog away. She said he had threatened to do that. But why would he give the dog to me? Maybe he wants to let me know that he has Lillian back and that he's in control again. I hate the thought of that whack job being anywhere near me. Hopefully, he did what he needed to do, made his warped statement, feels as if he's won in our little online argument, and is long gone now. I'm sure I'll hear from Lillian soon. Poor Lillian, poor Snowflake. Poor me, the conversations I have with myself can be so exhausting. Wish I knew where I packed my essential oil diffuser. I could use a hit of patchouli and ylang-ylang right about now.

I answer a flurry of texts from my kids, letting them know that the pets and I have settled in at the cottage just fine. I leave out all the worrisome parts about crazy exes and abandoned dogs and drunken mothers answering their doors half-dressed.

I hear a car door slam. Both dogs are barking. I know who it is by the high-pitched singing of one of the irritating hits from *Hairspray* complete with snapping fingers.

Florrie bursts in, now clearly hangover-free, with bags of baked goods and a warm asparagus gorgonzola quiche from her shop for us to enjoy. She's a dream. "Dinner!"

I release Snowflake from the bedroom, and both dogs throw themselves at Florrie and not just because she smells like food. Florrie is a dog magnet. She squeals over the fluffy white poodle-ish new addition to the household. "Oh my God! You're so cuuute!"

I do the intros. "Snowflake, meet your crazy new foster mommy."

"What kind of degenerate would dump a dog?" Florrie is super pissed, but her voice instantly switches back to baby talk when she scoops Snowflake up into her arms. "And one as sweet as you, tooooo." She breaks out into another track from *Hairspray*, "Good morning Baltimore," and swirls around the kitchen floor, tiny white dog tail swishing through the air and loving every beat.

"Nobody I want to know." Zoe presses against my legs, and I scratch her scruffy head. At ninety pounds, she doesn't make the best dance partner, but she's great at cuddles.

Florrie shoots a lethal side-eye. "Somebody I want to kill." She sets

Snowflake down on the floor. "I'll take this cutie for a while. No problem. But who do you think left him here, anyway? Why wouldn't they just drop the dog at the Humane Society in town if they didn't want him?" Florrie gets busy putting out the food. She's all about the food. Come to think of it, everyone in my family is all about the food. I'm extremely grateful for being born into that.

"I think they wanted me to have him." I put the kettle on, sample the sugar cookies with pastel-colored icing Florrie has already laid out on a plate.

Florrie looks surprised. "Why would you think that? Do you know who these lowlifes are?"

"I have a vague idea."

"Why would they want you to have him? And why wouldn't they just knock on your door and ask you to take the dog, then?" Florrie's eyes are narrowing skeptically.

I shrug. "Those are good questions, but I haven't figured out any of the answers yet."

"Have you figured out if there's anything good about any of this?"

I nod. "I'm thinking there's not."

Florrie pours us each a glass of rosé. "Yikes."

"Yup." My stomach flips. "And I've got the kettle on. I can't do wine."

"It's sparkling. You're fine."

I light the candles on the kitchen table, and we sit, Snowflake on Florrie's lap, Zoe on my feet.

The sun is dropping, but it won't be completely dark for another hour or so. The boastful sky struts its stuff with streaks of pink and purple, admiring its own reflection in the mirror of the Great Lake Huron. This magnificent occurrence is a regular cinematic display that has earned this sleepy tourist town a place in the Guinness Book of World Records for top three spots with the most spectacular sunsets on the planet. In an homage to the town's Scottish roots, on summer nights, a bagpiper in full uniform of kilt and blazer stands at the foot of the long fishing pier and pipes the sun down. The eerily beautiful sound of the likes of "Amazing Grace" playing against the backdrop of nature's otherworldly abstract art is one of the best things ever to calm a mind and ground a spirit. But I'm still unsettled. My thoughts are a jumble of knots laced with eeriness. I just can't turn them off.

Florrie serves up a large slab of warm gooey quiche onto two plates and nestles a colorful tossed salad next to both. I didn't realize I was hungry until the delectable smells of Florrie's gourmet cooking triggered my suddenly happy hypothalamus. We dig in.

I'm literally inhaling the food. "Thanks, gal, this is delicious."

Florrie is not focusing on her food, but rather is clearly bursting at the seams with curiosity. "Sooo . . . ?"

"So?" I'm not twigging at all.

"Sooo, how did it go with Hugh today?"

Shocked and speaking with my mouth full, coughing a few crumbs across the table, I answer, "I thought you were asleep all day. How do you even know Hugh was here?"

"The whole town knows Hugh was here."

"Oh my God. The aunts?"

"Between them and Iris. Word got around in about two seconds flat. Even the last couple of offseason tourists hanging out on the main beach know about it by now."

"Is that her name, Hugh's ex-wife? Iris? How has she not been arrested? She's stalking the man."

"That's true, but Hugh isn't one to make a fuss. He mostly just ignores her."

"I don't understand how he can. She sits in her car and watches him on his jobsites, did you know that? That's disturbing as crap." I pause only to shovel another oversized mouthful of field greens into my piehole. Stress eating. "I'll tell you one thing—I'm sure not going to ignore Iris if she tries to make a habit of hanging around my place. She wrote some nasty, quasi-religious post on my website today. Called herself Bible Babe. She's a card-carrying freak." Stress drinking the wine now.

"Half the town would agree with you—all those on Team Hugh. Hugh, however, believes Iris is harmless."

I'm astonished. "He's a traitor to his own team?"

"Sort of."

"I'm not so sure she's harmless, myself." Okay, sudden realization, I actually cannot do the wine, bubbles or no. I set the glass down, push it away, and pour the tea.

Florrie tops up my wine glass anyway. "Me either. She's definitely not good for business. She's got a gob that never stops gossiping. Spreading false rumors is her forte."

"About you and your bakery?" I'm shocked.

Florrie nods. "Iris led a campaign a few years ago trying to ban Easter chicks and bunnies in town. She said they were blasphemous. She wanted me to make cookies shaped like human hands and feet with strawberry jam oozing out of holes in them."

I involuntarily spit a cherry tomato across the table.

"I didn't cave to the reverent pastry push, so Iris no longer frequents my establishment, nor do any of her freaky church lady friends, and to be honest, I am perfectly fine with that."

"Did anyone in town make the scary Easter cookies?"

"Yup, the Silver Star Café. Small children ran screaming through the streets when they saw their window display. The crucifix cookies weren't a big seller, so Iris and her flock bought them all up to serve at coffee time after their Sunday church services."

Can't help it, my lips have curled in disgust. "How did Hugh end up with a dingbat like her?"

Florrie is slightly reprimanding. "You're not exactly one to point fingers."

Sadly, she's right.

"Hugh and Iris's messy divorce was the greatest drama to hit the shores of Sunset Beach since old Granny Sykes shot her husband in the foot for snoring too loud. Their break-up divided the town right down the middle. Iris spent two years actively recruiting team members for her side, but really the only followers she ended up with were the people from her whackadoodle congregation. And all the businesses they support. Hugh doesn't get any work from that lot, let me tell you, nor does he want it."

Florrie is having no trouble with ingesting more alcohol. "Speaking of

Hugh—what do you think? He looks like the hot guy from *The Walking Dead*, am I right? The guy with the smile. Do you know who I mean?" Florrie is getting excited. She points a finger in my face. "Oh, oh—he's the same guy Julianna Margulies sleeps with at the end of *The Good Wife*, too! Do you watch that?"

Fork drop for emphasis. "Cripes, we're not dating. He's working for me. And I've talked to him for a total of fifteen minutes since we met for the first time today."

My attempt to divert this line of questioning is failing. Florrie is still leaning across the table in my face, waiting expectantly for me to acknowledge the fact that my contractor does look like a hot Hollywood celebrity.

I acquiesce. "He does kind of look like Jeffrey Dean Morgan, though, you're right there. He was Denny in *Grey's Anatomy*, too. Do you remember him?"

Florrie's eyes instantly well up. "Oh my God! The gorgeous heart patient who proposed to Katherine Heigl and then died when she was at the hospital prom and then he came back later as a ghost and haunted her?"

"That's him." I nod somberly. That storyline was a real heartbreaker.

Florrie wails a little, "I can't!"

A respectful moment of silence for the dead fictional character and then a quick recovery. Florrie is nothing if not persistent. "So hypothetically speaking, what do you think of Hugh slash Jeffrey? Humor me."

"Hypothetically speaking, I am one hundred percent positive that the man is not interested in me romantically, nor will he ever be. I didn't exactly make the greatest first impression at our meeting this morning."

"Yeah, I heard."

"You've got to be kidding me, this town." Shaking my head in disbelief. "Anyway, Hugh's not quite the world's finest catch himself." Regardless, images of Hugh slash Jeffrey's broad shoulders and devilish grin flicker across my mind's eye.

Florrie disagrees emphatically. "What are you talking about? He's a great guy, and he's also hot as hell." Florrie lifts her glass to the hot contractor.

"He's also a hot mess, saddled as he is with that freaky ex-wife of his. That's one heavy piece of baggage I'm not willing to lug around ever, for anybody, nor stand by and watch anyone else lug around. I'm too old and wise to take on that crap. Thank God."

Florrie's voice has an obvious trace of sarcasm in it. "Everyone's got baggage, but yeah, I get that. Poor guy, though. Tragic that he's branded because of a crappy ex." Florrie looks pointedly, accusingly even, in my direction. "Bet Hugh might be able to say the same thing about you if he ever met your Lil' Dick." Florrie presses her half-empty wine glass hard against her lips, tries to suppress her laughter but then bursts out anyway, and I have to join in.

Lil' Dick is what I call my ex-husband in The Gal Guide books. "I guess you're fricking right there. Maybe Hugh and I do have a lot in common after all."

Florrie raises her glass. "A toast to all the twisted mofo exes out there. We've all got a few packed away in those old suitcases. Baggage be damned."

I raise my glass too, clink, and wink. "And some of us had to saw our exes into little pieces to fit their bodies inside those bags. I'm fairly sure that's what the aunts did with their husbands."

Florrie is nodding exaggeratedly. "I've seen those harmless-looking biddies at work in that kitchen of theirs. They've got some seriously sharp knife skills."

We both scream with laughter now.

The night sky has settled over the lake, and it's a dark one with the moon hidden behind a blanket of clouds.

Florrie serves up more of her amazing asparagus quiche. "Heard Hugh saw you in your underwear when you answered the door half-naked this morning. You decided to throw the third date rule right out the window, huh?"

"Oh, my frickin' God. Well, that has to have come from Bible Babe because the aunts sure weren't lurking around here at eight-thirty this morning."

A text alert sounds on my phone.

Florrie, "You can go ahead and check that. Maybe it's the kids."

"No, it's okay. It's the middle of the night in Europe now. I was texting with them earlier. They're all good. I'm absolutely stuffed, girl. That was amazing."

Leaping up, Florrie grabs a signature pink-and-mint box from her bakery off of the kitchen counter and holds it out to me. "Miso Chocolate Chunk cookie?"

"I have absolutely zero room for food but yes of course. Is that a trick question?" Me and desserts have a love-hate relationship. I'm pretty certain I have cow-like internal anatomy with a separate stomach for sweets. My name is Gina Malone, and I am a sugarholic. I'm too devoted to confections to ever give them up. This is evidenced by thirty-five solid years of failed New Year's Resolutions.

The text alert on my phone repeats and repeats.

Florrie raises her eyebrows. "That's a lot of messages. You'd better check them, Gina. Maybe it's Snowflake's owner trying to get a hold of you."

I hadn't thought of that. "That would be great." I stand to pick up my phone. "Just one message, sent five times." I open it and read it.

Florrie looks up at me. "Who's it from?"

I look out the pitch-black squares that the windows of my cottage have become since nightfall. "From someone who says they're watching us right now."

"What? Who is it? Iris?"

I look back at the phone screen. "The number's blocked."

Florrie scoffs, "No way. No one's watching us out here. Someone's pulling your leg. The dogs aren't even barking."

It's true the dogs are sleeping soundly, but I hold the phone out to Florrie, my fingers prickling with adrenaline. "They describe exactly what we're wearing and what we're eating. Even the cookie you just handed me. There's someone outside the cottage right now."

Chapter Ten

I t's so surreal I feel as if I'm in a daze, and I wonder why I'm not rushing to check the locks on the door and draw the curtains closed. Maybe I'm finally completely out of adrenaline. Maybe my fight or flight mechanism has fled my system once and for all. Who could blame it? It's been taxed to the max. I wish I could flee from me, too. FML.

Florrie jumps up, crosses to the window that looks onto the road. "What the heck do they want? Tell them to come to the door and show their face. I'd love to meet them with a cast-iron fry pan in my hand." Clearly, Florrie has enough fight in her for the both of us. Thank DNA for spunky genes.

Florrie is making an exaggerated Bring It sign with her arms in front of the window to anyone who may be watching. At last, the necessary hormones circulate through my veins. I find my feet, move toward Florrie, and push my way in front of her to close the curtains. Zoe is growling now. Snowflake joins Spook under the bed to shudder in unison.

Florrie crosses from the window to the door. "I'm going out there. This a-hole's ass is grass."

Rationale has settled over me, an imperative counterbalance to Florrie's feistiness. I grab the door handle before she can. "No, you're not." I twist the lock. My brain is back on track. Thanks for kicking in, limbic system.

Florrie gives her head a shake. Her common sense returns with a thump. "Yeah, okay, you're right. You don't bring a fry pan to a gunfight."

Okay, so not all her common sense has returned. It's up to me to de-escalate. I take Florrie by the shoulders to calm her down. "No one said anything about guns. The person probably doesn't have any sort of weapon.

74

Let's keep our cool."

Florrie's eyes are darting about wildly, her breathing quickening. "Who knows what this Peeping Tom is armed with? We'd better call Floyd at the station house."

I press my back against the door to keep frantic Zoe from scratching the crap out of it any further. "The cops aren't going to do anything. The guy will be long gone before they get here."

"It's worth a try. Maybe the cops will see him taking off and catch him. What else are we going to do?"

Florrie pulls out her cell. I notice that her hands are shaking, sort of like Snowflake's entire body. Her last bits of bravery are slipping away with each second that passes, thankfully my courage is returning and doubling down. We're a good team, I strengthen when she wavers, she feeds me when I waver.

Florrie's voice has risen an octave. Who would do this?"

The only thing shaking on my body at this moment is my head. I am truly perplexed. "The list of suspects is growing." I'm trying to gather my wits about me, but they split instantly when I see the next text that comes in.

Even the quiet ding of my phone makes Florrie jump. "Is that him again?" Florrie bites her bottom lip.

I nod and read the message aloud, "*You can let me in now or let me in later, but believe me when I tell you, you will give me what I came for.*"

Florrie moves to press her back against the door with me, her voice cracks. "Oh my God. Who is this maniac?"

My mind is cracking. "Okay, call the cops."

Florrie makes a few mistakes in dialing, has to correct, but moments later, her cell is ringing through to the police. We wait silently, the only sound a low and steady growl gurgling up from Zoe's larynx. Suddenly, the stillness is broken by a loud thudding on my door reverberating against the backs of our skulls. We both leap away from it, involuntarily shrieking. Florrie drops her phone on the floor. Zoe charges for the door, frantically barking as loud as she can, throwing herself against the old wooden frame. Florrie snatches a heavy pot off the top of the stove to arm herself.

I yell out, "What do you want?"

"It's Hugh."

Florrie and I look at each other. So confused. So shook. So pissed.

I can barely see. "What the hell?"

Florrie shakes her head wildly. "No, he wouldn't have done this. Not Hugh."

Florrie throws the door open, breathing heavily, deadly kitchen utensil in hand. "What were you thinking, Hugh? You scared us half to death."

Hugh smothers a snicker. "I'm sorry. It's not that late, but I wanted to let you know it was just me outside. Ryan couldn't remember if he locked up the bunkie, and we've got tools and materials inside, so I came back to check on it."

"That was not a funny joke." Florrie sets her weapon down with a thud.

Hugh's arms are out, palms up, professing his innocence. "What joke? What are you talking about?"

Florrie is absolutely livid. "Did you text Gina and say that you were watching us from outside?"

Hugh is offended by the question. "What? Of course not. Why would I do that?" And then he is immediately, instinctively protective. "Why? Did somebody actually text that to you?"

I nod. "Just a few minutes ago, and they described what we were wearing and doing. There was somebody here watching us through the window."

And with that Hugh is out the door at a breakneck pace.

Florrie yells after him, "For God's sake, Hugh, don't kill anybody." She slams the door shut. Then opens it again, calls out, "And don't get killed, either."

He yells back, "Lock the door."

She slams it again, locks it this time.

Hugh circles the house and moves through the surrounding woods using the flashlight on his cell to flush out the Peeping Tom. We watch through the kitchen window, then move into the bedroom, visually following him around the property. In one hand, his phone broadcasts his location like a beacon, in the other, a sawed-off two-by-four swings at the ready.

Florrie picks up her cell from the floor. "Should I still call Floyd?"

"Let's wait and see what Hugh finds out there."

A loud smash, like crushing metal, breaks the stillness of the night. A man yells out and tires squeal as a vehicle takes off down the road.

"Okay, call the cops!" With Zoe at my heels, I run outside, round the corner of my cottage, and smash headlong into Hugh. I scream, fall backward, but he grabs my shoulders to keep me upright and only just barely succeeds.

Seconds later, Florrie reaches me with her cast-iron pot held high and ready to swing. Hugh and I both throw our arms up in self-defense. When she sees us, Florrie drops her heavy pot. "Holy smokes, what happened out here?"

Hugh, "Indoors you two. Hurry up." Florrie picks up her pot. Hugh firmly guides us back to the door of the cottage.

All three of us and the dog rush back inside. I try to look around on my way, but there's nothing to be seen in the dark night.

Hugh locks the door behind us.

Florrie clasps her frypan tightly against her chest. "What was the crashing sound?"

Hugh's voice is steady and serious. "There was somebody out there alright. When I finally saw him, he was running for his car. He hit a tree backing up to turn around on the road. He's not from around here."

"How could you know that?" That's an important deduction that surprises me.

But Hugh is sure of himself. "Because he hit that tree. He doesn't know these roads."

It wouldn't make sense to an outsider, but I believe Hugh knows what he's talking about. "Are you sure it was a male? Could it have been Iris?"

Hugh looks shocked at that suggestion. "Absolutely not. I didn't see the face, but it was definitely a guy. Average height and build. He was driving a small black or navy car. Couldn't make out any other details in the darkness. He was moving really fast."

A small black or navy car. My blood runs cold. A small dark car is what my uninvited guest drove on the last night I spent in my house before moving.

It must be the same person.

Florrie paces, her nerves clearly worn thin. "Should we call Floyd now?"

Hugh's calm voice is comforting. "You can if you like. There's not much he'll be able to do tonight, but in the morning, there may be paint chips on the tree the guy hit. Maybe he even dropped some belongings out there. We'll be able to take a good look around in the daylight."

I really don't want to go over any more of this tonight. My nerves are shot, too. "It's late, Florrie. Let's wait for tomorrow. I'll go talk to Floyd in the morning. I need some sleep now. My head is pounding."

Florrie sags as if she's equally exhausted. "I'm staying here with you tonight."

"Won't argue with you." I was hoping she'd suggest that.

Then Hugh, too, offers his services. "I can hang out here, as well, if it makes you two feel better."

Florrie, without hesitation, "Sure. That sounds great."

Me, imagining tomorrow's headlines in the *Sunset Beach Tribune* if Hugh spends the night at my place, "I think we'll be okay, but thanks for the offer."

Hugh nods, smiles. He understands. "I'll be back at eight in the morning, then. If you need me in the night, if anything weird happens, or you just get creeped out, call. My farm's only a fifteen-minute drive away. I can probably make it here in ten if I have to."

I wave goodbye, smile back at him. "Thanks. See you in the morning." Smiling hurts my head.

"Lock it up tight." Hugh closes the door firmly behind him.

I do lock it up. And check it twice.

Still cradling her heavy frying pan, Florrie announces, "Going to sleep with this baby by my side tonight. Never a dull moment since you rolled back into town, Gina."

"Ugh. I've been thinking the same thing. Maybe I'm cursed." I pull the rest of the curtains shut and switch off the lights.

Florrie yanks an extra blanket off the couch, heads toward the second bedroom. "Ask the aunts. They'll be able to tell you if you've been hexed. Maybe Lil' Dick has put the evil eye on you."

"The aunts are probably the ones who brought the curse on me. One of their well-meaning love spells gone wrong." Too tired to pull the sheets back, I flop onto my bed.

Florrie's last words before she passes out for the night are still on the dark art of magick. "Wingardium Leviosa!"

One moment, I'm chuckling, probably a result of delirium, and the next, I'm unconscious.

* * *

My cell phone rings in the middle of the night, waking me from a dead sleep. I fumble for it, always a little panicked when this happens because there is the potential for horrible news when your phone rings in the middle of the night. Usually, it's not an emergency, but only a wrong number, and I always pin my hopes on that possibility. "Hello?"

No response, but someone is on the line.

Me again, "Hello?"

Him, muffled and menacing, "I saw the dog."

It's a man's voice. An angry man's voice.

"Who is this?" I check the screen of my phone, which reads Private Caller.

His scratchy voice claws at my ear. "You've got my wife's dog. Which means you know where my wife is. I was right about that. So, you wanna tell me where she is now, or you wanna tell me in person when I visit you next? To be honest, I wouldn't mind seeing you again. You're smokin'."

I'm sitting upright in bed now. "Listen to me. I don't know where Lillian is. She didn't give me her dog. Someone dropped it off when I wasn't home. I've never even met your wife."

"Okay, so just to be clear, I'm hearing you tell me that you are choosing option number two. Is that correct?"

My speech is getting way too loud, and I'm acutely aware that I do not sound unafraid. I'm trying to state the facts, but it'd be easy for someone to think I was lying since my voice has become high-pitched and my breathing shallow. "What are you talking about? I'm telling you that I don't know where your wife is. I can't help you."

The louder I get, the quieter he becomes, and the quieter he gets, the more sinister he sounds. "Okay, then, what I said. You're choosing option number two. I'll come back for another visit when your boyfriend isn't around, and you can tell me where my wife is when we meet in person. Fine by me. Actually, looking forward to it. You're pretty damn sexy."

I borderline shriek, "No, it's not fine, and I have absolutely nothing to tell you! Do not come around my home again. I will call the police next time and have you arrested."

The man laughs louder than he spoke, and then he hangs up.

I put the phone down and start when I notice a shadowy figure standing in the doorway of my bedroom.

Florrie shakes her head, her hand pressed tightly over her mouth in disbelief and fear, her eyes the size of dinner plates. "Holy moley. That guy sounds scary." She climbs into the bed and curls up next to me, her frypan lodged between us.

"Yeah, he does. We might need one of the aunts' banishing spells after all."

Chapter Eleven

One of the best things about waking up at a cottage is the sounds that wake you. Gently lapping waves, sweetly chirping birds, the welcome beep of the ready coffee maker. However, when one is renovating a cottage, one is regularly awakened by the shriek of saws, the pounding of hammers, the piercing squeal of drills. Such is my life. When it's not being threatened, I'm contemplating ending it myself.

I stumble out of bed, feeling my way toward the coffee maker. I've gone to the trouble of pulling on bottoms today, just in case my contractor comes banging on my door again and the paparazzi are about.

Pleasant surprise, Florrie has beaten me to the kitchen, has the coffee on and a lovely breakfast prepared for the both of us. Okay, life is not so bad after all. I'll give it another go.

I pull up a chair at the perfectly worn pine table. "Thanks for breakfast, girlfriend. And for the backup last night."

"Anything for you, cuz." Florrie passes me a buttery croissant and a bright little pot of raspberry jam.

I like watching the sunlight dance across Florrie's golden locks. She's strawberry blond with the perfect sprinkling of faint freckles across her nose and cheekbones. She's a pure Irish lass. She has our family's trademark wavy hair. Not a single female in our brood has straight hair, and every last one of us wishes she did. We're all athletically built, but Florrie is a little curvier, an extra ten pounds of softness that suits her perfectly. I got a heavy dose of the Italian genes, olive skin, green eyes, and a penchant for pasta. You'd be hard pressed to peg the two of us as blood relatives based on our physical attributes.

"So just to clarify, the guy on the phone at three a.m. was for sure the same guy who texted that he was outside watching us last night right?" Florrie pours steaming java into a large mug and passes it to me. Bless her.

I'm nodding. "He claimed responsibility for the peeping, so yes, same guy."

Florrie is nodding along with me now. "And this Peeping Tom is Snowflake's dad, your reader Lillian's husband, and he's threatening to come back to pay you another visit when you're alone. Correct?"

Me still nodding, eyes still only half-open. I happily swallow scorching-hot coffee, not caring that it burns because it's so damn good, and I need it so damn much.

Florrie seems intent on waking me up to more than just the day. "Okay, so that can't happen. You do know you need to file a police report, right? It's stupid not to. This is serious business. You should also stay in town until this guy has made tracks. I've got a comfy pullout and lots of room for the pets. So it's all settled, then. Pack your bag. You're coming with me."

I can't help but smile at my well-meaning cousin with her Great Lake of a heart. "Thanks for the offer. And I will think about it. I don't know that I'm going to file an official police report, but I will go in to talk to Floyd today about it all. I promise."

Florrie's normally sunny face looks more like a dark rain cloud at the moment. "It's not safe for you to stay out here until after the cops catch this asshole. If you refuse to stay in town, then I have to sleep out here with you, and to be honest, I'd prefer not to. It's freaking freaky around here right now."

"I hear you. I'm not going to put either of us at risk. I just need to sort some of this stuff out today. I'm going to go see Floyd right after I fuel up with another couple of mugs of your life-giving coffee."

Immediately, Florrie pours me more of the brew as if to hurry me up. "I think Floyd has gone fishing for a few days, but Lloyd will be manning the station house."

"Floyd and Lloyd, right. How many sets of twins are there in this town, anyway?"

Florrie dishes scrambled eggs and buttered rye toast onto a plate for me. "Way too many to not suspect that the water is off."

"Don't you have to be at the bakery early? Get going, girl. You cooked. I'll clean up."

"I've got a full crew on the morning shift. They work well even when I'm not there. They're scared to death of me. Go figure."

I point at her weaponized frypan from last night sitting on top of the stove. "Maybe you've been swinging lethal pots and pans around in that kitchen, too?"

"You can bet your ass I do." Florrie kisses the top of my head, attaches Snowflake's leash to his pretty rhinestone collar. "My new man and I are hitting the town."

"Have a great one."

"You too. Talk to you later." Florrie shoots me a serious stare. "And lock up."

I salute obediently and Florrie and her furry new companion bounce out the door.

It's suddenly very quiet. The saws stop momentarily, and the cat can finally now emerge from his hiding spot under the bed. Just the three of us again. Both the cat and the dog curl up at my feet, and I curl up around my coffee mug. Our first peaceful interlude since arriving. I need to think. I do my best to tune out the construction noises that rev up again, and instead, focus on how fabulous my new art studio in the refurbished bunkie will be a few weeks from now. It'll feel wonderful to get back to painting again. It's a soul need of mine that hasn't been met for far too many months.

The sun is strong for late September, and the lake glistens in the light. Once I'm fully caffeinated, I'll spend the day with my feet in the sand and a book in hand. That is, after I pay a visit to Floyd or Lloyd, or whichever doppelganger detective is manning the police station today. I do need somebody to do something about Lillian's lunatic husband. I'm definitely not looking forward to bumping into him in the night.

* * *

I'm feeling a sight better this morning than I did yesterday, which is kind of strange since my life is seemingly being directly threatened on this fine fall day. I suppose that's an exaggeration, and I don't want to hyperbolize. There's enough drama swirling around the atmosphere as it is. No need for embellishment. On one hand, Lillian's husband didn't exactly say he was going to hurt me. On the other hand, harm was implied in his tone of voice, and that's something that one must take into account when evaluating one's chances of survival.

Lillian's husband is definitely trying to scare me, and some people can die of fright. I wonder if I'm one of them. I've had some bad scares in my life, but I'm still kicking, so I reckon not. On the flip side, skydiving, bungee jumping, hang gliding, these things do not appeal to me in the least. I consider myself an adventurous spirit, but I draw the line at swinging, glass-bottomed suspension bridges hanging over bottomless canyons—a popular new tourist attraction in numerous Chinese provinces, I've read. I don't get it. How is that fun? I simply wouldn't want to live through the experience. So, I suppose it's quite possible that I'm one of those faint-hearted few who actually can be scared to death. I hope Lillian's husband hasn't deduced the same.

I pull on jeans and a T-shirt, brush my hair, and add a swipe of lipstick and a touch of blush. I don't want to waste too much time on my face. It's all coming off as soon as I get back from town and jump into that lake at long last. I plan on floating for a good few hours. Hope the water's not too cold, not that it would stop me going in. See? I am the adventurous type. I just set certain boundaries for myself, like heights over eight feet, speeds over eighty miles per hour, centrifugal force, and Tinder dates.

I meet Hugh on the driveway on my way out of the cottage.

He drops what he's doing, moseys on over to me. He looks like a gunslinger, a hammer swinging from one side of his tool belt, a drill hanging low on the opposite hip's holster. "You survived the night, I'm glad to see."

"Nothing gets by you, Sherlock." I wink friendly like, purposely not flirty, and throw my handbag into my jeep.

Hugh laughs. "I didn't want to wake you but wanted to let you know I checked out the tree the guy hit last night. He banged it up pretty good and took some bark off. His car must have one helluva ding on the back bumper, but I didn't see paint chips or any body parts laying around."

"Body parts?" Okay, now I'm alarmed.

Hugh chuckles. "Car body parts."

Relief. "Aha. Gotcha." I'm an idiot.

"There's a lot of bramble in front of the tree, which makes it hard to find much of anything. I'm sure a forensic team could come up with evidence, but Sherlock here isn't having any luck with it."

I shrug. "I'm pretty sure you're the lead investigator on this case. It would be tough to get a forensic team all the way up here for a victimless crime."

Hugh's phone rings. He checks it, but he declines the call. "Let's keep our eyes out for small dark-colored cars with dented rear bumpers, driven by an outsider. There can't be too many of those in town this time of year."

"The guy called my cell at three this morning, threatening to come back for another visit when you're not around."

Hugh's easy smile disappears. "What does this whacko want? Are you sure you don't know who he is? Could it be some bitter ex or some jerk you rejected?"

For some reason, I check over my shoulder before I speak. "I sort of know who he is, but I don't know him personally. His wife wrote into my column a couple of times for relationship advice, and I advised her. She left him some time afterward, and it seems that he blames me for their breakup. The problem now is he thinks I know where his wife is, and he wants me to tell him."

Hugh looks at me closely, ready to study my response. "Do you know where the guy's wife is?"

I shake my head. "Not that I'd tell him if I did know, but no I don't. Snowflake, the little dog that got dumped here, belongs to his wife. Her name is Lillian. That's really all I know about her."

Hugh is trying to follow the breadcrumbs. Not an easy task. "So, the wife Lillian, who wrote to you online, left her dog at your place for you to take care of?"

"That's what I'm thinking at this point."

"You gave your address to a stranger online?"

"No, I'm not thirteen years old. I don't know how Lillian found me, but her dog was left here the day after I moved, which is pretty quick detective work on her part. I have no idea how she tracked me down."

Hugh's bushy eyebrows distractedly dance about his nicely lined forehead. I think they must be pushed and pulled by the wheels turning behind them in his brain. "Could Lillian have followed you up here?"

"She would have had to know where I was moving from and to know that I was moving in the first place and"—I'm shaking my head, feeling even more confused by Hugh's logical questions—"she would have had to figure all that out within days of writing to me. None of it is very plausible."

"But she did find you here."

"She did." I shrug.

Hugh rubs the rugged stubble on his chin thoughtfully. "That part's a mystery, but at least some of the randomness is starting to fall into line. Sounds like you should definitely go into the station house and give the cops a heads-up. I'm worried this guy may not be going anywhere until he gets what he came for."

"Well, that's not going to happen. Not from me, at least. I'm heading into town now to talk to Floyd or Lloyd or whoever is behind the desk at the cop shop today. I'll see if they think I should file a report or if there's anything they can do to help. I suspect the guy is trolling me online, too. There are some weird comments on my social media pages. That's not entirely uncommon, but these ones seem a little more personal and angrier than usual."

"Hope that's not the work of Bible Babe."

My eyes roll involuntarily. "Is she still skulking around here?" I look over my shoulder again. Creeps all around.

"Not so far, but it's early in the day yet."

"I admit I'm in no position to judge anyone for having an unbalanced ex, but I'm curious—did you know Iris was certifiable when you married her?"

Hugh chuckles wryly. "It was a short courtship, but by the time I figured it out, it was too late to make an easy escape."

"There were no red flags?"

Hugh shakes his head. His remorse is palpable. "Iris was the new girl in town, and nobody knew much about her. She moved down from Kapuskasing and got a job at the flower shop here. She claimed to be an expert in funeral flora."

"Impressive." I laugh. "That's an unusual talent."

Hugh laughs with me. "I mistook weird for interesting."

"Cold Ethyl?" I question half-jokingly, kind of afraid to hear the answer.

"Sometimes." Hugh winks at me. "Iris sure liked me and all the same sorts of things that I liked to do. She also dialed the intense religious stuff way back when I was around. I came to realize that she'd studied me, learned my interests—cased me like a house she planned to rob. I broke it off then, but on the heels of that, she told me she was pregnant, and I did what I thought was the right thing."

I'm surprised. "You two have a child?"

Hugh shakes his head. "She faked that, too. I was outta there within a year, but it took four more to get unhitched. And that's when the rumor mill started. Iris made fanning those flames her full-time job."

I feel for the poor guy. "That really sucks."

Hugh shrugs good-naturedly. "I have my people and places in town—Happily Napoli, The Bakehouse, the King's Landing pub, the lumber yard and hardware store. And I know where I'm not welcome—the Silver Star Café, Bitch 'n' Stitch, or the Salvation Army shop, but I'm okay with that."

I can't help but giggle. "Too bad about the Bitch 'n' Stitch."

"I'm content to do my knitting at home and complain to my cat." Hugh winks. "Back to work." He turns to head back toward the bunkie, waves goodbye to me.

I climb in my jeep. "See you later."

I start the engine, shift into reverse, but the vehicle doesn't move. I try again, step harder on the gas. The engine revs, but the wheels don't spin. Hugh has heard and turns around, crossing back toward me to offer assistance.

I unroll my window. "I don't know what's wrong with it. I had it serviced a couple of weeks ago. Could it be the transmission?"

Hugh walks around my jeep, kneels down on the ground at the rear end. When he stands up, he's looking grave. "Your back tires have been slashed."

Chapter Twelve

Two hours later, Hugh has removed my slashed tires and replaced them with new ones he picked up for me at the garage in town. My hero. I reward Hugh and his man, Ryan, with Florrie's leftover quiche and croissants since they missed their lunch break in order to rescue me. Beyond that, I feel nothing, I say less, and I'm acutely aware that everything I'm doing is robotic.

Outside once again, I calmly climb back into my jeep and attempt for a second time to leave the premises. I'm very grateful for Hugh's help, but I'm not sure I'm adequately expressing that in my current borderline catatonic state. "Thank you so much, Hugh. Really." I can't even muster up a smile.

It seems as if Hugh understands where I'm at. No offence taken; no judgment made. I appreciate that.

Hugh doesn't try to mask his concern, though. "I'm happy to help. That's no big deal. But this stuff is getting serious. I mean it could have been my nutter ex, but more likely it was the guy hanging around here last night who did it. He obviously didn't want you getting away from him in a hurry."

I. Just. Can't.

Better to make light and get myself alone as quickly as possible so I can think all this madness through and try to make some sense of it. "Some welcome committee this town has got. I'll see you later, and thanks again. Truly."

Hugh tries to hold my gaze in a temperature-taking kind of way. It's uncomfortable for me, and I break it after a couple of seconds. A fake smile, a quick wave, and I'm outta there.

* * *

According to the clock, it took me ten minutes to drive downtown, but it felt like ten seconds. The thoughts in my head, hurling around tornado-like, wreak havoc on my mental state, and I'm able to make sense of nothing by the time I arrive in the police parking lot. The station house is the last building on the main strip. Good thing because it looks like a tooth growing in next to the stately brick establishments on the street proper. I walk inside the blocky 1950s building in a daze and find it empty except for Lloyd and the friendly ginger cop shop cat, Charlie.

Even though it's been a few years, jolly old Lloyd recognizes me, and though this mountain of a man's gray hair is thinner, and his skin is deeply lined, and his paunch is paunchier, I'd know him anywhere. He immediately pours us coffee and, as etiquette dictates in this part of the world, we spend almost fifteen minutes catching up on friendly small-town small talk before I can turn our conversation to the business at hand.

I set down my coffee and spill all of the bizzarro that I have brought back to my hometown with me and inflicted upon unwitting friends and family. I tell Lloyd about Lillian and her threatening husband and his small dark car that I suspect followed me from my old house to my new one. The emails and the texts and the phone call and the tires and the wounded tree. I tell him about heroic Hugh and fabulous Florrie and bonkers Bible Babe and my stalker of an ex, and I don't cry at all until I get to the part about my best friend, Sinead, passing away, and then I can't figure out how I got to there in my story, but Lloyd's comforting arm wraps around my shoulder, and he takes the reins in the conversation and thankfully brings me back to the matter on the table. And finally, I breathe slowly and deeply, and I can focus again.

Lloyd is genuinely concerned for both Lillian and me, and he springs into action, signing in to the provincial database on the police computer. "You know this Lillian's last name or her address?"

"Nope. Don't even know what town she lives in. But it can't be too far away. Her dog got to my cottage hours after I got there."

"Got a photo of her?"

"Just her dog, Snowflake."

"Did Hugh get any read off the guy's license plate?"

"No, it was dark, and the car was moving fast."

Lloyd shakes his head. "Not much to go on, I'm afraid."

"Yeah, I know. He did threaten to come back, though. I'll try to get a picture of him or his license plate if he does."

Lloyd points a stern finger in my direction. "No, you won't, missy. If that guy returns to your cottage, you need to get the heck out of there and call me ASAP."

I love that Lloyd is exactly like the fictional, caring cops I used to watch on my black-and-white TV when I was a kid. "Don't worry. It's easier to think brave thoughts when I'm standing in a police station in the middle of the day than when I'm alone at my cottage in the middle of the night with a frying pan for protection."

"We're all heroes in our heads. That's not such a bad thing." Lloyd searches through the computer files for a while longer. "At this point, I don't think I'd get the go-ahead for RCMP IT to start looking into the IP address of the computer that's been posting the comments on your website. They're nasty, but the comments aren't directly threatening. Their cases are backlogged by about six months. The alarm's got to be pretty loud to get them to jump in."

Lloyd waves hello to a couple of uniforms who enter the station house. "All we have to go on so far is that we know we're looking for an out-of-towner driving a small dark-colored car with a dent in the rear bumper. That's going to be our best bet for finding this guy presently. We know he's from out of town, so he could be staying at one of the motels or the housekeeping cottages in the area. Most of those places are near empty at this time of year. I'll take a drive through the parking lots and see if I spot anything, and I'll tell the uniforms to keep their eye out for vehicles that match the description. If he's cruising around town, someone will spot him, guaranteed."

I'm not ready to give up on the databases yet. "I wonder if the husband would have filed a missing person report on his wife, Lillian? Are you able to check?"

"Based on everything you've told me, I don't think it's likely, but I'll pull up all reports filed in the province over the past week. We think the wife is in her thirties or forties, right?"

"Probably. The husband's voice sounds about that age on the phone. She didn't mention any children, so I don't think they have any. Oh, and she said in her first letter to me that they'd been married for ten years, so yeah, I'd guess she's maybe thirty to forty."

"There's upwards of three hundred missing person reports filed every week in this province. Half are kids. Eighty-five percent of those reports are removed from the files within a week."

"Because eighty-five percent are found?"

"Usually. Some of them the families give up on. That's going to leave us around fifty, half of those are adults and half of those adults are male. So, we've only got a dozen or so adult females to check through." Lloyd scrolls through photos and descriptions in the provincial database. "Not seeing any new reports for females that age from the general area. There's a few from way up north, Timmins, Kenora, we're talking an eighteen-hour plus drive from here. A couple from the Ottawa area and further east, but they're in their early twenties. You're welcome to take a look, though."

I look over Lloyd's shoulder while he scrolls through the pictures of people who have disappeared lately. Lloyd's right. I don't see pictures of women who seem as if they could be Lillian. "None of them seem like possibilities."

Lloyd exits the database. "The truth is our guy hasn't committed a crime yet. It's not against the law to drive your own vehicle into a tree unless you're under the influence or unless you're damaging a tree on private property, which our guy did do, but which we have no way to prove at the moment. Trespassing and being a Peeping Tom are illegal, but we're not going to be able to prove either of those misdemeanors with what we've got to go on so far. You can't go around slashing people's tires, but presently we don't have any evidence of who did that to your car. And according to what you've told me, it sounds like there could be a few people on that suspect list."

"How about the guy is harassing me? Isn't that a crime?"

"Unfortunately, the way the laws read; this guy's not even close to being in danger of being charged with criminal harassment yet. It's got to go on for quite some time and be pretty regular before there's any sort of a case to be made. You've also gotta have hard evidence like copies of texts or emails or traceable phone calls."

I'm feeling frustrated, but not with Lloyd. He's being as helpful as he can be. I can't hide the irritation in my voice, though. "Our effed-up legal system strikes again."

Lloyd's voice is laced with genuine empathy. "Is there any other information about the wife that you may have neglected to mention? It's incredible how the tiniest details can often turn out to have the biggest impact on a case."

I shake my head. "Can't think of anything else. I know so little about either of them. On the phone last night, though, Lillian's husband said he saw the dog at my place and said that's how he knows I'm in contact with Lillian. So, it obviously doesn't sound like he's the one who dropped the dog off in my yard."

Lloyd swivels in his chair to face me. "If that's true, then who else could have left the dog on your property?"

I shrug. "Only Lillian, I suppose."

Lloyd gets up from his desk. "Well, that's good news then because at least that would mean the wife is fine and probably just getting herself set up in a new living situation somewhere far away from her domineering husband. She'll likely come around to collect her dog from you as soon as she's sorted. Unfortunately, her husband has probably figured out the same thing, which is why he'd be watching you, waiting for his wife to turn up."

"Good news for Lillian but bad news for me."

"I'd say so." Lloyd pours two more coffees into our small Styrofoam cups.

Worst coffee ever, but I drink it anyway out of politeness. "I just don't know how Lillian found out where I was. I mean I only moved there the day before."

Lloyd throws back the stale brew, pours himself another. "It's frightening, but the truth is with technology these days, anybody can be found, and it doesn't take long. There's not a human being on this planet with enough money to hide out forever, anywhere."

My head is pounding. "Why did she choose me to give her dog to?"

"She trusted you. People act on their gut instinct a lot especially when they're backed into a corner, and it's not such a bad thing to do. Look, she was right to trust you with her dog, wasn't she? You're making sure the pup is well taken care of just like she knew you would. And when this Lillian is ready to pick up her pet, you're going to happily hand it over to her."

"I like to think Lillian wouldn't have picked me if she knew she was siccing her menacing ex on me."

Even in a town this tiny, Lloyd has seen his share of desperate people doing desperate things. "Obviously Lillian made some good choices, but I doubt she thought every detail through. Even when people have been contemplating running away for years, they usually end up leaving in a hurry when the right time to split actually presents itself. Best laid plans and the like."

I rise to leave. "I guess you're right, Lloyd. Thanks for all your time today."

Lloyd takes my elbow and gently guides me toward the door. "I'll fill out a report on everything we've discussed just so there will be a record of what's gone down so far."

"Appreciate it."

Lloyd holds the door open. "You take care of yourself. Call me right away if anything happens, if you remember any details that you think might be important, or even if you're just feeling a little nervous. I'll swing by or send a uniform over to have a look around. Don't be a hero."

"No danger of that happening in real life." I step out the door, take a few paces along the sidewalk.

And then, mere moments later, I have a mini panic attack. I've spent the last six years being stalked by my ex, thinking, *What is he capable of? Is he out there watching me now? How far will he go for revenge?* I've been lucky to stay safe, despite never getting the help I needed. My gut tells me Lillian has not been granted that same luck.

I spin around to head back inside the station house, catch Lloyd in the midst of his picking up the phone to take a call, and I pre-emptively blurt,

"What if Lillian's husband has already found her and done something to harm her, or worse? What if Lillian is dead?"

Lloyd hangs up the telephone mid-call, his face professionally expressionless. He uses his calming police-academy-trained voice to alleviate my worries. I know Lloyd isn't being condescending. He's just doing his job. "The most helpful thing you can do for yourself and for this Lillian is to stay calm and rational. The vast majority of female victims of homicide are killed by their partners—but don't be jumping to any unfounded conclusions here, missy. It's too early to go there. So far, there's nothing whatsoever to indicate foul play, is there? Not even a missing person report."

If I were Lloyd's young daughter, he'd be tucking me in for the night now, patting me on the top of the head, turning off the light, and firmly closing the bedroom door. No more nonsense here.

I was that kid who could never settle until I had turned over every rock and bugged every adult to find the answers I was seeking. I'd defiantly be out of that bed with the light switched back on and the door flung open in two seconds flat. "Nothing to indicate foul play so far, no. Just a psychotic ex hunting down his runaway wife. What could possibly go wrong?" I know my voice is sounding snippy, but my stress levels are rising incrementally. None of the information, or lack thereof, that Lloyd has provided has made me feel any better. In fact, I can feel a low-grade hysteria stirring in the pit of my stomach.

Lloyd picks up on my tension, being the ace detective that he is. Perhaps it's my expressive eyebrows that give me away, which I'm quite certain have purled themselves into a full-on cable-knit sweater of stress across my forehead.

Lloyd takes another shot at mollifying me. "Most crimes are solved in the simplest of ways. The obvious conclusions are almost always the correct ones. Except on TV. Crimes get complicated on *CSI* and the like that's for sure. And every one of them is pure rubbish. You'd be surprised how careless people get. A slip with the tiniest little detail can bring a whole house of cards tumbling down. If this bozo sticks around town for more than a minute, we'll find him, guaranteed. Keep your eyes and ears open, but don't take any chances with yourself."

I pet Charlie the cat on my way back out, and the little critter is surprisingly grounding for me. "Thanks again for your time, Lloyd. Say hey to Floyd for me."

"Will do. Hopefully, he'll bring back a big bucket of pickerel for our dinner tonight. Bet you haven't had a good fish fry since you left for the city."

I smile and wink, too. "Actually, I haven't had one since I became a vegetarian."

Lloyd scoffs. "Bet the aunts don't think much of that."

"As a matter of fact, they take it as a personal insult and are never going to forgive me for it."

Lloyd's laugh trails after me as I head out the door.

I climb into my jeep, sit for a few moments with my eyes closed. I need to get centered. I need to stay calm. I need to figure out a game plan for myself. Lloyd means well, but I don't know if he's going to be of much help if things take a bad turn. I suppose the bad turn has already occurred. I should say if things take a turn for the worse.

I don't know whether anyone will be able to help me if Lillian's husband is determined to get me alone with him. The thing that's making me feel most vulnerable right now when I think about this ominous man is that I don't know what he looks like. He could be watching me in plain sight at this very moment, and I wouldn't even know he was there. He could sit at the table next to me in a coffee shop, share a bench with me at the beach. How will I know it's him?

At least my spiteful ex has to do his lurking in the shadows, so he's not usually able to get all that close to me. And Hugh's ex, well it looks as if she thinks we can't see her behind those goggle-sized shades. I can just picture her covering her eyes with her puffy hands, thinking she's disappeared, her toddler voice squeaking, *Bible Baby Bye-Bye*. Holy crap, she's a freak. What Stephen King could do with that character. Willies up and down my spine.

It's only been forty-eight hours, but I'm seriously questioning my decision to return to my roots. Maybe it's true that we can never go home again. Perhaps attempting to go backward in any way is always a mistake. I was expecting a sleepy little town, but instead, I've encountered a creepy little town. I guess we'll see what the next forty-eight hours bring. I'm not feeling overly optimistic. I'll keep my bags packed in case I decide to make a quick exit.

I pull out of the station parking lot and turn onto the main strip of downtown Sunset Beach. It's lunchtime, and High Street is surprisingly busy. I'm glad for the shopkeepers. It can be rough getting through the off-season months when the tourists retreat to the city.

I stop at a crosswalk. A man on the sidewalk catches my eye, and I stare at him for what feels like a really long time. He's not looking back at me. Something is registering in my memory bank, but my brain is not wrapping around the visual, not dialing in. Like seeing someone you know out of uniform for the first time in an unexpected location and not being able to place them. Is my mind playing tricks on me, or has it switched into a state of denial?

I'm looking at the back of his head as the man reaches the other side of the road. Now the driver in the car behind me is honking—definitely a tourist. Locals would never be so rude. Screw him.

The man I can't place turns to look in the direction of the honking horn, and I'm still looking at him, and he's so familiar, and I think I know who he is, but I have to be mistaken because why in the hell would my ex-husband be here in my hometown?

Chapter Thirteen

The impatient honking behind me carries on until I finally step on the gas, drive along the road, and pull into the first empty parking spot I find. The sight of my ex-husband, Dick, walking the main street in my little town has me so shell-shocked that I'm full-on hyperventilating and can barely see. I grab the steering wheel tightly, breathe deeply.

I need to calm down. I need to think this through. I need to locate that ultra-rational part of me that jumped ship when I saw my ex standing in front of me and realized he'll never ever leave me be, that I'll never be rid of Dick in this lifetime. At least, not until one of us is dead.

I feel sick to my stomach, and I think it's hate that's making me ill. And that concept makes me feel even worse. If it's not hate, then it's rage, and I know that is not healthy. I need to cool off, to regroup. I need to get my act together. After years of having to contend with exorbitant amounts of stress, and finding ways to cope and survive it all, I may officially be losing it after all, and that is seriously scary.

I pull back onto the street and point the jeep in the direction of my cottage. My hands are shaking on the wheel. I have to focus on the road enough to get home in one piece. I tell myself to keep going, that I'll feel better once I get to the cottage, and I can collect myself and make sense of what's happening.

Deep down, the truth is I don't believe anything will ever really be okay again. It's been so long since I felt safe that I can't remember what that's like anymore. And right now, feeling safe is what I want more than anything.

* * *

I'm still panicky when I arrive home and park in the laneway of my cottage. Hugh and his hired man aren't here, probably gone for afternoon coffee break. At least I don't have to attempt to conceal my white-as-a-ghost complexion, which is apparently how my body reacts to encountering the poltergeist that is my ex-husband. On the other hand, I'm not totally down with being alone at the moment. I hope Lillian's husband isn't planning on popping in just now. I lock up my jeep. I normally wouldn't bother to, outside of the city, but it seems like the prudent thing to do with so many pests out of the woodwork.

I cross quickly to the cottage, lock that door behind me, too. The dog and cat are elated to see me, but I can barely muster a response to their playful greetings. I'm numb, mechanical. Ticket for one on the bad-pet-parent guilt trip, please. I feed them, open the door to the screened-in porch so the cat can get some fresh air and curl up in the warm sunlight.

It's a gorgeous sunny day, and I am considering holing up in the cottage on lockdown for the afternoon and stewing in suspicion—loser. I feel so angry with Dick and Lillian's husband for scaring me and with Hugh for not being here and most of all with myself for allowing myself to be bullied. I promised myself I'd never do that again. Screw 'em. Feel the fear and do it anyway. Sinead would tell me to pull on my big girl panties. I pull on my bathing suit instead and grab an old towel from the linen cupboard.

Zoe and I make the one-minute walk across my scrubby lawn to the beach. The sand between my toes is soft and warm while the sheltering cedars keep my bare shoulders cool. When we reach the lake, both of us plow straight in without stopping. I can't tell whether the water is cold or not, for my numbness, and I don't care. I want it to freeze my brain. I want it to carry the stress away. I want to slip below the surface and stay there. Forever.

Lake Huron is shallow for a long way out, and the soft, sandy bottom rivals any Caribbean beach. Stretching out on my back, my bare flesh meets the rippled sand, and I take one breath before submerging my body and head completely. I open my eyes, look up at the blue sky and white clouds, distorted through the watery lens of the lake. It looks dreamy, and I want to sleep here. I close my eyes and stay submerged.

My legs float up, but I use my hands to keep myself under. I'm slowly running out of air. It's getting uncomfortable, but I don't think I care. Now it's even starting to hurt my lungs a little bit. Normally, I'd panic at having this sensation, but I'm not now. I want to get away from Dick, and maybe this is a way.

A few moments later, the dog is pouncing on top of me, and I bolt upright, sitting chest-deep in the water and gasping for breath, deeply sucking in glorious oxygen.

Zoe is all over me, shaking the water from her fur, and she makes me laugh despite myself. I may hate Dick, but I love my kids, my pets, and myself more. Also, this lake, that sky, and chocolate are extremely lovable and worth fighting for. That's right—I'm the kind of person who would resort to fisticuffs for chocolate if it came to it.

I pull myself onto the beach and sit down on my worn terry towel. It's a favorite that's been in the cottage linen cupboard since I was a kid. I marvel at the expanse of the endless horizon and the lighthouse in the distance. That same lighthouse guided four generations of my family home to this safe harbor, year after year, helping them navigate through even the worst of storms.

Perhaps it's guiding me now, too. Maybe I've sailed back into this port because I'm supposed to be here. Perhaps it's only wishful thinking.

I realize I'm floundering a little in the midst of all the change right now, but when it comes down to it, I do know what I want. I'm looking for smooth sailing and calm waters. I don't want to battle stormy seas anymore. I'm done with that. The restorative waters of this Great Lake have done their job. They work to heal me. I am slowly, gently, starting to feel a little better.

The breeze is cool on my wet skin, but the sun is warm. Zoe curls up next to me on the threadbare towel. I try to ignore the thick clumps of sand stuck to her sopping fur and hope that at least half of it will drop off outside the cottage.

I'm alert and centered now. I'm here. I can think this through. I don't have any answers to my questions, but I trust they'll come to me. I can do this.

Dick knew I was moving. I saw him driving around my neighborhood, likely watching for the Sold sign to go up. And he's always creeping the kids' and my social media. The kids had posted about saying farewell to their childhood home. It's possible that Dick was my late-night visitor on my last night in the farmhouse. He often borrows different cars to drive around in so one of them could have been a small dark vehicle. In all probability, a burglar would have split as soon as they realized the house was empty and there was nothing for them to burgle. Teens looking to party would have booked it at the first sound of the barking dog. I'm certain Lillian's husband would have taken off, too, if he was able to find me that quickly to begin with—unless he is a total psychopath, which is a definite possibility. A random serial killer would've had me exactly where he wanted me and definitely would've followed me into the woods.

If it was Dick at the door that night, why would he come around then? Because he can't stop himself, that's why. Because before new owners took over the property, it was his last chance to set foot on it, to be at the house that he believes I stole out from under him in divorce court. And because Dick is always trying to remind me that he'll do whatever he wants, that he refuses to answer to me or even to Orders of the Court.

Dick is obsessed with me, and it's got nothing to do with love. It has everything to do with vengeance. With control. With winning. As my best friend Sinead used to say, "Dick is like a dog with a bone. He'll never let go." I am the bone. How romantic.

When I think about it, it's not such a stretch that Dick would deduce that I'd move to, or at least visit, my hometown and family cottage. But I would've figured that if he was going to stalk me up here, he'd do it on the down-low. He usually watches me under the cover of darkness. He doesn't want people to know he's an obsessive who hasn't moved on with his life after six years. Today Dick was openly parading down the main drag in my old hometown. He would know that, in a place this small where half the people are my blood relatives, someone in my family would spot him and tell me. I can only assume that he wants me to know he's here.

The question I'm wrestling with is why doesn't Dick care about people knowing that he's stalking me now? Could it be because he's not? Could he be in town for some reason other than me? If so, I can't imagine what it could possibly be. Oh God, please don't tell me he's bought a place up here.

I'm feeling the chill in the air now as the sun slides behind a patch of dark clouds. I'm looking forward to the sun setting on this very long day—I just don't want to be alone for it. I know I can always stay with Florrie, but I don't want to be driven out of my home by some thug. Again. The dog and I make our way back to the cottage. I rinse the sand off my feet in the outdoor shower and manage to flush a good five pounds of sand off of Zoe's coat with the hose.

Inside the cottage, my cell phone rings as I'm pulling my jeans back on. It's the aunts. The aunts don't talk on phones—they yell into them. I have to hold the device away from my ear to keep from being deafened. Their voices are garbled. They're both talking at once, and they're speaking more Italian than English, so I'm not quite grasping everything they're saying, but I do understand from their tone that they're not too happy with me. I hear *tu mangi*, and *tea*, and *chiromante* (palm reader), and I remember that I was supposed to stop by their flat today for lunch and tea so they could take another stab at reading my stars to tell me my fortune. I'm late.

"Okay, okay, so sorry. I'll be there in an hour."

The last word I hear them say is *stupida* before they hang up on me.

* * *

A pickup truck pulls up in front of the cottage. I expect it's Hugh returning from his three o'clock coffee break, but I peek out the window to make sure. The crew is back on the job, filling a bin with rotting posts and floorboards that they're ripping out of the battered old bunkie.

I check the messages on my laptop before I head out the door. There are a lot of letters from lonely hearts and confused minds. Like attracts like. Tonight, I'll devote a few hours to replies after I return from my psychic reading. Hopefully, the aunts don't exhaust me completely. Also hoping the tarot doesn't throw me down another hand of death, doom and destruction—ordering up a Ten of Cups and The Lovers card, please.

Hugh calls down from the roof of the bunkie as I climb into my jeep, "There's a couple of things we need to go over. You have to tell me where you want the sink and toilet for the plumbing rough in. Does first thing tomorrow morning work to discuss?"

"Sure, I'll be here with coffee on. See you then."

Hugh smiles. "Have a good night. Call if you need me for anything."

* * *

Driving back into town, I keep a lookout for a small dark car with a dented bumper that may or may not belong to Lillian's husband. I don't know what Dick drives, so I'm checking out every driver I pass for him. Not exactly a relaxing trip, but there aren't that many cars to inspect. The streets are quiet. I notice a small silver vehicle driving behind me in the distance, nothing out of the ordinary.

A light rain begins to fall enough that I have to switch my wipers on. Storms blow in quickly across the massive lake but often blow over just as fast. The clouds are thickening and closing in, and the sky abruptly grows extremely dark for this time in the afternoon. Hugh will have to call the day early on the construction. Zoe's not a fan of thunder. I'll try to get home to her as soon as I can.

The clouds open up, and all of a sudden, the rain is near torrential. The silver car has pulled up closer to my rear bumper than it should especially in this weather. I slow down. They can go around me if they're in such a hurry. Unless they've got a kidney in a cooler and they're rushing to the ER, they can screw right off.

The silver car is not slowing down. In fact, its headlights are filling my rearview mirror. The driver is way too close. This is effing dangerous.

The rain is driving down so hard I can barely see beyond my windshield, but at the very last second possible, I do manage to see a suicidal squirrel dash across the road right in front of my jeep. I scream and slam on my brakes to spare the rodent and simultaneously hunch my shoulders and squeeze my eyes shut as my body instinctively prepares to be smashed from behind by the car tailgating me.

The squeal of my brakes is echoed by the screeching tires of the silver car. It swerves onto the dirt shoulder of the road to avoid plowing into my trunk and only narrowly misses my bumper. The vehicle slides forward on the slippery gravel until it halts directly beside me. I know I missed the squirrel, but if those jackasses hit it, I'll be the one rear-ending them in a few seconds.

I catch my breath; turn to see who these colossal idiots are. The rain is lightening up enough for me to make out two people in the front seat of the car. I can't see the passenger very well, but it looks like a male. The driver, however, I'd recognize those oversized knockoff Ray-Bans and that bleached-to-straw hair anywhere. Puffy faced Bible Babe looks at me with an ugly crooked smile, and I stare back at her in shock as the silver car spins its tires then squeals off down the wet street ahead of me.

I sit for a minute, waiting to see whether this is an absurd dream I'll wake up from. Unfortunately, that doesn't happen.

The rain clouds are blowing over already, and it is only sprinkling now. I climb out of my jeep with dread to look for the squirrel. If he's been hit, I hope he's dead, so he doesn't suffer. I check around. No sign of the reckless little bugger. Looks like we've both defied yet another near-death experience. The squirrel and I are batting a thousand, and I'm thankful for that, but I'm also totally aware that no lucky streak lasts forever.

Chapter Fourteen

Who do I tell about this unfortunate event? Lloyd? I couldn't get the license plate of the silver car with the rain and the speed and the shock, so I guess there's not much he can do with the information. Do I tell Hugh? I guess I'll further impress upon him the extent of his ex-wife's unstableness, but he and at least half the town seem already to be aware that Bible Babe is bananas. Basically, there seems to be no option other than me suffering in silence, and that is almost never a good idea. Thank God for Florrie. I'm looking forward to her and a bottle of wine and a venting session sometime soon.

I center myself and practice some mouth yoga. I hope it's true that the act of smiling sends signals to the brain tricking it into believing that you're in fact happy. Feels a little like putting the cart before the horse, but I'm willing to give anything a shot at this point. I cannot cancel on the aunts now, and I have no time to process what just happened to me on my drive, and I don't want to give in to my current overwhelming urge to curl up in a ball on the floor and cry for days. Instead, I'm going to persist with the mouth yoga, and drink a few glasses of the aunts' homemade wine, and hope their own brand of idiosyncratic sweet and sourness is enough of a distraction to get me through the visit. If they detect any significant level of distress from me, I won't get out of their place until they've exorcised it out of me with either crystals or cannoli.

I park on High Street in front Happily Napoli.

My zias are waiting for me to arrive, and before I have a chance to knock on the door, they throw it wide open and excitedly usher me inside and up to their second-floor apartment. These old women can be super annoying, but it's also impossible not to feel their love even when they are thoroughly pissed off with me. Being in their presence is already lifting my spirits. I feel a wisp of my mom around.

Speaking of spirits, the aunts' apartment hasn't changed one iota in forty years. It looks like one of those religious gift shops you have to exit through after you visit the big cathedrals in Europe. So many Blessed Virgins, so many Saints. So many floral prints and lace doilies. So much plastic-covered upholstery. Except, mixed in amongst the crucifixes are decks of tarot cards and palmistry maps of the hand. There are sticks of incense and piles of dried herbs everywhere. A Northern Ontario Italian version of a New Orleans Voodoo parlor. Gotta love it.

The aunts run a thriving business telling fortunes from their flat. The numbers in their restaurant may drop when the tourists leave after the summer, but they have a steady cash flow year-round from clients hungry to hear what the cards and stars have in store for their future. And those people come from far and wide to hear these old witches' uncannily accurate predictions.

Identical twin Chihuahuas, Peppita and Peppeto, attack my calves upon my entry into the apartment and basically never stop attacking my legs until the aunts finally give them tiny bowls of homemade spaghetti to distract them. I'm totally amazed that the dogs can tell the aunts apart, and the aunts can tell the dogs apart. They're actually more like quadruplets, and I mean that in the nicest of ways if that's possible.

They fuss over me and lead me to their dining table, a brown-and-gold laminate number with brass-colored curlicues at the legs. They serve up Spezzatino, a fabulous stew with peppers and zucchini that they assure me is meat-free after I pick through it searching for evidence of dead animals, and eggplant parmigiana in marinara sauce on fresh ciabatta. Heaven.

They rush me through the meal even taking my plate away from me mid-mouthful. I object, tell them I'm still eating, and they begrudgingly give my food back to me but impatiently snatch it away again a few minutes later.

It's tough to hide my annoyance. "What is wrong with you two today?

What's your hurry?"

Zia Rosa, "No hurry. *Tu mangi.*" Eat up.

Zia Ange, "Why you so slow? *Sbrigati.*"

Sbrigati means *hurry up*. Usually, these two don't want me to leave, and now they're giving me the bum's rush. What's up with them?

"Do you have a client coming here soon? Is that why you're rushing me? That's fine if you do. I can come back again later in the week."

The kettle whistles loudly, and they both jump up to run to the stove. They return with a china pot of tea and a flowered cup and saucer for me. None for them. They're both wearing Cheshire cat smiles. Now I get it. I am the client. Again. They're anxious for a better outcome this time around. Can't say I'm not. Come on Ten of Cups.

The aunts clear my dishes and pull their chairs up way too close on either side of me, invading my personal space and not giving two hoots about it.

Zia Rosa pours. "Drink."

I do as I'm told.

Ange, "Make a wish."

Rosa, "Leave a little bitty in the cup."

I follow their instructions exactly, wouldn't dare not.

"Now flip the cup upside down on the saucer and turn it tre times like the clock."

I'm not sure about that one. "Like the clock?"

"The wise clock."

"Oh, gotcha." I rotate the cup clockwise three times.

"Other hand!" Zia Ange shouts, exasperated with my lack of expertise.

I switch to my left hand. Rosa snatches the cup from me, turns it right side up and begins her examination of the mystical patterns left by the wet tea leaves. She swirls the cup around and stares intently into it.

Rosa is very serious. "The bird is flying."

Ange is excited. "Oh, that's a good luck."

Rosa, "You're going on a journey. Far, far away…"

Ange is nodding knowingly. "Oh, probably to visit the bambinos in Europa."

Rosa's eyes darken. "The money's not so good for you. You're spending a lot of money."

She stops, looks up at me to berate. "Why you spending so much money? You *stupida?*"

Ange is trying to be positive. "That's okay. She's fixing up her house. That costs a lotta money. That's probably where the money is going."

Rosa returns her gaze to the teacup. "Okay...there are two lovers, old and new, good and bad. You need to be careful. This one's got the horns. The devil's horns."

Ange is horrified. She makes the sign of the cross over herself and gasps. "Oh no, Madonna!" Her hands fly up to hold her cheeks.

Rosa lowers the cup, shakes her head, delivering the dire news. "He's the Dick. Your ex-Dick."

I'm trying not to laugh. That's such a good way to describe him.

"He's coming back, and you need to beware. He's no good. No good. No good for you. No good for nobody."

Ange moans in distress at this news, looks skyward, her hands in prayer pose, begging for mercy.

"Thanks for the info, but I already knew that Zia." I smile.

"Husha!" Rosa picks the teacup back up. "The other lover is good. He's a good man for you."

Ange's face lights up. Has heaven just answered her prayer? She wants the deets. "What's the name? You see a letter in there? Is he Italian?"

I'm raising my voice now. This Italian push always confounds me. "Dick the Devil was Italian, Zia. Italian men haven't worked out so great for me. I think I'm going to try out a different nationality next time if it's okay with you."

Zia Angela protests, "Your exa-Dick doesn't count. He was from the north. They speak the Gallo-Italian up there. They more like Irish than Italian."

Zia Rosa agrees wholeheartedly, "You can no trust the northerners. They eat the cheese fondue in the north. What do they know?"

Zia Ange shudders visibly at the thought of a cheese fondue.

Rosa turns her attention back to the cup, inspects it very closely for a long moment. "No letter. There's crisscross and a dress."

Ange is perplexed. "Crisscross and a dress? *Che cosa?*"

It's slowly dawning on me. I wait a bit, but the aunts aren't twigging. I throw them a clue. "Crisscrosses like plaid? And a dress like a skirt? Maybe like a kilt?"

"Si! Si! He's the Scottish."

Zia Ange is crushed by that news. "Oh no, not the Scottish. That's worse than the Irish."

I don't get that. I would think she'd lump all the British Isles together. "Why is Scottish worse than Irish, Zia?"

Ange, "The skirts."

I laugh. "I kinda like a man in a kilt, Zia."

Ange scoffs. "But they maybe no like you." She winks knowingly as if she's got the inside track on gay men.

I can't help but laugh out loud.

Zia Rosa, "No it's okay. This one's a good man. He's the good one for you, the Scottish. But you be careful around the devil's Dick. He's coming back again. He's got the owl on his shoulder. He's going to bring the trouble."

My well-meaning aunts want me to take their dire warnings seriously, and I convince them that I do. After a lovely cappuccino and some amaretti cookies arranged around a dish of pistachio gelato, I get up from the table, thank my comical caretakers for their fabulous food and entertainment, kiss all four cheeks, shake a couple of irritating Chihuahuas off my ankles, and gracefully make my exit. And I'm truly thankful for all of the above. These eccentric old gals have successfully distracted me from my troubles for two full hours, and that is no small feat. They have also sent me on my way with a week's worth of pasta and vanilla panna cotta.

No Italian host would dream of sending a guest home without buckets of leftovers. If one dared try, any self-respecting Signora would be in their right to take it upon themselves to stuff their purse full of linguini and cannoli. That's the law.

* * *

It's just after dinner hour but already dark by the time I step outside. There's a chill in the air, the nights quickly becoming colder as autumn approaches. Only the odd person is still on the street, and they are hurrying to their cars. The stores stay open later in summer, but most close by six in the fall and winter. It's after seven now.

I turned off my cell while I was visiting the aunts but switch it back on before I reach my jeep. There are six missed calls from Florrie and a bunch of texts. Before I get a chance to dial her back, she rings again.

I answer, "Hey."

"Oh, thank God. Where the heck have you been, and where the heck are you now?"

"I was held captive in the aunts' apartment. I made a break for it, and I'm standing outside of their place and yours now."

"You scared me half to death. I thought Snowflake's evil stepdad had done away with you."

"Still in one piece, but the night is young."

"I can see you." Florrie is waving to me from the second-story window in her flat above her bakery across the street. "You're sleeping here tonight."

"I can't. The dog and the cat are at the cottage, thanks though. I'll be fine. Really." Secretly hoping Florrie protests.

"As if. I'm going to stay at your place, then."

Selfish relief. "No, it's okay—" I can see the lights turning off in Florrie's apartment room by room. Sixty seconds later, she is standing across the street from me, Snowflake in her arms, hollering happily as she climbs into her car, "I'll follow you."

I know there is no sense arguing with this one, and in truth, I'm grateful I won't have to sleep alone tonight. I get in my truck, pull out, and Florrie, my fearless protector, falls in behind me. Our mini convoy heads back to the beach for the night.

* * *

There are even fewer cottages with lights on than there were when I arrived in town two days ago. The sidewalks really have been rolled up for the winter. No cars are parked in any of the lots that line the public beaches, and none are to be seen along my stretch of the road, either. That is a good thing, no unwanted visitors detected.

Florrie pulls up right behind me in my laneway. Zoe barks at Florrie's vehicle. I should have kept a light turned on outside when I left to go into town earlier, but I didn't plan on getting home this late. Will have to remember to do so in future.

Snowflake is on a leash, and Florrie takes him to a bush to let him piddle. He seems to be adjusting to his new circumstances quickly, but then, who wouldn't fall for Florrie? I unlock the cottage door and release a very happy Zoe to relieve herself in the tall beach grasses. As soon as we're all inside the house safe and sound, the doors are locked up tight and the lights and kettle switched on straight away. The cat curls himself around my calves, looking for attention. Or maybe food. I give him both to cover my bases.

Florrie is looking extremely anxious, jittery even.

I squeeze her arm. "Thanks for coming to stay with me again. I know it's a lot. If this kooky crap doesn't get sorted soon, I think I'm going back to the city. It's too hard on everybody here, especially you."

Florrie pours us both tea, perches nervously on the edge of her chair. "No, it's only hard on you. Everyone else is fine. Listen, I have to tell you something, and I didn't want to do it over the phone."

"I know already."

She's surprised. "You do? And you're this calm?"

"Not at first, I wasn't. I was totally thrown. I completely freaked out. But I pulled myself together after a long swim and a good cry. I don't know why Dick is in town, but I know it can't be good."

"Is that all you know?" Florrie is biting her lip.

Instant dread on my part. "Oh my God. What else is there to know?" I brace myself for the delivery of even more distressing news. "Please tell me he didn't buy a place up here?"

"Oh crikey, I hope not." Florrie's hand flies up to her heart. "Cordelia called me. She saw Dick in the Silver Star café today. He was having coffee

111

with…Iris."

"Iris? Hugh my builder's ex-wife, Iris? Bible Babe, Iris?" My vision starts to go. I think my brain may be cracking from the overwhelm. This feels like one of those ten-thousand-piece puzzles that I detest with a vengeance, where every minuscule, anxiety-inducing piece looks like it has the identical fall foliage printed on it. It's impossible to sort out. I can't do that, and I can't do this.

"Hugh's ex-wife was having coffee with Dick? I'm so completely confused right now. How do they even know each other? Is she the reason he came up here? How does this make any sense? Oh my hell, are they dating?"

Florrie picks her phone up. "I don't get it, either. Maybe they met on a dating site? Do those kinds of coincidences actually happen outside of Jennifer Lopez movies? It's more than weird. I think we should talk to Hugh. Maybe he knows something. I'll message him."

"Hugh's ex nearly ran me off the road in the rain today. A man was in the car with her, but I didn't get a good look at him. Frig, maybe it was Dick." I've never felt a more acute pain in my skull before.

Florrie is stunned. "No freaking way."

We are both reeling mentally, and then an assault on our senses ensues when I notice something stuck on my lakeside window. "What the hell is that?" A large piece of paper is taped to the outside of the glass.

Florrie shrieks. "Oh my God!" She spins around, covers her eyes with her hands in fright, only peeking through her fingers to see.

I cross to the window. Stare for a long moment, waiting for the familiar image to register.

It's a photograph of me. Zoe and me lying in the lake earlier today. Taken from the yard of my cottage.

A message handwritten across it in marker reads, "I've got my eyes on you."

Chapter Fifteen

Lillian's husband kept his promise. He came back just as he said he would.

Florrie is frantic. "Is it the maniac from last night?"

I am nodding. "I have to go outside to get the picture so I can show it to Lloyd."

Florrie is nodding also. We're both doing a lot of nodding. Robotically.

Florrie is shaking her head now. "No, you can't go out there. What if this lunatic is outside waiting for you to retrieve the note? We can get it in the morning when it's light."

"No, it might be gone by then. Lloyd said I need physical evidence to be able to charge the guy with anything. I have to get it now."

Florrie grabs my arm to stop me from leaving. "Let's call Lloyd and have him get the note."

"No, I'm not doing that."

"Okay, we'll go together, then. Take Zoe with us." Florrie locks her arm around mine in human-wall style.

We both try desperately to drum up the courage we need to do this thing as we inch toward the door. The progress is very slow. And then, at the exact moment, we reach it and I touch the handle and begin to turn it, a heavy banging reverberates through its oak planks.

Both of us scream leap backward. Zoe instantly morphs into rabid Cujo and starts slamming her snarling, drool-spewing face against the door.

Hugh calls out, "It's me, Hugh." I can't tell from his voice whether he's amused or afraid. Cool cucumbers are hard to read. But basically, I don't care. I'm pissed off that he's caused this uproar. Again. Plus, there's no one else around for me to be pissed off at, and I need to lash out at somebody.

I swing the door open, breathless. "It's freaking you again? You show up unannounced in the dark of night again and scare us half to death? What is with you? What were you thinking?"

Zoe is thrilled to see that the intruder is actually her new best friend. Hugh rubs the dog's ears vigorously. Snowflake and Spook also come out from their hiding spots to greet their favorite fellow. Traitors all.

Cool cucumber is neither amused nor afraid. "Florrie texted me fifteen minutes ago and told me to get over here right away, so I came."

My pounding heart slows, and I remember that detail all of a sudden. "Right, right. Forgot about that. I'm sorry."

Hugh looks around. "Why are you two so wigged out? What the heck is going on here, anyway?"

Florrie closes the door. "So much."

I open the door. "I have to go outside to grab something."

Florrie points to the paper in the front window. "A threatening message taped to her house left here by Lillian's lunatic, that's what she's grabbing."

Hugh turns instantly steely. "I'll get it. I'm going to take a look around outside, too, in case the guy's still here." Hugh steps in front of me, goes outside himself, closes the door behind him. "Lock the door."

We do. Hugh's gone for at least ten minutes, but it feels like an hour. He returns with the photo and carries his two-by-four weapon inside with him.

"There's no one out there that I can see now. No vehicles, either." He reads the message scrawled across the photograph when he steps into the light over the kitchen counter. "This is next level. You think it's the same guy from last night, then? It has to be, right? You don't have more than one madman following you around threatening you, do you, Gina?"

Florrie cringes. "Actually, there are a few possible suspects. Your ex-wife for one."

"No." Hugh is astounded. "Iris is buggy but she would never do anything like this."

Florrie raises an eyebrow. "Would she run someone off the road? Because that's what she almost did to Gina today."

Hugh drops the photo on the counter and looks between us. "What are you talking about?"

I open my mouth, but Florrie launches in again. "True story. Gina saw Iris driving a silver car, probably her vehicle, and it nearly rear-ended her. On purpose. A man was in the passenger seat."

Hugh turns to me. He's alarmed and apologetic. "I am so very sorry, Gina. I will handle her. I promise. All of this garbage is going to stop now once and for all."

I'm skeptical. "I won't hold you to that promise. I don't know if I believe that people like your ex-wife can be controlled. I know my ex can't be. Anyway, this note was definitely written by the guy from last night, Lillian's husband. That's how he signed the letters he posted on my website: 'I've got my eyes on you.'"

"When was the picture taken?"

"Today."

"So, this guy was at your cottage twice today, then. Once to take the photo and once to tape it to your window. I never saw anyone while I was working here, but I left a couple of times. He must be watching the place and timing his visits carefully." Hugh looks absolutely furious. "The cops need to see this. They're going to have to do something right away. Enough of this sicko. They have to find this guy and lock him up. It's not safe for you to stay out here, Gina. Why aren't you guys sleeping at Florrie's place?"

Florrie crosses her arms and gives me a look, obviously wondering the same. "Yeah, tell me again why we're not sleeping in town tonight?"

I'm trying to put up a brave front, but my resolve is weakening. "Because it's late, and I'm tired, and this is my home, and I don't want to be pushed out of it. I grew up here, and I never felt scared a night in my life in this sweet place, and I'm not going to let some asshole ruin that for me. I came here to find peace and tranquility, and goddammit I'm going to find it. Even if it kills me."

Florrie is visibly cringing. "I don't think you should say that out loud."

"I didn't mean that last part." I hope the Universe registers my cancellation.

"Takebacks are allowed." Florrie is reading my mind. "Staying at my place would just be temporary. No one is going to force you out of your home. Maybe you could look for that peace and tranquility you're after once this stalker is behind bars? And maybe Iris, too?"

I'm wavering between illogical and irrational even though the line is thin. "I don't know. Maybe I'll stay in town tomorrow night, then. It's late, and I'm so exhausted."

Hugh's voice is rife with concern. "You two should go now."

I'm still protesting, but more in an effort to convince myself than the others. "Florrie is sleeping here with me tonight. And we have the dogs. And you said the guy is gone. And I'd have to bring the pets to Florrie's, and the cat will freak out, and it is so much work, and I am so bloody worn out. I'm sure we'll be okay here for one more night."

Florrie is biting her bottom lip nervously. "There's no one around to hear us scream." The dramatics are increasing exponentially.

Hugh takes a seat at the table. "Maybe none of us can protect ourselves against a guy like this. I guess it depends on how far he's willing to go, but if you gals are staying here tonight, then I am too."

Florrie's face brightens. She's obviously in favor of this proposed arrangement.

I object, but perhaps not with total vigor. "No, you're not. I can't ask you to do that."

"You're not asking. I'm telling. And first thing in the morning, you need to go back to the police station with this note and demand that Floyd and Lloyd take action. This is seriously heavy, and it's got to stop. And you can't stay at this cottage anymore until after the guy has been picked up. It's way too dangerous. We don't know what he's capable of."

Clearly planning on staying put for the evening, Hugh takes a seat at the kitchen table. He leans his two-by-four against his chair.

My resolve, what little was left of it, has dissolved completely. There's no fight left in me, and I'm secretly grateful for Hugh's presence on this strangest of nights. I pull out a chair and sit down across from him.

Florrie puts the kettle on then tentatively broaches the other subject. "I actually messaged you asking you to come over before we found the photo on the window."

"What for? Don't tell me there's more crap happening?"

Florrie winces. "There is. Hopefully, you'll be able to explain it to us. It's about Iris. And Gina's ex-husband."

Hugh seems almost amused but also totally perplexed. "This is getting interesting. And confusing. What's the connection?"

Florrie is fussing with teacups. "Cordelia saw them in town at the Silver Star today. Together. As in, sitting-at-the-same-table-having-coffee-and-chatting-together together."

Hugh is genuinely shocked. "Iris and Gina's ex? Is he from around here?"

I shake my head. "No. He lives in Toronto."

"What's he doing in town?"

"I have no idea."

Hugh leans in across the table to study me closely. "How do they know each other?"

I'm at a complete loss. "No clue. We thought you might know more."

Hugh's face is grave. "Was he the man with Iris in the car that almost hit you today?"

I shrug. "It's possible. Maybe even likely, but I didn't get a good look at the passenger, could just tell it was a male."

Hugh is tugging at the thick wavy hair on the top of his head as if his brain is hurting. "This is getting harder to swallow by the minute."

The more stressed Florrie gets, the busier she gets. Usually, this involves preparing and serving food, which opportunists such as myself gladly take advantage of. Florrie hands me a strong cup of black tea. "We're wondering if the two kooks coincidentally hooked up on a dating site."

Hugh, "That would be one hell of a coincidence. I can't see Iris on a dating site unless it's for Christians only."

I know for a fact that Dick wears many masks. I've seen most of them. He's never able to don the likable ones for long. "My ex is a con man, so he can be a Christian for a while if it serves his purpose."

Florrie hands Hugh his mug of tea. "There's a niche dating site for absolutely everything, so there's probably one for middle-aged wackos obsessed with their exes. They could have found each other online. Star-crossed stalkers. How many of those can there be out there?"

I can testify to this fact from the abundance of letters The Ex-Whisperer receives on a daily basis. "There are lots of them out there, believe me. I hear from them every day."

Hugh is getting up to speed quickly. "What's your ex-husband's name?"

Florrie jumps in. "Lil' Dick."

Hugh roars. "No, for real. What's he called?"

I back Florrie up. "He's called Lil' Dick by us and in my books, but his ID says, Richard Valentino. He goes by Dick."

Hugh is still chuckling. "I've never understood that. Even if your parents called you Dick when you were a child, after all the name-calling any kid named Dick would have been subjected to, why wouldn't a grown man named Richard go by Richard or Rich or Rick? What's up with that?"

I quote Shakespeare somewhat, "A dick by any other name would smell as funky."

Florrie sets out a plate of soft brie, sharp Dublin cheddar, seedy oat crackers, and olives. "Lil' Dick and Bible Babe have found each other. A match made in hades. May they live miserably ever after."

His face serious, Hugh leans backward balancing on two legs of his chair, the wheels in his head turning. "The idea that the two of them hooked up randomly is too big a stretch. The mystery here is how these two twisted sisters met."

My tea is already cooling off, but I sip it anyway. "Two stalkers stalking in the same location bump into each other? A cute meet. Stalker serendipity. How romantic."

Florrie giggles.

Hugh leans forward on the table again. "You could be right. We know Iris was watching me working here at your place. If Dick came to town looking for you . . ."

It's beginning to make sense to me, too. "...Dick spent loads of summer vacations here with me and the kids. He could have been creeping around, trying to figure out if this is where I moved to."

Florrie points an accusatory finger in my face. "Or after Iris saw you hitting on her husband…"

Hugh leaps to his own defense, corrects Florrie. "Ex-husband."

I also attempt to defend myself. "I was not hitting on him. I merely answered my door in a disheveled state."

Florrie does her best trial attorney impression, paces back and forth across the kitchen floor dramatically, then spins around on one heel to address me sternly, "That's your biased version of events, madam." She swings her prosecutorial finger around to point at the other defendant, Hugh. "And you, sir, may be divorced, but clearly your ex-wife is not aware of that matter. In fact, it is common knowledge that Bible Babe still wears her wedding ring and continues to use her former husband's, being your, surname, Mr. McTavish. After Iris saw Gina hitting on her husband by answering her door half-naked with that sexy, just-rolled-out-of-bed tousled hair look—"

I interject with an objection of my own, "—You mean that un-brushed hair and unwashed face look you get when you're too drunk to clean up before bed and too hungover to give a crap about how you look when you answer your door in the morning?"

Florrie is trying hard not to break up laughing. "Let's just agree to disagree about the styling deets and call it homewrecker hair, shall we? And anyway, there's no denying that you got caught red-handed answering the door in your underwear, so you are guilty as charged regardless. And the fact is, that act alone would have been enough for Iris to go on the offensive to protect the sanctity of her marriage, delusional as she is regarding her relationship status."

Hugh is exasperated. "Oh, for god sakes. We're not married anymore."

"Immaterial. Overruled." Florrie uses a wooden spoon on the countertop as a gavel, continues with her theory. "In the irises of Iris, you are still man and wife. It would not have been difficult for Iris to figure out who the owner of this cottage and Hugh's minx of a new client was. Everyone in town knows that Gina is The Ex-Whisperer and Bible Babe wrote that freaky letter on the same day the defendant answered her door naked."

I bury my face in my hands, protest weakly. "I wasn't naked."

Florrie ignores me. "It is, however, a little surprising that Iris found a way to connect with Gina's ex-husband so fast."

Hugh finishes his tea. "It's surprising because Iris isn't actually all that bright."

"Iris is on the ball but off her rocker." Florrie laughs at her own joke.

Hugh nods in agreement. "She is persistent, though. I gotta give her that."

None of this seems improbable to me. "Persistence will take you a long way in life. I guess all Iris really had to do was stop in for some lasagne at Happily Napoli and ask the aunts a couple of questions about me and she'd have had all the info she needed to commence stalking."

My phone is pinging repeatedly. Someone is clearly trying to reach me. With trepidation, I pick it up, relieved to read only numerous messages from my kids, updating me on their news and asking how my first few days at the cottage are going. I respond with little white lies to keep them from fretting.

Then I notice that my Inbox is bursting at the seams. Eighty-eight messages. I'm definitely falling down on the job. I scan the list of senders, hoping I don't see any from Lillian's husband. Hopes dashed.

Dear Ex-Whisperer,

You look great in a bikini. Next time, I'll join you in the lake, and we'll do some deep-sea diving. I've got a thing for brunettes. Is your hair curly everywhere or just on your head? Be seeing you soon.

Eyes on you.

The skin on my back crawls up my spine and settles at the base of my neck, the muscles tightening with a vice-like grip that's not going anywhere in the foreseeable future. "Lillian's husband sent me a message a couple of hours ago. Around the time he left the note on the window, looks like." I read it aloud to Florrie and Hugh.

If Florrie's nerves weren't bare to the air before, they sure are now. "This guy is scary. At least we have proof now that he was definitely the one who took the photo of you at the beach and stuck it on your window. Is that enough for Lloyd to charge him with something?"

"I doubt it. Lloyd said the harassment has to go on for a long time."

Hugh is clenching and unclenching his fists. "That's utter rubbish. This guy is smart, though. We know he's being threatening in the message, but he's careful to make sure it's not blatant enough to get him arrested."

Florrie is on her feet and nervously busying herself at the stove again. "Deep-sea diving? I wonder why he'd write that. Does that mean something I'm not getting?"

I have heard every sort of sex talk on the planet referred to in every way imaginable in the letters I receive as The Ex-Whisperer. I know what Lillian's husband means, and I know he doesn't mean it in a "You're hot. Let's hook up and have some fun" kind of way.

His message is a violent one that isn't lost on me. "Deep-sea diving means oral sex. He's threatening to assault me."

Hugh's complexion turns a shade paler. "Or maybe to drown you."

Chapter Sixteen

Hugh is fuming. "I hope I find this guy lurking in the woods out here tonight. I'd love to have five minutes alone with the bastard."

Florrie is terrified. "I hope he's hell and gone and never coming back. Oh my God no wonder his wife ran away from him. What a monster."

I'm shaking. I'm pretty sure I've reached my stress-test limit and am about to implode. "Guys, I can't do this anymore. I'm done."

Florrie reaches her hand out to comfort me, squeezes my shoulder. "Of course you are sweetie. What do you want to do? You tell us." Her voice is gentle.

"Option one, flight. I need to get in my truck right now and leave this place for good."

"I don't know if that's the best idea, Gina. This guy found you up here without any trouble. He may find you wherever else you go." Hugh's logic is steadying.

A very worried Florrie, "And if that happens, you won't have us and the rest of the family around you. And Lloyd and Floyd, at least they're cops who'll listen to you and who care about you."

I go on, "Option two, fight."

Hugh speaks quietly, "I like that option better."

Florrie's voice is shaky. "I don't like either option."

"I don't know which one is best, but I need to take a break from all this intensity for tonight. Hopefully, my batteries can recharge so I can formulate some sort of plan to deal with this madness in the morning. I know I can't handle any more right now. I'm just so damn tired. And confused. And I hate to say it out loud, but I'm afraid, too, and that's not me. I need to get my angry back so I can fight this goon."

Florrie jumps up, instantly energized as if to lead a cheer. "Okay, I vote for option two. Let's fight this creep—in the morning. Tonight, Hugh is staying with us, and we're safe here, and we don't have anything to worry about. And in the meantime, we're going to take a mental health break, and we're going to have some fun."

I interject, "And get drunk."

"That's a given. A proven way to forget your troubles." Florrie is already popping the cork on a bottle of Merlot.

Hugh is game. "The troubles aren't going anywhere. They'll still be there waiting for you in the morning, but they'll look different by then, and sometimes that's enough to be able to get on top of them. I vote for option number two, also."

Florrie fills three wine glasses. We empty them, and they're refilled just as fast. We're definitely all on the same page. There's a long silence while we focus on the alcohol and try not to mention the elephant in the room.

I break first, point out one of the pachyderms. "I gotta say, it's eating away at me trying to figure out how Dick and Iris got together."

Florrie tops up the glasses. "Hey, we're supposed to forget all that garbage for tonight. Let's talk about movies. What was the last one you each watched?"

Me, "*Sleeping With The Enemy.*"

Hugh, "*Cape Fear.*"

Florrie, "Both stalker flicks. You guys suck at this changing-the-subject thing." Florrie downs her wine.

The mystery of how my ex and Hugh's ex found each other is still niggling at the back of my brain. "I just can't let it go. There's so much that's off about it."

Florrie shrugs. "I think the dating site theory is the best one we've come up with."

Hugh shakes his head. "Too big of a coincidence."

Florrie offers up theory number two, "Okay the aunts' liberal information sharing is how the two stalkers found each other, then."

The bottle of Merlot is already drained. I grab a second one. "There are a few ways these two could have connected. It's really strange that they did, but I guess the *how* doesn't matter all that much. I think I'm more concerned with the *why*."

Hugh is clearly naturally unaffected by most things that would send lesser mortals into full stress-mode meltdowns. He shrugs the connection theories off. "I don't think you have to worry about those two fools. So what if they've found each other? Seems like they've got a lot in common, and maybe they will start dating. Good for them."

Florrie's lips curl at the thought. "Bizarro."

Hugh continues, "If it takes their attention off of us, I'm all for it."

I'm shaking my head. "That's not going to happen. Dick has been losing against me in the courts for years. His mission is to be the winner in the finale even if it kills him, or me, which is why this circus never ends with him. I'm sure their obsession with you and I will be the glue that holds Dick and Iris together."

"Krazy Glue." Florrie is still doing her best to keep things light.

I manage a half smile for her. "Their craziness levels will only ramp up if the two of them start feeding off each other."

"Such a gross image." Florrie's lips are curling again. "Two vengeance vampires sucking the crazy out of each other. Yuck."

Hugh is clearly an expert on his own ex. "Iris lives for attention. She'll take it wherever she can get it, which is why I do my best to ignore her. It's the most effective strategy in dealing with her. If Dick is willing to listen to Iris's tall tales of a messy marriage and her blameless victimhood, then she's going to be all over that."

Likewise, I know my ex pretty well. "She's going to have to give him equal time—rehashing all that crap turns his narcissistic crank, too."

Hugh snickers. "Let's say the two of them are going to feed off their mutual obsessions and whip each other into even greater frenzies than they usually run around in. If that's the case, I don't think there's anything any of us can do to stop them."

My internal cringing is manifesting as external, full-on physical shudders. "Dick's got the whole Italian grudge, vendetta thing going on when it comes to me. And probably a dozen other people too. That kind of bad blood never disappears."

Florrie rolls her eyes. "The guy's not even really Italian according to the aunts. He's from the north."

I explain for Hugh, "Anyone who's not from the toe of the boot, or Sicily, is not really Italian according to the aunts. Either way, revenge is a full-time job for Dick."

Hugh is unwavering. "I don't think we should give Dick or Iris any more of our attention."

Florrie protests, "Dick is scary. He refuses to be ignored. He could hurt Gina. Or worse."

Hugh turns to me, concerned. "Has he hurt you in the past or threatened to?"

"Does trying to scare me to death count?" I get up from the table.

Hugh smiles. "No, it doesn't. You're too tough for that."

I fill a glass of water at the kitchen sink to pace myself with the alcohol. "He regularly threatens to kill himself on my doorstep. I have to admit, that does freak me out a little."

"That could be the happy ending we're all hoping for. Lil Dick is a blight on the world. A waste of oxygen." Florrie is unapologetic.

I drink my glass of water while staring out the black square that is the window onto the lake on this dark night. The tape has left glue residue on the glass where my watcher posted the photo for me to find. I trace the outline of it with my finger. Who is this person spying on me? Did he notice this afternoon that I held myself underwater for too long and emerged from the lake gasping for breath and clutching my chest? Did he know why I did that? Does he think it's because of him? I wouldn't want to give him the satisfaction of thinking he's getting to me. I need Lillian's husband to think I couldn't care less about him, that he has no effect on me. That's how I fight this freak.

I tune back into the conversation at the kitchen table.

Levelheaded Hugh, with his calming voice, is keeping things grounded. "I know it's not easy, but we need to forget about Dick and Iris for the present time. I'm more worried about this other demented dude who's been photographing you in your bathing suit and full-on threatening you. Lillian's husband is definitely the more immediate danger."

It's obvious that Florrie hasn't been pacing herself with the vino. She's had an epiphany and jumps in, spinning the conversation in another direction. "You know what I just realized? If we put their names together, Dick and Iris, they'd be Dickiris." Florrie is choking on her oat crackers. "Can we please call them Dickiris from now on? I love it!"

I snort. "Like Brangelina but not cute sounding."

Florrie is roaring. "Use it in a sentence. I'll go first. 'Dickiris is ridiculous.'"

Hugh accepts the challenge. "Dickiris got cocky, flew too close to the sun, their wax wings melted, and they ended up swimming with the fishes."

"We can only hope." Florrie is wiping laughing tears from her eyes.

My turn,

"Hickiris, Dickiris, dock,

Lil Dick had a wee lil cock.

Bible Babe lost her mind,

Two nuts of a kind,

Hickiris, Dickirus, dock."

We're all laughing. Maybe we're all starting to lose our minds. We plead temporary insanity.

After a few moments, our laughter winds down, a weighty silence settling back in the room. The welcomed distraction of the momentary lightness has completely disappeared, and the air in the cottage feels incredibly heavy again. All the levity has left the building.

Hugh steers us back to the serious matter at hand. "The most Dickiris can do right now is annoy us, and we don't even have to allow that into our space. Iris is a bad driver, worse in bad weather, but so far that's as dangerous as it's gotten with them today. I'm sure they weren't trying to hit you with their car. Even Iris isn't that stupid. We don't want to waste any more time on those two losers. Let's not get distracted by them. What's scary here is the guy who left the note on your window and the dog in your yard. We need to know what he wants from you and how far he's willing to go to get it."

Florrie and I look at each other and shudder in unison.

Hugh picks up the photo left taped to the window and studies it again. "This is serious, and this is where we need to be putting our attention. This guy is trespassing. He's spying. He's threatening. That officially makes him a stalker. You need to bring this to the cops."

Of course, Hugh is right, and I'm in complete agreement. "I'm going to take it to Lloyd in the morning."

"Let's take a few deep breaths here." Hugh attempts to collect and organize the facts, "This guy is looking for his wife, and he thinks Gina knows where she is."

"Correct," I answer through a mouthful of dry crackers, accidentally blowing some crumbs through the air that reach all the way to the end of the table where Hugh sits. How attractive. "And he's a nasty bugger to boot. His wife made it plain that her husband was very controlling and that she was afraid of him."

Hugh wants to list the established points. "And this Lillian ran away from him to a shelter, right?"

I shrug. "I advised her to, and I assume that's where she would have gone. She said she had no friends or family who she could turn to for help. But I've never heard from her again, so I can't say for sure where she disappeared to."

Florrie perks up. "Can you check with the women's shelters?"

I shake my head. "I don't know what area she lives in, and anyway, the shelters don't release information about their residents to anybody. It's not safe for the women."

Florrie nods. "Yeah, of course, that makes sense."

Hugh, "Is there anyone else who could have left the dog in your yard for you to find?"

I've already gone there. Repeatedly. "There aren't any other players that I'm aware of."

Florrie passes Snowflake a cracker under the table. "I think it had to be

Lillian who left Snowflake here. She loves her dog, but a pet can make things complicated if you're on the run. I wouldn't leave my dog at a pound if I knew of a good-hearted person and trusted they'd take care of it for me. I'd definitely take my pet to that person for safekeeping."

Hugh gets it. "Sounds reasonable. But how would this Lillian have known where Gina moved to? How would she have found out so quickly?"

I answer, "Lloyd says it's easy for anybody to track a person down these days, social media, GPS, and all that."

"God, I hate the thought of somebody knowing where I am all the time." Florrie grimaces.

Hugh hands her a reality check. "Florrie, everyone knows where you are all the time. You own The Bakehouse in town and live above it."

"I guess you're right." She crinkles her nose.

I'm thinking out loud. "I considered the possibility that Lillian's husband dumped Snowflake here to let me know that he had Lillian back at home with him. She told me he threatened to punish her by getting rid of her dog."

"Brutal. What a bully." Florrie is appalled.

I carry on, "Initially, I thought maybe the husband was sending me a message to back off, to let me know he was in control. He blamed me for putting the idea into Lillian's head that she should leave him. But then he called and said he knew for certain I was in contact with his wife because he saw her dog at my cottage. It sure didn't sound like he was the one who dumped Snowflake in my yard."

Hugh's furrowed brow eases as if the pieces are starting to fall together for him. "So, if it wasn't him, it had to be her. Like you said, there are no other players in the game. The husband is watching your place because he knows his wife will return at some point to collect her pet. Or you'll take the dog and meet up with Lillian. Either way, he wants to make sure he's around when his wife shows up."

Florrie is thrilled. "Great! Problem solved since he's got to figure out soon that Snowflake isn't staying here anymore."

It's all starting to make sense to me too now, too. "He might think I took the dog elsewhere just so he would leave me alone."

Florrie is suddenly even more nervous than before. "Uh-oh. When he realizes his wife's dog isn't here anymore, he'll try to figure out where Snowflake went. If he drives around town long enough, he's sure to spot Snowflake at the bakery. That's going to have him thinking that I know Lillian, too, and maybe I know where she is. Yikes. Makes sense that me trying to rescue an animal is the way I'd end up leaving this world."

Hugh looks at Florrie, trying to reassure her. "Or he'll think that Lillian showed up and got the dog already and that he missed her, and he won't go looking for the dog in town at all. In which case, he'll likely leave you both alone and leave town to go searching for his wife."

I'm not feeling comforted in the least. "We could hide Snowflake, but I'm not so sure Lillian's husband will take off once Snowflake is gone. If I was him, before I left town, I'd be wanting to ask me where Lillian and her dog went. He thinks I'm still in communication with her. He'd assume that Lillian would have told me something about where she was headed. I'm his best lead for finding his wife. And he's not going to ask me nicely and then bid me adieu when I tell him I don't know anything." I take a deep breath before I lay this one on the table. "And I have another theory."

Florrie covers her ears. "I don't know if I want to hear this one."

It's been nagging at me all day. I have to say it out loud. "Maybe Lillian's husband only wants us to think that his wife left her dog with me because she's fleeing her marriage and couldn't take her precious Snowflake with her."

"I don't get it." Despite herself, Florrie is all ears now.

"Maybe her husband wants us to think he's trying hard, that he's desperate, even, to find his beloved wife."

"Because…" Hugh's eyes meet mine.

"Because he's killed her, and this is how he's covering up her death. Maybe Lillian's husband wants everyone to believe she's alive and, on the run and hiding out from him. And that he, the worried husband, will do anything to find her. But he's never going to find her. No one is."

Florrie gasps. Hugh listens without reacting. Naturally.

"Lillian could be a missing person forever. And her husband could get away with murder."

Silence.

Hugh, "That's a stretch."

Me, "I don't think it is. Why hasn't she contacted me? Why isn't she coming to get her dog that she loves so much?"

Florrie's phone rings, and we all jump at the sound.

Florrie catches her breath, answers the call, "Hey Sarah how you doing?... Oh my God, you're kidding. Are you okay? What did he look like?...Did he leave a name?...Did you see what he was driving? Thanks, and don't answer the door again. Keep it locked up." She hangs up.

"That was my cleaner, Sarah. The bakery's closed, but a man was banging on the door half an hour ago, asking if anyone had seen his lost dog. He showed her a picture of Snowflake."

Chapter Seventeen

Lillian's husband is conducting his business in broad daylight now. What's changed that makes him comfortable being out in the open? His boldness is unnerving. I need Florrie to tell me everything she heard on the phone call from her employee. "What did Sarah tell this man?"

"She told him that the dog was found and that I had Snowflake with me. She said I was staying at the lake for the night but would be back with the dog in the morning, and he could come back then to talk to me."

I'm so annoyed. "Oh my God. Why did Sarah give out information about you? Why didn't she just take his information? He's a complete stranger. Is she stupid?"

Florrie is protective of her employee. "No, she's young. She didn't tell him where on the lake I was staying, of course."

"There's only a handful of cottages on the lake inhabited right now." It's clear that Hugh is also unimpressed with Sarah's decision to share so much detail with a guy she didn't know who pounded on the locked door of a closed establishment in the dark of night. "If it's our same guy, then he saw you here last night when he was watching the two of you through the window. He already knows where to find both of you." It's also clear that Hugh is far calmer than me.

I shouldn't have snapped at Florrie. She's not to blame. I'm the reason everyone is having to deal with all this stress, including her employee, Sarah. "I'm sorry, gal. It's not your fault or Sarah's. Hugh's right. It's not like the guy learned anything new. The dog was here yesterday, and it's back here tonight. Did Sarah say what the man looked like?"

Florrie is unoffended. "Shaved head, tattoos, average everything else. Except she said he seemed weird because his voice sounded nice, but his eyes looked angry."

I know his type well. I was married to his type for two-and-a-half decades. "Great. We're dealing with a sociopath after all."

"Oh, and she said he was wearing a red T-shirt that said IDGAF."

Hugh, "What does that stand for?"

We pretty much all swear like sailors, but for some reason, Florrie silently mouths her answer to Hugh, "I Don't Give A Fuck."

There is a loud knock on the door of my cottage. All three of us startle, and the dogs go berserk. The poor cat shoots back underneath the bed. Snowflake follows.

Hugh crosses to answer the knock, holds Zoe back by the collar. "Who's there?"

Lloyd calls back, "It's me, Lloyd."

Hugh throws the door open. When Lloyd lets Zoe smell his hand, she calms down, and he pats her head.

Lloyd looks surprised to see Hugh in my cottage at this late time. "You're putting in long hours on the job, Hugh. Getting to be like me." Lloyd winks at him.

By way of explanation, Hugh, "There's a lot of weirdness going on around here, Lloyd. Glad you stopped by."

"So I hear." Lloyd turns to Florrie and me, his voice calm and even. "You two doing okay?"

"Been better." I hand Lloyd the photo with the creepy message scrawled across it. "I was going to come in to show you this in the morning. Found it taped to the outside of my window when I got home from town tonight. It's from Lillian's husband. I know it's him because he signed his online letters to me the same way, 'Eyes On You.'"

"The guy driving the small, black vehicle with the dented back bumper who was snooping around your place last night? This is the same guy who left this note? You're sure?"

I nod.

Lloyd inspects the photo. "No one's seen a car matching that description anywhere around town yet. I've had the uniforms checking all the parking lots and side streets. That's what I came over here to tell you. Also wanted to come around to keep an eye on you. I was going to suggest that your Peeping Tom must have left town, but I guess I would have been mistaken based on the calling card he left for you here." Lloyd looks at the photo more closely. "When was this taken?"

I know exactly when Zoe and I went for our swim. "This morning just before lunch. He was obviously here watching me, but I never saw him."

Lloyd looks over at Hugh.

Hugh shakes his head. "I never saw anyone around, either. I was gone at lunchtime and left again around three to pick up materials and coffee."

Lloyd begins pacing across the kitchen floor. "Son of a gun. What is this troublemaker up to?" He can't stop looking at the photo, studying the frozen image as if there's an answer in it that hasn't yet jumped out at him.

Florrie puts the kettle on for Lloyd. "My cleaner, Sarah, just called and said a man came around tonight asking if anyone had found his lost dog. He showed her a picture of the dog that was left in Gina's yard. This little guy, Snowflake." Both Snowflake and the cat have emerged from under the bed.

Weary, I rub my sore head and try to remember how many weeks this headache has lasted. I think I'm going to have to measure it in months. "Snowflake is his wife Lillian's dog. There's no doubt."

Snowflake is jumping up on Lloyd's legs, and he absently bends down to scratch the dog's ear. "Did Sarah recognize the man? Is he from around these parts?"

Florrie shakes her head. "She'd never seen him before."

Lloyd's lips purse as if he's figuring. "I'm sure my people would have spotted his car if he was driving it on the high street today. This guy must be using another vehicle around town now. Or he's got it parked in some remote location, and he's clocking a lot of miles on foot. Either way, that's not a good sign. It shows a heck of a lot of determination. He's going to an awful lot of trouble to find a woman who apparently doesn't want to be found. And he's not too shy about it anymore. He's ballsy, out in public for the world to see, also not a good sign."

Florrie pours Lloyd's tea, and her hands shake slightly but enough for me to notice. Florrie's eyes meet mine, and she puts the kettle down quickly and smooths her top over her hips, grappling for composure. "And, unfortunately, this creep is focusing an awful lot on Gina."

Grateful for the hot beverage, Lloyd smiles at Florrie. "He must figure Gina is his best lead to his wife."

After my conversation with Lloyd in the police station this morning, I'm not expecting him to be open to my theory that Lillian's husband may have done away with his wife and is actually going to all this seeming trouble to find her in a well-planned effort to cover up foul play.

I give it another shot but approach the topic gingerly. "I guess when Lillian's husband was on my property today, he realized that Snowflake wasn't here with me any longer, so he went looking for the dog in town."

Lloyd sips from his teacup. "It's amazing how many people don't take notice of other humans but remember every dog they ever see."

Florrie pipes in, "That's me."

Lloyd continues, "I'm sure this guy wants to know where the dog is because, if he finds the pooch, he'll find the wife if she turns up to reclaim her pet. And there's a good chance neighbors will notice a cute little pup like this one whereas they might never take notice of his wife." Lloyd pets Snowflake again.

I'm trying to present my idea to Lloyd in a subtle way in the hopes that, with some gentle prodding, he may come to the same conclusion on his own. I try again. "Up until last night, this guy was sneaking around in the dark, running his car into trees just to avoid being seen. Why do you think he would suddenly show his face to the locals in town today, connecting himself to his missing wife by asking about her dog in public? I mean Florrie's employee is a witness who can identify him."

Puzzled, Lloyd looks at me. "Witness to what? He's just looking for his missing dog."

I'm not so great at subtle. "Looking for his missing wife's missing dog."

Lloyd is shaking his head emphatically. "His wife is not officially missing.

134

No one has filed a missing person's report, so no one is looking for her. Adults of sound mind are allowed to take off and disappear for a time if they want to. They're not legally obliged to tell anyone where they've gone, not even their spouse."

"So, you're saying this guy still hasn't committed any crime?" Hugh sounds a little irritated.

"None that we can prove at present."

It's becoming difficult to conceal my outrage. "What about this invasive photo he took of me? And the intimidating message scrawled across it? He's had to trespass to tape it to my window. He's made me feel extremely unsafe. Surely he's broken some laws there."

Lloyd is trained in keeping tempers cool, and he attempts to do so now. "It's not that simple. First of all, if someone secretly takes photos of a person, you have to prove that there was a sexual purpose to the act. Usually, that means the person being photographed was in some state of undress. We live in the digital age. Everyone's got a camera in their phone, and virtually everything is recorded. Strangers are in the background and foreground of other people's photographs all the time. An individual is allowed to take pictures of people without their consent. They just can't publish them or use them maliciously."

Florrie pipes in, "Okay well he was trespassing. Isn't that a crime?"

Lloyd lifts his arms helplessly. "Secondly, a person is allowed to enter someone else's property if they're delivering something. That's not trespassing. There might be grounds for a mischief charge here because the message seems unpleasant, but it's unlikely. The courts usually just order a fine if you can make anything stick to begin with. It's hardly worth pursuing. And still, we'd have to prove that this guy is the one who wrote the note. It's not so easy."

Florrie is exasperated, "I can see why people end up taking the law into their own hands sometimes."

"The system sucks." I'm extremely frustrated as well, and the fact that, apparently under the law, Lillian's husband hasn't done anything wrong confuses me. I'm second-guessing myself. Have I been overreacting to all that's gone on?

I'm pacing now. "Lloyd, please tell me if I'm understanding the situation correctly from a legal standpoint. After trolling me online and sending me numerous threatening and aggressive letters, some strange man creeps around my yard in the dark, watching me through the window, then texts me to tell me what I'm wearing and eating to prove to me that he is, in fact, outside my home watching me from the shadows. Later, he calls me in the middle of the night and threatens to pay me a visit in person so he can question me face to face about his wife, who was so afraid of him she was planning on fleeing to a shelter and has either done so or has plain disappeared, willingly or not."

My voice is getting louder and higher with each point I rhyme off. "Today, the same man is on my property again without my knowledge or consent, photographs me in my bathing suit, and later returns to stick the picture on my window with a scrawled message letting me know he is still watching me and makes a veiled threat of sexual assault. And even with all that so far, this man's behavior isn't even close to being labeled as harassment because, while frightening, the threatening acts haven't carried on for a long enough time period. So, since this maniac hasn't yet assaulted or killed me, he hasn't technically broken any laws, and I'm just going to have to learn to deal. Do I understand the legalities here correctly, Lloyd?" I may or may not be screeching at this point.

I notice the louder I get the more stoically silent Hugh becomes.

Lloyd exhales slowly. "The way you state the facts makes the situation sound pretty terrible, and I'm sorry to say that your explanation is, unfortunately, accurate. What this man has done so far would certainly warrant the police paying him a visit and giving him a stern warning to stay away from you and to refrain from further contacting you or making you feel uncomfortable in any way. I've been looking for this guy, and if I find him, I'll be giving him a warning myself that would put the fear of God in anybody. You can be sure about that. As far as the law goes, I can't even say if you'd be successful in obtaining a peace bond at this point. I don't think the courts would do much with this. I'm sorry Gina. That's the way the laws are on the books right now. And you're right, in lots of ways, the system does suck. But the reality is, the existing legal framework is all we've got to work with right now."

Florrie is disgusted, and her voice is strident. "Well, the damn laws need to change."

Lloyd concurs, "Can't argue with you there."

My tolerance level is boiling over. "I guess I'll have to wait until this guy physically harms me before I can count on the law to help me out then, Lloyd. That's basically what you're telling me."

Lloyd still maintains his calm, professional demeanor. "We're not going to let that happen, Gina." He rises from the table. "I'm gonna get back out there and try to find this perp. You three take care of each other and let me know right away if you hear anything from this guy again. Gina, I likely don't need to tell you that you probably shouldn't be staying alone right now. You probably shouldn't be staying at this cottage at all. Can you stay in town? You've got at least a dozen family members who I'm sure would be happy to have you visit."

"I'll consider it. I don't want this creep thinking he's winning by driving me out of my home."

"Don't waste your time trying to deduce what an angry, desperate person might be thinking. You'll never figure it out. Most times, they're not thinking at all. They're driven by the basest animal instincts. There's no winning here, Gina. There's just keeping you safe until we apprehend the bugger."

Hugh holds the door open. "We're sticking around. Gina won't be alone. Night, Lloyd. And thanks for stopping by."

Lloyd picks up the photo from the kitchen table to take it with him. "Night. Thanks for the tea." He accepts the biscuits that Florrie presses into his hand. "And the cookies." He tips his hat, winks, and is out the door. "Lock it up."

After Lloyd leaves, the three of us share long glances across the stillness of the room, but there's not much more to say tonight.

The loudest noise in the cottage is the pounding in my head. "Let's take the dogs out for a pee and get some sleep. It's late."

When we come back inside, I hand Hugh a pillow and some extra blankets, and he makes up a bed for himself on the couch.

The night is dead quiet, and I think between the wine and the sheer mental exhaustion, none of us have much trouble falling asleep.

* * *

I can tell morning has come because I see pink instead of black through my closed eyelids, which feel heavy as velvet curtains. My mind is slowly waking, but my body is seriously lagging. The cottage is completely silent, the others still asleep. I'll lie in for a while longer, so I don't disturb either of them.

Juggling four kids and their dozens of activities was always fun for me, even when exhausting, but being married to a workaholic is a lot like being a single parent—it takes its toll. Being married to a narcissist who spins a web of lies so tight it nearly chokes the life out of you is next level. I've burned out once or twice in my life, and I remember the feeling vividly. It sucks hard. The recovery process takes a long time, and I assume the older one gets, the longer it takes to make oneself whole again. I'm beginning to worry that I may be on the verge of burnout now. The verge is a warning signal. It's not so bad yet, kind of like the soft shoulder of the road when you're driving tired, and your vehicle drifts a little off the pavement and catches the gravel. You're supposed to correct, stop, rest, and make sure you're firing on all cylinders before carrying on with your journey. Burnout is a total car wreck. When you're only on the verge of burnout, you still have a chance to steer yourself back on course and prevent the crash from happening. I'm going to try my best to do that.

I'm thinking coffee and the beach is a good cure for me just now. I must have gained a hundred plus pounds this week because it feels like I'm dragging a three-hundred-pound body out of my bed. Two and a half of me (okay, maybe closer to two of me). I pull on my jeans and a T-shirt, tiptoe quietly toward the bathroom, trying not to wake Hugh or Florrie.

I know I shouldn't peek. It's not very respectful, but I'm curious to see what Hugh looks like when he's sleeping. I let my eyes drift in his direction as I cross through the main room.

The couch is empty, the blankets folded neatly on top of the pillow. He's gone. I check out the window and see that Florrie's car is also missing. Snowflake, too. Jeeze, how did I not hear either of them leave? How dead asleep could I have been? What time is it? I check.

Damn. Ten o'clock! I don't think I've slept in this late in years. When I come out of the bathroom, Spook is wrapping himself around my legs, but Zoe just looks up from her cozy dog bed in the corner. She can't be aroused to get up this morning, either.

There's a note from Florrie on the kitchen table. "Good morning, Sleeping Beauty. You were so peaceful we didn't want to wake you. Coffee's on, and there's a fruity yogurt parfait with your name on it in the fridge. Call you later. Have a great day!"

In fact, the coffee is not on. It was on, but after two hours of waiting for me to wake up, even the coffee pot gave up and shut itself off. I flick the switch back on. Hours-old coffee will do fine for me this morning. I accept it as my punishment for being so sloth-like.

At ten-fifteen, coffee break is over for Hugh and his man Ryan, and the saws and drills start up again around the bunkie. I even slept through those one-hundred-and-twenty-decibel level sounds earlier.

The pets and I move into the screened-in porch. Fall is in the air this morning. There's a cool crispness that gives my bare arms goosebumps. The dog and cat find shards of sunlight on the painted wood plank floor to curl up in. I set up my laptop and coffee on the wicker table facing the lake. After too many minutes of staring at the rolling waves, I finally check my messages. Yikes, so many. I'm days behind in responding. I scroll through The Ex-Whisperer letters and choose a couple of interesting ones to publish.

While I'm working, another letter comes in that catches my attention.

Dear Ex-Whisperer,

I heard about you from a friend of mine. She told me how much you helped her out. It's actually her that I'm writing to you about. She is such a sweet person, quiet and shy, doesn't have many friends. I met Lillian at our local library. She was always there three or four days a week, as am I, but I don't know her all that well. We belonged to the same book club for a time, but her husband made her quit. From what she told me, he sounded extremely controlling, and I believe she was afraid of him.

Sometimes he would wait on the street for her to leave the library and yell at her when he got a hold of her outside. She said her husband took her computer away from her because she had written to you. The last time I saw her, she was using the library computer to reach out to you again.

I'm concerned with Lillian's safety. She was talking about ending her marriage and said you advised her to go to a shelter. She hasn't shown up at the library in over a week, which is unusual for her. I'm hoping she's safe and sound at a shelter now. Have you heard from Lillian? Do you know whether she's okay or not? I hope her husband hasn't done something to hurt her. Or worse. Please do not publish this letter on your website or column. I wouldn't want Lillian's husband to read it.

Sincerely,

Friend of a friend.

Chapter Eighteen

At least I'm not the only one who's got a bad feeling about Lillian. I quickly forward a copy of the letter to Lloyd to keep him up to speed. Not that it's going to help much. It's not as if there's an investigation going on into Lillian's disappearance, and it's not as if this letter would prompt the police to launch one. The letter doesn't have any clues or answers in it, nor does it implicate Lillian's husband in her disappearance in any way.

The letter does confirm that Lillian believed she was in some degree of danger and that her husband was the person posing it. It also confirms that I'm not just imagining or exaggerating my fears about Lillian. My suspicions are not unfounded, and I'm not alone in having them.

We already knew Lillian's husband was a controlling jerk, which in my books should be reason enough to lock someone up and throw away the key. Unfortunately, others don't agree.

Perhaps Lillian's friend can help me identify who Lillian is. She'll be able to tell me what town she's from, at least. And maybe we can even get a copy of Lillian's library card that would have her last name and possibly a photo of her on it. I'm sure Lloyd could get Lillian's address from the library or from the book club she was a member of. The privacy laws are tough these days. It's difficult to get information on people if you attempt to go through legitimate channels. Like Lloyd said, you can find anything on anybody, including where a person is hiding out, if you're willing to go around and behind those proper channels.

If Lillian is alive and well and staying at a shelter, or if she's on the run from her husband, then she wouldn't want to be found, and certainly wouldn't be pleased with me attempting to track her down. Maybe the best thing I can do for Lillian is to let all this go. For some reason, that's not what my gut is telling me to do. And even if I wanted to, Lillian's husband isn't letting me walk away from the situation right now.

I'm fully aware that Lillian's husband is most certainly reading all the letters and responses on my website and in my column looking to see whether his wife contacts me or whether I reach out to her. I edit her friend's letter and post it, giving just enough information to catch her husband's attention. Then I respond to Lillian's friend. Maybe her husband buys it maybe he doesn't.

Dear Friend of a Friend,

I too am concerned for Lillian and have not heard from her since the last letter she wrote to me. I hope she went to a shelter and is getting back on her feet again. I am going to envision our friend Lillian safe and sound in my mind and send her good thoughts because those are the only things I can offer her now.

Affectionately yours,
    The Ex-Whisperer

I hit Post

I also send a private message to Friend of a Friend.

Hey Friend,

I'm glad you wrote to me about Lillian. I'm seriously worried about her also. I'm trying to find some information on her that I can share with the police in case she's in trouble and needs assistance. Can you please tell me what town you live in and what library branch Lillian attended with you? Do you know her last name or maybe even her address? Anything you can share would be helpful.

Thanks again for making contact,

The Ex-Whisperer.

Florrie calls to check in. "Morning, sleepyhead. How's the day going so far? Bet it's better than yesterday."

"Nearly every single day of my life has been better than yesterday. Did Lillian's husband come into the bakery looking for Snowflake again?"

"No, but there was a small black car parked across the street for a long time with a guy in it. Average everything sort of guy, just like Sarah's description. Didn't look like he did anything other than watch the strip. I called Lloyd to tell him, and he said he was sending someone over to talk to the guy. A few minutes later, the car was gone."

"At least he didn't bother you if it was Lillian's husband."

"I know, right? That's one good thing. Also, Iris and a flock of sheep from her Jonestown Church were parading down the sidewalk today, looking like they had some pressing business. Probably just praying at people without their permission. Lil' Dick must have drunk the Kool-Aid, too. He was in the middle of the crowd craning his neck to see if you were in the bakery, I think. He wouldn't dare step inside here. He knows he'd get a face full of meringue on the house. Anyway, Dick's sure not concerned about anybody knowing he's up haunting these parts of the country. He's definitely out of his stalker's closet for now."

"The good thing about that is he probably wouldn't do anything too weird right now because everyone knows he's around and there are enough people watching him."

"True. Look at us cheery optimists today, finding the silver linings everywhere we look."

I'm trying. "Yeah. I'm in serious need of upsides right now."

"I've got another one for you. Hot contractor Hugh has got the hots for you."

Ugh, I can't deal with silliness at this early hour. "That could not be farther from the truth. Also, hooking up is the absolute last thing on my mind and worst thing that could happen right now."

Florrie offers a reminder of my woes, "Not quite the worst thing. You forgetting about your secret admirer freak?"

"*Freaks* plural thanks for the reminder, and on that note, I shall bid you farewell."

"And I shall stay cheery all day. Cheerio and toodle-oo!" Florrie hangs up.

As soon as we disconnect, Floyd, Lloyd's identical twin, and fellow police chief, calls through.

Floyd is even more chipper than my last caller. "Top of the morning to you, Ms. Gina Malone. It's Floyd, here. Lloyd's turn to try to lure in a few fish upriver, so I'm taking over the shop."

"Hey, Floyd. That's nice that Lloyd's got a bit of time off. Did you catch any, or did all the big ones get away on you?" I engage in the de rigueur small-town small talk.

"Oh, I managed to bag a bucket or two. Stop by, and I'll fry you up a fillet."

I laugh. "Thanks, Floyd. I'll probably be seeing you soon what with the series of unfortunate events parading around."

"Lloyd filled me in on what's been going on with you lot. And it's a lot, indeed!"

"Too much. Florrie said there was a car matching the description of Lillian's husband's vehicle parked outside the bakery this morning. Were you able to speak to the driver?"

"We were, but it doesn't look like he's our guy. Small black car, but his rear bumper was clean, no dents. Could have been repaired recently, but the uniform wasn't able to discern that visually. We'd have to take a closer look at the bumper, and the stop didn't warrant that."

"Was he bald with tattoos?"

"Wearing a hat and long-sleeved jacket so they couldn't tell for sure. The man said he was in town to do some hunting and was on the high street waiting for his buddies to arrive. He had a shotgun in the trunk, a hunting knife, and some rope and canvas. Looked legit according to the uniform."

"Well, if it was our guy, the fact that he's got a trunk full of weapons and restraints doesn't make me feel so great."

Floyd chuckles. "Understood, but it doesn't seem that this one was our guy. Half the vehicles in town have got hunting gear in their trunks at this time of year. We recorded his plate just to be safe, though. Don't you worry, missus. We're keeping our eyes and ears peeled. We'll call you if we catch wind of anything at all."

"Thanks, Floyd." I hang up.

* * *

A long hot shower brings me some much-needed balance and calm followed by Florrie's fabulous yogurt parfait layered with tart raspberries and crunchy maple granola. I'm feeling way more centered and stronger than last night. *I got this.* My new mantra.

I brush my still-wet hair, put on a bit of makeup. Through the bathroom window, a number of voices float in from the road side of my property. Zoe hears them, too, and starts barking. I look out the window to see who's here.

Two men and a woman, middle-aged and well-groomed, if overly conservative in a righteous sort of way, are standing next to the bunkie speaking with Hugh. He seems to know them. There's a lot of aggressive arm-waving going on, and the voices grow louder. Especially Hugh's. In fact, Hugh is starting to look thoroughly pissed off. I can't make out what they're saying, but I do notice that the woman is clutching a bible against her chest.

Really, if they're Jehovah's Witnesses out on a neighborhood mission, I think Hugh would be better off politely telling them to shove off. I refuse to argue with those people when they knock on my door. They're all extremely annoying and frighteningly weird, but I get rid of them quickly when I tell them I'm a professional psychic.

Uh-oh. Things are going downhill quickly. Hugh's voice is now clearly projecting a demand to the trio to get the heck off his jobsite and not come back. I take Zoe on her leash and step outside, round the corner of the cottage to watch them pile hurriedly into their soccer-mom van. They all look straight at me but don't smile, nod, or wave, so I respond in kind with a stone-cold glare. Hugh turns his back on them and returns to working on

145

the bunkie, but right after they depart, he walks purposefully toward me.

"You don't happen to have any whiskey, do you?"

I'm surprised by his request. "I don't. And by the way, it's only three o'clock. You know that, right?"

By Hugh standards, he's looking extremely stressed, his cheeks flushed in anger. "It's been a very long day, and those zealots just capped it for me."

I want to help. "There's a half bottle of the red wine left over from last night."

"That's not gonna cut it today. Times like this call for something stronger. Want to go for a ride, pick up a bottle of Crown Royal?"

I'm even more surprised now. "I don't drink the stuff."

"You might start after I tell you what that visit was all about."

"Oh God."

"You guessed right."

Hugh's already got his truck keys out. "Bring the dog. She can come for the ride." He holds open the back door of his pickup and whistles. Zoe leaps inside it. He opens the front passenger door for me. "Hop in, and I'll elaborate."

Hugh calls out to the young man working for him, "Ryan, I'm running into town to pick up some supplies. You can shut it down, lock the tools up. I'll see you in the morning."

"Awesome." Young Ryan is thrilled to be knocking off early.

I climb in the black pickup. "I've braced myself for the worst. Give it to me straight."

Hugh is exasperated. "Frickin' Dickiris." He closes my door for me, slides in behind the wheel.

"What are those two mutants up to now?"

Hugh pulls onto the road, heads into town.

"The gruesome couple have outdone themselves. They've gone way over the top even by their weirdo yardstick."

"Oh no. Maybe I need to work up to this slowly. First, tell me who those people were. They looked like Jehovah's Witnesses."

"Good eye. Like Johos, but even worse. They're from Iris's church. The mystery of how our two exes hooked up has now been solved."

"That's good to know. Fill me in."

"Iris researched you online, figured out who your ex was, and contacted him. What she lacks in smarts she makes up for in bulldoggedness."

"I believe that. She looks a little bulldoggish."

"She told Dick about you and me."

"You and me? What's to tell? You mean she told him that I've hired you to renovate my cottage?"

"Told him that we were having an affair. As in cheating."

"Cheating on who? We're both single."

"The three dingbat delegates from her church told me both of us are still married in the eyes of God and always will be."

"Yeah, well, my God don't roll that way. Also, you and I are not involved with each other."

"They know I spent the night at your place, so they're not buying that story."

My voice is rising in tandem with my blood pressure. "They don't need to buy anything. We don't need to sell them on anything. Nothing we do is any of their business. Why do we even need to care? Why are we having this conversation? Why can I feel blood pounding in my ears because of people who know nothing about me and mean even less to me?"

"Because they know how to get under our skin. And they're working very hard at it. Iris invited Dick to come to town for a special, emergency, church meeting, and he was more than happy to oblige."

"Of course he was. He'd be drooling if he thought he could get any dirt on me. But Dick is a lapsed Catholic. He hasn't gone to church in years."

"From the way they were talking, it sounds like maybe Dick found the Lord yesterday at the meeting. Iris is taking full credit for his being born again."

"How convenient. What a conman—he'll be a fallen angel by the end of the week. I guess being invited to come to town explains why Dick didn't feel the need to hide in the shadows. He had a valid reason to be here as far as he was concerned."

"They called in all the big guns, the elders and church council."

"A meeting of biblical proportions."

Hugh chuckles. "They called in the big guns because, apparently, it's a big issue that needs to be dealt with."

"What is?"

"We are. Iris told them that you're a witch and that you put a spell on me. Dick corroborated her stories. They're on a mission to protect the whole town from your wickedness now."

"Oh no, he promised he'd never tell anyone about my baby-eating habit."

"Iris asked them to try to save me and her marriage, which is why they came to talk to me at your place. They're all as looney as she is. They told me in the meeting they held hands in a circle and prayed, asking God to cast you out of my life and out of town."

"Gotta love neighborly Christians. Maybe I'll sic the aunts on them."

Hugh scoffs. "Some of these hypocrites are regular customers of your aunts, and they don't go there for the spaghetti. They sneak in the back door of Happily Napoli to get their fortunes told. Those old gals have gotta have the goods on everybody around here."

"We might have to ask them to use it one of these days. For now, this church meeting was held in a public place, and these nasty gossips defamed my character in public. That's slander. I think I'm going to let my lawyer handle this one. He can send out letters warning these no-good do-gooders to cease and desist. Scare the righteousness out of them."

Hugh pulls off the highway. "Sounds like the right thing to do. Put an end to their misguided mission before they get the tar and feathers cooked up."

We drive up in front of the liquor store.

Hugh parks. "Coming in?"

"Should we be seen together in public? At the liquor store of all places?"

Hugh hops out. "You betcha."

In we go.

"So, what's your poison?"

"I wish I could say I was a scotch on the rocks gal. I aspire to be one. It sounds cool when you order and goes great with a little black dress, but I'm actually a super sucky drinker. Other than wine, a brown cow or Baileys is the most I can handle."

Hugh is laughing. "That's incredibly unimpressive."

I elbow him. "Hey, I know already. Don't rub it in. It's embarrassing, but there's nothing I can do. I just don't have the stomach for it. Truth is, I'm a gummy girl at heart."

Hugh looks surprised. "That actually is impressive. And it's legal now."

"That's right. I can consume cannabis-infused candy out of the closet now."

Hugh picks up his Crown Royal and grabs a bottle of Baileys, too. He pays for both. "You wanna stop by the pot shop?"

"No, I'm good with the Baileys for tonight, thanks."

As we cross through the parking lot back to the truck, my neck prickles with the feeling of someone behind me, and I answer the urge to turn toward it. Someone in a silver vehicle is taking photos of the liquor store through their open car window. Hugh unlocks the truck doors.

Correction, they're taking photos of us in front of the liquor store. "Is that your frigging ex with the camera over there?"

Hugh whips around to face the silver Nissan, throws the paper booze bag onto the seat of his truck, and books it in the direction of the paparazzi.

Iris's mouth drops open when she realizes Hugh is jogging toward her. She looks totally shocked that we've spotted her, what with her being incognito wearing her ridiculously oversized dark sunglasses and all.

Iris doesn't have time to roll up her window before Hugh is on it, stretching his long arms through it—If it was anyone other than Hugh, I'd think he was reaching for her throat.

Chapter Nineteen

I ris throws her camera down, starts reversing, but Hugh has his entire head and shoulders inside the open driver's window. Such a bad idea. An eerie squeaking catches my ear—it's emanating from Iris's mouth, her B-movie starlet version of a scream. It's loud, not pretty. Kind of like the sound Dudley Do-Right's damsel in distress girlfriend made when Snidely Whiplash tied her to the train tracks every week—overly dramatic and not believable.

Hugh grabs Iris's keys out of the ignition and throws them onto the ground a good fifteen feet away from her vehicle. Then he pulls his body out of Iris's car.

Hugh is telling his ex-wife off real good. People passing by turn to stare but don't stop to intervene. Likely because all of them know both Hugh and Iris, and no one wants to get involved in their messy theatrics.

I stand next to the truck in the parking lot, immobilized and mesmerized by the Italian opera scene playing out before me. I can't make out everything Hugh is saying because all the commotion is causing Zoe to bark her brains out in the back seat of the pickup, but it sounds as if he's getting a whole lot off his chest. When he's finished, Hugh spins around, strides back to his truck, and holds the passenger door open for me. We climb inside in silence.

Iris exits her car and crouches down to retrieve her keys from across the lot. Meanwhile, Hugh takes long deep breaths, bringing himself back to center, coming down from the adrenaline rush and the stress attack before he turns the key in the ignition. He doesn't look good and doesn't speak.

I offer quietly, "Can I say that probably wasn't the best approach?"

"I know. It's no good for my health. She's no good for my health." Hugh starts driving.

We travel halfway back to the cottage without talking. I hope Hugh is self-reflecting.

I break the silence. "You know, if you'd written into my column about this messy situation and I was responding to your letter, I'd tell you that you just inadvertently gave your ex one of the best gifts she's had in forever."

"You mean by telling her she's a delusional, vindictive piece of work?"

"What Iris wants more than anything is to engage with you. She'll obviously go to any lengths to get your attention. You know that. Like a naughty two-year-old, even if all Iris can get from you is an angry reaction, that's still preferable to being ignored by you. She won, and you lost because she feels good right now and you feel like crap after your encounter, and that's how this scenario will play out every single time you entertain her melodramatics."

"Sage advice. I should probably start reading your column. Truth is I've been successfully ignoring Iris for ten years, and it's not very hard for me to do even though she's constantly in my face. I don't usually react. I'm kind of surprised with myself by how she's been pushing my buttons the past few days."

"You've probably been repressing your feelings for a long time, and you finally blew. That's normal. It happens to all of us."

"I don't think it's that. At least, it's not only that. I guess I really don't like her messing with you."

"I get that. You're working for me right now, so when she's messing with me, she's screwing with your business, your livelihood. I'm sure you're not used to your ex-wife attempting to sabotage your relationships with your clients."

Hugh looks over at me. Pointedly. "It's not that. You're not just a client."

We are both silent for the moment, both aware that we just crossed over into new territory. For the next few minutes, it's not too late to cross back. If we stay quiet and wait, one of us can say something that pulls us back to where we were a moment ago. I can say something like, *It's great that we've got each other's backs in this working relationship. I think the project will be more successful because of it.* He can say something like, *You're not just a client—I see you as a true business partner in this endeavor, and even as a friend.*

Waiting. Waiting. Neither of us is saying the thing that will erase the implications of Hugh's last words. Soooooooo…are we silently agreeing to enter into this new territory, then? This great unknown where relationships deepen and love can blossom, or just fun and sex can be had, and you never know how things will play out, but that's okay because it's all good and mostly unavoidable anyway and is simply humans being human?

Finally, we turn to look at each other, and both talk at the same time.

Hugh, "I'm sorry if I spoke out of turn and made you feel uncomfortable."

Me, "I'm sorry if I left you hanging there and made you feel uncomfortable."

We both stop talking. Look at each other with unreadable faces for a long moment, then burst into laughter. Now my blood is pounding in my ears for a different reason. A much better one.

Hugh pulls up in the laneway of my cottage. His man Ryan is gone, and all the equipment has been locked up for the night as Hugh instructed.

I get out of the truck then open the back door and release the beast. Zoe bounds around outside for a bit.

Hugh holds up the bag of liquor.

"Are we still going to have that drink?"

I'm smiling. "Sure."

Hugh visibly relaxes and gives me an easy smile of his own.

I have absolutely no idea what's going to transpire between the two of us this evening. I'm equally excited and terrified out of my mind. But more than anything, I'm undyingly grateful that I shaved my legs before I went for a swim yesterday.

I unlock the cottage, and the three of us step inside.

Hugh pulls the whiskey and Baileys out of the paper bag, sets the two bottles down on the kitchen counter. I cross in front of him to reach for two glasses from the cupboard. My arm brushes against his firm shoulder. He turns to face me. And this new thing between us fizzes and pops in the air.

"McTavish. You're Scottish, right?" *Ladies, watch how it's done. Not.* I cringe inwardly. It's been too long. I suck at this.

"Aye. Even wear a kilt once in a while."

The bloody aunts and their tea leaves. How did they know?

A whole world of reasons not to move forward on this possibly emotionally reckless path flashes before me. We're about to jump off a cliff, and there's no net below to catch us.

We could be screwing ourselves so royally here. We're working together.

What if things go sour between us romantically when we're only halfway through the project and it's impossible to continue our professional relationship?

What if I feel as if I can't speak up to complain about something that he's built in the cottage because I'm worried it will affect our intimate relationship?

What if he's bad in bed and I want to get out of this real quick?

What if—

What if he's the best kisser I've ever had the pleasure of experiencing?

What if I melt into his long, sinewy body and lose myself there for weeks at a time?

What if his kisses remind me that I'm more alive than I've felt in years, and what if I feel as if I've kissed him a thousand times before in a thousand different lifetimes? What then?

When I return to the moment, Hugh smiles knowingly as if he heard every question I asked myself and has all the answers. He bridges the small space between us by brushing a stray curl from my face.

Our lips lock. Hugh holds my face between both of his large, square, rough hands and kisses me deeply, longingly.

I don't know which of us is pushing and which of us is pulling, but our tangled, frenetic bodies are moving through the space toward my bedroom, and we can't seem to get there fast enough. Our eyes are closed, and we stumble over furniture and fumble with zippers, but nothing slows us down.

And then the room tilts. Hugh falls backward, flat on his back onto the floor with a loud thump and a crash, taking a table lamp and me out with him. I flip above and beyond him, arse over teakettle, screaming in shock as I go down in flames of shame. How monumentally unromantic is this? What in God's name? Zoe is immediately on top of us, leaping and play biting and barking with glee for the roughhousing game she thinks we've invented just for her.

Hugh sits up, holding the back of his head. He reaches out to help unpretzel me. I can't see anything for the hair in my eyes.

Hugh, "I tripped over this box and these papers spread all over the floor."

I push the hair off my face. "What the...? How did those papers get there?"

The cat rubs against Hugh's side, and Hugh rubs the other side of his body, which has to be sore from the fall. "The cat knocked it over?"

I hoist myself up to a standing position. I'm sore, too. "No, that box was on the floor in the spare bedroom. The cat couldn't have dragged it into this room. These are my work papers. Copies of the letters my readers send in and stuff like that."

I go out to the screened-in porch where I was working before I left. All my papers have been thrown around, strewn about the floor. "Someone's been inside the cottage. They've been riffling through all my work material."

I run back in to check the coffee table. "Damn it! My laptop's been stolen!"

Chapter Twenty

Floyd is at my home in less than ten minutes. He's brought a young female officer with him. "This is Constable Griffin. She's going to take a look around to see if the perpetrator left any evidence behind that may help us out."

The young officer nods, begins moving through the rooms to inspect the place. Spook won't leave her alone, which tells me she's sweet.

Hugh paces back and forth. "They must have been watching the house closely to know the exact timing of when Gina was out, had taken the dog with her, and Ryan and I weren't working on the site. There was only a window of about forty minutes when the cottage was empty. We weren't gone any longer than that."

"There were no cars parked nearby so he had to have been on foot. Waiting and watching in the woods." No pacing for me. I barely have the strength to stand. "That was the only time since I arrived here that there wasn't somebody, Zoe at least, in the cottage. Spook was here but he's not talking."

Floyd is noting everything down in pencil in his little black book. "Definitely sounds like the perp was casing the joint waiting for the perfect opportunity to get inside here and rummage around."

Hugh is still pacing, and it's beginning to agitate the crap out of me. "We know it wasn't my lunatic ex-wife because she was busy being buggy in town with us when the break-in occurred."

Floyd jots down that detail, too. "Looks like whoever it was went through the place in one heck of a hurry, but they were obviously looking for something very specific since they left most of your belongings behind.

Clearly, they were searching for something in your files. Did they take anything of value other than your computer?"

I'm at a loss, "Nothing else that I've noticed. They've gone through my work papers, but there's no way for me to tell if any of them are missing. There's just too much there, and it's all jumbled up now. The files are valuable to me, but I can't imagine they'd be worth anything to anyone else. Other than my laptop I didn't have anything of much value in here. Almost all of my things are packed in storage until the renovations are finished."

"No unpublished manuscript for a *New York Times* bestseller laying around?" Floyd winks at me.

"That blockbuster's all up here." I tap my finger against my temple.

Floyd is serious again. "If we hadn't had the recent goings-on with the stranger hanging around your place, I'd assume it was just kids messing about. Happens on the regular especially this time of year when the cottages empty out." He seems to be thinking out loud. "But the likeliest scenario is that our guy in the small dark car returned for another visit. And he's looking for information that he thinks you might have that could lead him to his wife who's gone AWOL."

I already knew that, of course, but still hate hearing it said out loud. "I don't have any of the communications between me and Lillian printed out. No reason to, so there was nothing for him to find here."

Floyd looks at me expectantly, "The letters to and from you and the guy's wife are all on your missing computer?"

I'm nodding. "They're all online posted on my blog. He didn't need my laptop to see them. He's not going to find anything on the computer that he hasn't already seen online."

Floyd is still jotting. "But our disgruntled hubby wouldn't know that until he checks your computer out for himself. He may be thinking you and this Lillian are messaging privately."

Then I remember. "I did receive a letter from a friend of Lillian's who is worried about her and hasn't heard from her in a week. I forwarded it to Lloyd. The friend asked me not to publish her email and I didn't. He'll find that one if he looks."

"Yeah, I saw that letter. Did the friend ever give you any personal information to help us figure out who this Lillian lady is? Her surname or address?"

"No. I asked her to tell me whatever she could, but I never heard back from her again. I find that super strange."

Hugh stops pacing. "I wonder why she wouldn't want to help us find her friend if she was so worried about her that she went to the trouble of writing to you about it?"

Floyd shakes his head. "That's typical. People are curious, maybe she was just being nosy. You'd be surprised how many good Samaritans hightail it in the other direction when it comes time for them to get involved in a matter in a way that would actually be constructive. It's the know-it-all next-door neighbor syndrome, people hoping they get their fifteen minutes of fame on the six o'clock news. Most people are full of dog doo-doo."

That theory's not sitting well with me. "She sounded like she knew a lot about Lillian, and she seemed genuine. To be honest I'm surprised she hasn't tried to help. Maybe I'll hear from her yet."

"Don't hold your breath."

Constable Griffin, Spook at her side, enters the room. "Didn't find anything, sir. Nothing at all. I think the perp must have worn gloves."

"Okay, take a look around outside before you leave."

"Will do." Constable Griffin pets the cat goodbye then exits the cottage. Spook looks sad, follows his new friend from window to window watching her outside.

Floyd tucks his notepad and pencil away inside his coat pocket. "I had one of the uniforms call around to the auto body shops to find out if any out of towners with small dark cars had dents in their back bumpers ironed out in the past week. Harve over in Northampton had one on Tuesday. The owner paid cash. Sounds like he could be our guy."

Hugh perks up. "Did Harve give a description of him?"

"Said there was nothing remarkable. Just your average Joe. But he was in a heck of a hurry. Said he had to get back to the city for work. Harve bumped a couple of other customers to get this guy in early. He paid extra for the rush service."

Now I perk up. "But he didn't go back to the city. The man sitting in front of Florrie's bakery for all that time this morning could have been the guy we're looking for. Your officers talked to him and took down his license plate. They'll be able to give us a description of him. That's great."

Floyd crosses to the door. "It's possible. That's what I'm hoping for. I'll let you know just as soon as we have anything that cross references. In the meantime, I don't think I need to tell you that you shouldn't be staying out here alone, Gina. Dog or no dog."

Floyd leaves. Constable Griffin drives out behind him.

My head killing me, I slump back onto the couch. Hugh and I are alone again. We could pick up where we left off, but no sane person would be able to.

Hugh, "Well that was a real buzz- kill."

Me, "Extremely memorable first kiss."

Hugh laughs. I can't. FML.

Hugh sits down beside me on the couch, turns to look at me, points at my face. "You've got something on your forehead."

My hand goes up to touch a sore spot. "Ouch. What the...?"

Hugh, still looking, "Yeah that's definitely a golf-ball-sized lump swelling up there."

"That would explain my throbbing headache."

Hugh rubs his hair. "Think I've got the same coming up on the back of my head. That must be where our skulls connected in the tumble."

"Look at us. Bringing sexy back."

Hugh jumps up. "Still down for that drink?"

"Down for the whole bottle."

"Let's do it." Hugh pours my Baileys and his whiskey. "Shall we rewind?"

We both laugh now.

"Where should we start?"

Hugh looks at me wryly, leans toward me, and kisses me gently but with conviction. It's nice, and it makes me shiver.

We both take a swig of our alcohol.

Hugh holds his glass up in a toast. "To sexy acrobatics."

I laugh, spit some of my drink out. Once again, I'm just so goddamned attractive, I can hardly stand it. "God, how funny would it be to see that video?"

Hugh is laughing, too. "We could have uploaded it to the Rough Sex category on Pornhub. Might have been a Most Viewed."

"Maybe if they have a Slapstick Sex category."

Hugh refills our glasses.

I'm not going easy with the Baileys. It's helping to dull the pain of my forehead and also my bruised ego. "I'm going to have to get another computer right away. Anywhere I can buy a laptop in town?"

"There's a repair place. They sell refurbished ones but not new. I think you'd have to drive to Owen Sound. They've got a good-sized shopping mall."

I check the time on my phone. "Damn, I guess they're closed now."

"You shouldn't be thinking about work tonight, anyway. You need to take it easy."

"Distraction is powerful medicine."

"Alcohol is stronger." He pours us both another double shot.

Hugh sits down next to me. "You don't have to do it now, and you probably should give yourself a bit of time first, but you need to decompress and process all the heaviness that's gone down. Your home was broken into, your personal papers trashed, your computer stolen."

I lift my glass. "And that's just today's events."

Hugh is super serious. "This guy is a scary dude, and he takes a lot of risks. He wants something that he thinks you've got, and he doesn't seem like the type to leave empty-handed."

"Ticks all the boxes on the psychopath checklist. We've got a few of those hanging around right now."

"Our exes have nothing on this guy. I don't want to see you go, but I think it's time for you to consider your option of leaving town for a while. You'd have to be very careful and secretive about where you head and stay off social media. But it's definitely not safe for you around here anymore."

I rub my aching forehead and flinch, forgetting about the large, painful, and wholly unattractive lump, which is continuing to expand across the entire width of my face, "This is all so screwed up."

A car pulls up in front of the cottage.

Hugh jumps up to look out the window. "It's Florrie." He sounds a little disappointed.

I deflate, too. "So much for a night of wild sex."

Hugh laughs. "Seems like it wasn't meant to be."

Now I'm disappointed. "Yeah, we hear ya, Universe."

He turns to me. "I meant it seems like it wasn't meant to be tonight. I'm game to try again anytime you are." He kisses me quickly then points at my forehead. "Maybe after the swelling goes down." He winks.

"How about tomorrow?" I wink back. That hurts my forehead, too.

Chapter Twenty-One

Hugh and I smile in secret agreement at our scheduled hook-up date, but I can already feel my momentary sexual bravado draining away. The chances of me chickening out of our erotic rendezvous are rising exponentially with each self-critical thought that shoots through my aching head. Scheduling sex is usually reserved for parents of toddlers. Spur-of-the-moment intimacy is easier to deal with because there's no time to think about cellulite or to count the days since the last gym visit and berate oneself for slacking. Anticipation, on the other hand, can be brutal on the ego. Self-love why have you forsaken me?

Florrie and Snowflake bound through the door. The three pets greet each other boisterously.

Florrie stops in her tracks, takes in the scene. "Well, you two look cozy." She looks at us with that accusatory glare that moms of teenagers wear when they walk into the basement rec room and their kid and their kid's "friend" shoot to opposite ends of the couch at warp speed. "Am I interrupting anything?" Florrie suppresses a giggle.

Me, "No, the break and enter that occurred earlier pretty much killed our plans to ravish each other."

Florrie does a double take. "What the heck happened to your forehead?"

"Like I said, a break and enter."

Florrie is instantly alarmed. "For real? Like a home invasion? You caught a guy breaking in here, and he hit you?"

Hugh shakes his head. "No, no. Someone rummaged through Gina's papers and stole her laptop, but he was gone before we got back here. Floyd and a uniform looked around but didn't find any evidence that would point to a specific individual. It's not the kind of crime where they search for DNA—the guy would have had to leave some belonging behind."

Florrie's mouth drops open. "Your laptop was stolen? Holy Moley! Do you think it's our same guy?"

I nod. Nodding also hurts. "Maybe. Probably."

Florrie turns back to the door to lock it. "I mean cottages get broken into in the offseason all the time, and a laptop is the kind of thing a burglar would take with them."

"It's possible it was random, but with all the other stuff going on, it's unlikely." I try to push my bangs across my forehead because I can see Florrie is beginning to zoom in on the widening welt.

"So how did you get that bump on your head?"

"I fell."

Florrie's eyes shift back and forth between Hugh and me skeptically. "Bull."

I rally in an effort to change the subject. "Looks like the guy sitting in front of your bakery this morning might be our watcher-in-the-woods after all. Floyd is looking into it."

"Wow. I'm only gone for a few hours and look how much excitement I miss. We're bunking at my place tonight, right?"

My white flag is waving. "Looks like it."

Florrie drops a huge pink-and-mint paper bag from her bakery onto the kitchen counter. "We can head out after we eat. I brought dinner."

Hugh, "Awesome. Smells amazing."

Florrie, "So does your whiskey."

Hugh leaps up to pour her a glass.

Getting up, I squeeze Florrie's shoulders. "I think I'd have forgotten to eat entirely this week if it wasn't for you, cuz. Thank you for taking such good care of me."

"No such thing as a free lunch. I'll collect at some point. With interest." Florrie grins. "Also, your aunts have been calling me ten times a day, asking me if you're eating, what you're eating, if I can feed you, and when you're going to their place next to eat." She flicks the stove on. "Anyway, fill me in.

162

What else did I miss?"

"So much." My cell rings.

I pick up and hear a cheery Floyd on the other end. "Will wonders never cease, we got your laptop back."

"You're kidding?"

"Nope. Old Mrs. van Dorn was going through the garbage bins again, looking for glass bottles to cash in, and she found the computer. She could have made a lot more money on the computer than the bottles, but she was afraid it might have something illegal on it, so she brought it in to us."

"Wow, lucky for me, my laptop was found by a paranoid Samaritan." I'm relieved for me, sad for the woman who found it. "I should give her a reward, especially if the poor woman is that hard up for cash."

"Old Mrs. van Dorn is the wealthiest woman on the entire Bruce Peninsula. Also, the cheapest. No need to worry about her."

I put Floyd on speaker. "Our guy either got what he was looking for, or he found nothing. Either way, when he was done with your computer, he dumped the thing in the trash bin right outside your aunts' restaurant. Not sure if there's any significance to the location or not."

"Me either." I'm surprised at the coincidence, but I'll take it. "The aunts don't miss a beat. They spend half their time peering out their windows. Maybe they saw the guy outside their place. I'll call them now to find out."

"I thought of that, too, but it's kind of late for them. I was going to wait till morning to ring them up."

That's a tough one. "I don't want to wake them or keep them awake all night worrying, but I don't think I can wait on this."

"Your family, your decision. The computer was wiped clean of prints, by the way. You'll have to go through it yourself to see if the perp has screwed with any of your files, and of course, you'd better change all your passwords and such right away. If he did find anything he wanted to keep he would have downloaded it onto a USB."

"Of course, will do."

"I'm sending Constable Griffin over to your place to drop the laptop off to you now."

I thank Floyd and hang up.

Florrie, "Cripes! They found your computer already?"

Me, "Yup. And dumped in front of Happily Napoli."

Seeming as perplexed as I am, Hugh ventures, "Is the guy trying to send you a message like maybe letting you know that he knows everything about you, including who your family members are and where they live?"

"I hope not." I dial the aunts.

Florrie offers a theory, "Maybe it's Dick. He's been to the aunts' place a hundred times."

"Pronto." One of them picks up the phone, but no one, not me, nor their husbands, has ever been able to tell them apart.

"Hey Zia, it's Gina."

"Madonna! Somebody died? It's the middle of the night."

I can hear the other aunt reacting to the conversation with alarm and a barrage of questions in Italian about which family member has been killed.

"Zia, it's only nine-thirty. I know you're still up watching the news. I can hear your TV on."

"We thought you went back to the city. You disappeared. We never hear from you."

"I saw you one day ago, Zia."

"Two days. What have you been eating?"

"I've been eating, don't worry about me. Listen—I have to ask you an important question. Did you or Zia see somebody outside your restaurant in the last few hours dumping something in the trash? Something that looked like a computer?"

"Why put the computer in the trash? Who's gonna put a computer in the trash?"

"Zia, just, please answer me. Did you see anything that looked like that?"

"Sure, there's some people in the garbage can. Signora van Dorn takes the beer bottles every day. She no need the money. She's *fuori di testa*."

That means *crazy in the head*. I try to keep Zia on track, "Did you see a man maybe?"

"I see a man in the trash, but I don't know if he put a computer. Wait and

CHAPTER TWENTY-ONE

I go look."

"No Zia, no, it's okay. Just, can you tell me if—Zia? Zia?" I can hear both their heavy footsteps receding.

I take the phone away from my ear, turn to Hugh and Florrie. "Oh God, I can hear the two of them. They've put the phone down and both gone outside to check the trash bin for the computer." I wait.

It's a good four minutes before the aunts pick their landline back up. "No computer in the garbage."

"What did the man look like Zia?"

"What man?"

I breathe in and count to four… "The man you saw around your trash can."

"How am I supposed to know what he looks like?"

Three, four…"You said you saw him."

"I got the bad eyes. I can only see the man shape." She talks to Zia Ange, "Ange, you used the *binocolo* last night when you looking out the window?"

The aunts are serious about their snooping hobby—they regularly use binoculars when they watch passers-by through their windows.

Zia Angela is snippy. It's past her bedtime. "How many times I gotta tell you the *binocolo* broken? They being fixed at the camera shop."

"No worries, Zia. Sorry for disturbing you. I'll try to come by tomorrow to visit. *Buona notte.*" Just before I end the call—

"But there was a man on the computer in the restaurant tonight. Your friend."

I switch my phone to speaker so Hugh and Florrie can listen in.

"What do you mean *my friend*? Who was it?"

"He says he's married to your friend. But his wife not with him. He's alone. He doesn't know where she is. She's a missing people. Did you know your friend is missing people? He says she's gone away, so he has to eat in the restaurant for dinner."

"What did the man look like, Zia?"

"I told you, he's married, Gina. Why are you asking me what does he look like? He's got a wife already. You need to be looking for the Scottish like we told you in your teacup."

I dive onto the phone, fumble for the button to turn the speaker off. It takes too long. "The Scottish is the lover for you. The man in your tea leaves."

Speaker off. Three sentences too late. Have now been officially stripped of the very last shreds of my dignity.

Florrie is trying to stifle her laughter and doing a horrible job. She's actually snorting.

Hugh raises his arm high. "I'm Scottish," he volunteers proudly.

Florrie bursts out now. Hugh smiles broadly. I cringe, am considering joining Spook underneath the bed.

"This man not the one in your tea leaves. He's no Scottish."

Can a person actually die from embarrassment? If so, I am a code blue, but I can feel that my cheeks are a flaming red. "Great, I really hope he's not the one, Zia. I just want to figure out which friend he is. What did he look like?"

"He's got the shaved head, but he looked like nobody, like everybody look. The same. Nothing special. Except for the eyes. He's got the mean eyes. I no like his tattoos."

"What kind of tattoos did he have?"

"Snakes and skulls. *Un cattivo presagio.*" *A bad omen.* "I no like him. But he like you."

"What do you mean?"

"The man he orders the lasagne and wine, and he works on his computer all through his meal. I tell him it's no good for the digestion. He says he's too busy, can't stop working on the computer. He says he loves your books. He tells me say hi to The Ex-Whisperer. And tell you his wife Lilliana says hi to you too. Everybody knows you, Gina. My niece she is famous. I'm so proud of my *piccola nipote.*"

Chapter Twenty-Two

I'm in shock and trying my best not to let Zia Ange hear the strain in my voice. I don't want to worry her. I just can't believe that the person who is stalking me—correction, one of the people who is stalking me—sat in my aunts' restaurant and talked to them about me, while he was going through my personal computer, which he stole from me when he broke into my home a few hours earlier.

Not only is this guy not afraid of people knowing who he is or of getting caught committing crimes like break and enter or theft, he actually wants me to know that he doesn't give a rat's ass about anything. Except for finding his wife. Or making people believe he wants to find his wife.

A full-blown psychopath has infiltrated my personal life. I'm completely aware that I have absolutely no tools to deal with this situation. The time to fight is over. I'm ready to take flight.

My voice is shaking when I say goodnight. I hang up the phone, look at the others. "If he does anything to hurt my aunts, I swear I will kill this creep."

Florrie is stress eating, picking all the sunflower seeds out of the quinoa salad she is tossing and eating them one at a time. "The guy had the nerve to tell your aunts to say hi to you? He's taunting you. He wants you to know he's all over everywhere."

Hugh is pacing back and forth across the room again. "What the hell? His wife says hi? What does that mean, that he's found her and she's back home with him now?"

I'm just throwing out possibilities. "Not necessarily. Maybe he just wanted me to know it was him talking to my aunts."

"The guy has the balls to walk into your family's place of business and tell them to let you know he was there." Hugh throws back a shot of whiskey, pours another for Florrie and himself, and points to the Baileys questioningly. I shake my head. "I know this guy is out of his head, but this is next level. He's not afraid of anything. He's not afraid of getting caught. That's what's really scary."

I remind the two of them, "He doesn't have to be afraid of getting caught. Remember what Floyd and Lloyd said? He hasn't committed any crimes."

Florrie objects, "He broke into your home and stole your computer, so he's broken the law now."

I'm struggling to keep my breathing steady. "Floyd and Constable Griffin didn't find any evidence here to link this guy to the break-in, and we can't prove the computer the aunts saw him using at their restaurant was mine. The aunts didn't get a good look at the man who dumped the laptop in the trash, and it was wiped clean of prints. This guy is being reckless but not when it comes to leaving incriminating evidence lying around. He's extremely careful not to do that."

Inside me, the anxiety is building up, and I need to keep it at a manageable level. I leave my Baileys untouched. I need a clear head to think through these latest developments. I don't want to slip underwater again. I'm afraid I might not come up for air next time.

Perhaps Hugh is picking up on my energy, or maybe we just happen to mentally be at the same place at the same time. He's visibly distressed but is clearly working at dialing it back and getting himself to that calm space he's used to inhabiting. He's strongest there. He makes a concerted effort to stop his agitated pacing, leans on the back of a chair with both hands as if to anchor his body still. "There's got to be something we're missing. Nobody is this reckless without slipping up somewhere. If the cops can't tie this bastard to a crime, we'll find a way to do it ourselves. We don't need to send him to jail. We just need to send him packing."

Florrie is surprised at what Hugh seems to be implying. "You mean like planting evidence? Framing the guy? Whoa there, buddy, we don't want to end up in jail ourselves."

Hugh's voice is darker than usual. "I mean like doing whatever it takes to keep Gina safe and run this maniac out of town."

I try to offer a bit of comfort to Florrie. "It's not like there's any action we can take at this point, anyway. We don't know this guy's name, or where to find him, and we barely know what he looks like, so all we can do is wait for him to show his face to us. Maybe he's smart enough to have bailed already."

"Wishful thinking?" Florrie's voice is skeptical. She pulls the wild mushroom and parsnip ragout out of the oven and portions the entrée onto three plates, next to it she artfully arranges whole roasted sweet potatoes stuffed with her quinoa salad..

"Self-preservation. I keep having nightmares about the guns and knives and ropes he's got rolling around in the trunk of his car."

"Eeeeewww." Florrie shudders. "Remember we're sleeping at my place tonight. We should head out right after we finish eating."

Hugh agrees, "I'll follow you two into town and make sure you get to Florrie's safely."

Florrie finally sits. "I meant to ask, have you heard from Lillian's friend again?"

I shake my head. "No. So weird. I just don't get that."

Clearly starving, Hugh wolfs down Florrie's scrumptious stew. "Floyd is probably right on that one. The world is full of nosy people who stir shit up and disappear when it starts to hit the fan. Damn this is good, Florrie."

Florrie beams.

I pick at the hearty, fragrant dish, wishing I could work up an appetite. "Maybe we just need to hold the guy at bay until enough time passes without Lillian showing up. At some point, he has to figure I'm a dead end as far as finding his wife is concerned, and he'll pick up some other trail."

Florrie tastes her own food. "Needs salt." Then, she salts the food on our plates without asking. "What I don't get is this guy has been showing his face all around town, so he obviously wants everyone to know he's here and what he's looking for, but why didn't he lay low and just stay in the shadows, waiting to see if his wife showed up to collect her dog or reached out to

Gina?"

Hugh answers as if he has the guy figured out, "It's the intimidation factor. If he can scare Gina enough maybe, she'll spill. Also, I think he's growing impatient. It has been three days now. He's getting worried. With each day that goes by, it gets harder for him to hang around here without alerting the cops. He's getting desperate, so he's getting reckless."

This talk is not making me feel better at all. "The more desperate he gets, the more dangerous he gets."

Hugh looks at me with a steady gaze. "We're not going to let anything happen to you, or Florrie, or Snowflake, or me. But you're right, and that's the reason why we can't let this go on much longer. If Lillian's husband doesn't come out into the open of his own accord, then we're going to have to do something to draw him out so that we can see that prick's face and run him out of town."

I put my fork down. "How do we do that?"

Hugh keeps eating. "We'll come up with something."

Florrie turns to me. "Do you still think Lillian's husband is only pretending to be searching for his wife so the cops and everyone else thinks she's missing when in reality she could be wrapped up in bits of butcher paper in a meat locker somewhere packed between the ham hocks and the short ribs?

Hugh chokes a little. "The stew was tasting excellent until you put that image in my head, Florrie."

"It's vegan. You're fine." Florrie scoops some more onto Hugh's plate. He shrugs, doesn't slow down. It is delicious.

I'm at a loss. Nothing feels probable or improbable anymore. "I don't know what I think this guy is doing now. Is he looking for his wife, or is he covering his bloody tracks? Maybe I was just letting my imagination run away with me. That's my usual MO, and I don't think I've ever felt more confused about more things at once in my entire life. I shouldn't legally be allowed to advise anyone on anything in my current state. Good thing I'm not managing to get much work done lately."

Florrie shakes her head. "There's going to be a lot of disappointed Gal Guide fans if that's the case. We better get the Ex-Whisperer back in form and on the job ASAP before the lovelorn are lost forever."

Hugh is sticking to his guns. "We don't have to figure out what Lillian's husband did. We can leave that to the cops if they ever get around to it. We just need to get rid of him. To scare him off."

Now Florrie chokes a little on her own vegan dish. "If we think he might be a killer, then we should just focus on trying to keep ourselves from ending up as cutlets in his deep freezer."

Clarity is beginning to settle in on me. Now I just need some courage to accompany it. "I'd rather be hunting this guy than be hunted down by him. Maybe we do need to turn the tables and actively pursue him, instead."

Zoe alerts us to someone on the property. Three hearts leap out of chests before Hugh answers the door to Constable Griffin. The friendly officer drops my computer off and politely hastens out when she receives a radio call.

Immediately, I open the laptop, and the other two anxiously watch the screen over my shoulders.

Florrie is excited. "Can you tell what he got into?"

"My email for sure. My password isn't working. He must have changed it." I reset and grab my phone to retrieve the new password code, enter that, and I'm in.

Hugh is leaning over me, his firm midsection pressed against my upper back. So distracting. A powerful current flows from my shoulders down to my butt—the energy curls around my hips. The muscles in my thighs tighten.

Hugh's mouth is way too close to my ear. "Has he deleted any files?"

I shift a few inches away from him so I can concentrate. "Not that I can see. It will take me a while to know for certain."

I'm not sure why, but Florrie's demeanor has brightened. "This is good, isn't it? Maybe he didn't find anything he was looking for. You said you posted all of Lillian's letters on your website, right? Maybe the guy will know that you haven't talked to his wife since then and he'll go away to look for Lillian somewhere else now. Maybe him stealing your laptop was the best thing that could have happened."

Oh, that's why she's so chipper. She has a point. "I didn't post the one from her friend saying she was concerned Lillian's husband had harmed her, though."

Hugh sounds hopeful too. "Yeah, but he'll be able to see that her friend hasn't written you back, either. This is really good."

Palms slapping behind my head make me jump. Whisky-induced high-fiving? Personally, I think it's too soon for that. I still haven't finished scouring my computer.

Florrie tops up the whiskey glasses and adds ice to my warm, untouched Baileys. "A toast."

I'm leery. "That may be premature. We don't know for sure the guy is going to leave us alone now."

"There's a good chance he will." Hugh's smile says he's ready to celebrate. "If he'd gotten the opportunity to talk to you in person like he wanted to and you told him this same information, he never would've believed you. Now he knows for sure you're not communicating with Lillian."

It occurs to me one of us has to drive, and I'm the only one who hasn't imbibed yet. "Hey, didn't we decide to sleep at your place tonight, Florrie? I guess I'm the DD. You want to put the kettle on for me, please?"

Florrie, "Do we have to go now? The guy has probably already hightailed it back to wherever he came from. Especially if he knows the cops are actively looking for him."

I hate to be the skeptic but... "I think we're getting ahead of ourselves."

"Hugh and I are way ahead of you. You've got some catching up to do." Florrie pushes my glass of Baileys toward me. "We've got this strapping sentry to guard the door." She points at Hugh, who flexes his muscles like the Hulk. "Let's live dangerously, have a wee nip, and camp out here."

I give Florrie a long look. "Oh, now you want to live dangerously? You go for it, girl. I need a clear head to check through my computer and have the ability to pour you two into my truck if we need to make a quick escape."

Playfully pouting, and at the ready, Hugh flexes his muscles at me.

I relent, throwback my drink. "Okay, let's think positive, then—we're safe and sound here for the night."

Florrie sets three lovely slices of cake on the table. "I don't usually serve Rhubarb and Ginger Cake with whiskey, but it's a night of living dangerously, so let's take our palate for a walk on the wild side."

The confection is delicious, and while we eat it, I quickly change all my passwords, banking, social media, my website, and access to my column. Where passwords are concerned, speed matters. But there's something I need to check next because a distant dread is niggling at me.

I open my sent emails folder.

Sure enough, there's one written just hours earlier while Lillian's husband was sitting in my aunts' restaurant, eating my family's lasagne, toying with their heads, pretending to be my friend, attempting to scare me silly and breaking into my computer.

The email was sent to Lillian from my address. I open it.

Hi Lillian,

I'm writing to you from my private email to keep your secret safe. Are you okay? Did you go to one of the shelters I recommended? Let me know where you are and if there's anything I can do to help. I've been worried about you. Also, I'm sorry to tell you this, but it's about Snowflake. He was hit by a car and may not live unless the vet performs a very expensive surgery. I don't want to do that if you don't want your little pup anymore. It would be more humane to put him down. You need to tell me what you want me to do with your dog.

Please write back quick. Or better yet, come see me. I don't know how much time your little Snowflake has left. He's really suffering, and you might want to say goodbye to him in person.

Gina Malone

(The Ex-Whisperer)

Chapter Twenty-Three

I show the email to Hugh and Florrie. Buzzkill.

"Talk about cruel and unusual punishment! Torturing someone with a fake story that their dog is dying? This guy is sicker than I thought." Florrie is beyond horrified.

Hugh is visibly disappointed. "I guess our guy is not quite ready to leave town after all."

I fill up my glass and down another Baileys. Why not? I've got some catching up to do, and I really want to dull the nerve endings sparking up and down my arms and legs like an electric eel. "You got that right. Our friendly neighborhood psychopath is not going anywhere anytime soon. He's going to stick around to see if Lillian shows up now that there's an emergency with her fur baby."

"And Lillian is definitely going to show up for Snowflake after she reads that email. I would." Florrie scoops Snowflake up into her arms as if to protect the little critter from the negative story in the letter.

I think Hugh is staring at my arms while he talks. I'm pretty sure he can see the voltage my nerves are generating. I hope I don't spontaneously combust. That would be embarrassing, but not the worst thing that's happened since I met the guy. I'm trying to remember whether I've had a single encounter with Hugh where I haven't ended up totally mortified. Can't think of one. I'm certain this does not bode well for any future relationship between me and this man. Your message is duly noted, Universe. Please back off before I burst into flames in public.

Hugh's still staring. "He must know his wife pretty well. He's probably picked the perfect lure. What we know for sure now is that Lillian's husband hasn't killed her. He is trying to find her."

I think about the gun and the knife and the rope in his trunk. "In which case, if he finds her, then he's going to kill her." I pet Zoe. Maybe she'll help calm my nerves. "But I'm not sure we can lay the previous foul-play theory to rest just yet. The email to Lillian could still be part of an elaborate setup to make it look like he thinks his wife is hiding out from him. Most psychopaths are extremely intelligent."

Florrie whines, "Oh my God, a smart psycho, please no. Smart and crazy is such a bad combination. I've dated smart and crazy before. At least we know his sign. He's gotta be a Scorpio. Why did we start drinking tonight? I don't want to live dangerously anymore. Let's call a taxi to take us to my place." Florrie's distress is ramping up by the second. "Do you think that's why the guy stole your computer? So he could trick Lillian?"

The theorizing has exhausted me completely. "Anything's possible."

"But why would he dump the computer? Why not keep it to check for Lillian's reply?"

"He doesn't need my laptop anymore. He thought he could log onto my email account from anywhere since he created a new password. And he doesn't know we've found the computer, either. But he will as soon as he tries to check for a reply and finds his new password has already been replaced."

"Thanks to good old Mrs. van Dorn, dumpster diver extraordinaire." Florrie knows everything about everyone in town.

Hugh crosses to the couch, flops down on it. "This guy wouldn't want to hang on to your laptop any longer than necessary in case he got stopped by the cops again. He stole the computer so he could find out if you and Lillian were in communication with each other. After he came up empty on your email account, he got resourceful and sent one to her."

"I don't think any of this is going to help us find this guy, and I can't do any more thinking tonight. My brain needs to have its plug pulled."

Hugh stands up, stretches. "Agreed. It's nearly midnight. I've got to get up for work in the morning, or we're never going to get your gorgeous little cottage reno'd. I'm going to call it a night. This has been one heck of an eventful day."

I take Zoe to the door to let her out before bed. "You don't have to stay, Hugh. Florrie is here with me. We're fine."

Florrie jumps up, takes Hugh's keys off the table, and sets them aside. "We've all had a few too many snifters, Gina. None of us are getting behind the wheel."

"You're right, of course. Don't trust me to think straight anymore tonight."

"I'll take the dogs out." Hugh opens the door, and Zoe bounds through it. He fastens Snowflake's leash and carries the wee one outdoors.

I retrieve the extra bedding from the linen cupboard, set the blankets and pillow on the end of the couch for Hugh.

Despite her exhaustion, Florrie throws a devilish look my way. "You don't need to put up appearances on my account. You can let Hugh sleep in your bed with you."

"Honestly, Florrie, that's not happening. And to set the record straight, nothing has happened nor likely ever will."

Florrie bends down and rubs the stubble on my calves with the palm of her hand, "Eeewww, yeah, I can see why. You'd better get into Midge's spa for a waxing before you let anybody touch these gams."

I laugh despite myself. "I've got bigger things on my mind than sex."

"Reset your priorities, girl. Hugh is hotter than hell. And you will be, too, once you ditch the sasquatch costume."

We both laugh in that sleep-deprived, stress-induced, high-pitched, hysterical way that gets otherwise-sane people committed to institutions. And we can't stop when Hugh walks back inside with the dogs. He smiles but looks slightly weirded out, and I know we sound way too frantic to make anyone else laugh along with us. We've crossed over into Vincent Price movie evil cackling.

In truth, Hugh looks a little frightened as if we've finally become unhinged—and perhaps we have, but his sketched-out expression makes us laugh even harder. Finally, both of us come down. And then there's a long, awkward silence.

Florrie, "Wow I think that's called delirium."

Me, "Let's get to bed before Hugh calls the sanatorium."

He chuckles. "I'm okay with temporary insanity. Sleep well, you two."

Florrie taps Hugh on the shoulder as she crosses to go into the spare bedroom. "G'night. Guard the door."

"The dogs and I are on the job. I'm the only boogie man getting in here tonight."

Before I walk into my room, Hugh touches my elbow, speaks quietly. "I know you can take care of yourself, Gina. You're one of the most capable people I've ever met. I'm just here because there's safety in numbers."

"I don't know how to be the damsel in distress, nor do I want to learn."

"I don't know how to be the knight in shining armor. The only character I know how to play is me, and that's all I'm doing here."

"Thanks, Hugh. You're a good friend. Good night." Even though we're exhausted, the air between us fizzes and pops like it did earlier in the day. Regardless, I squeeze his arm and retire to my room.

Lights out.

I hope I can turn everything off in my brain so gentle sleep will find me. I climb under the cool sheets in my comfy bed, and I'm wholly aware that it feels so damn good to be alone in it. I hope Hugh and I can go back to simply being new pals who happen to be working together. I'm fairly sure we dodged a bullet by not falling into bed with each other. I'm in no shape to begin a relationship, even a purely sexual one, and clearly all the signs are telling us to divert the disaster we'd likely become as a couple.

Hugh is a great guy, though, and I genuinely believe we could be friends forever. I just have to stop gawking at his forearms and large square hands and tracing the outline of his ridiculously broad shoulders in my mind whenever he stands in front of me, and I'll be just fine.

* * *

When morning arrives, Hugh, Florrie, and I rouse at about the same time and stumble into the kitchen to ingest much-needed caffeine. Brilliant Florrie put the timer on before bed, so the coffee pot is ready to pour as soon as we are up.

As host, I try not to let my offer sound half-hearted, but I'm hoping it's declined because I am just that tired. "You guys want toast, eggs?"

Hugh downs his java. "No, thanks. I'm heading home to change and grab a few tools that I need for the day. I've got to get back here to work before Ryan shows up at eight."

Florrie gathers up the new doggie toys strewn about the floor that she bought for Snowflake and attaches the little pup's leash to his collar. "I'll grab something at the bakery. Gotta fly. I'm training a new girl this morning. Let me know if there's any more excitement today, but let's hope for boring for a change. Snowflake and I will be back tonight for another sleepover party unless we decide to stay at my place, which gets my vote."

"You won't be alone here for long, but maybe you should come along with me, Gina." Hugh looks grave.

I feel guilty. I am putting so many people so far out. "You guys have lives. I can't keep doing this to you."

Florrie laughs as she walks out the door. "It's Sunset Beach, remember? There's never anything eventful going on. We barely had a pulse until you showed up."

I hug my wonderful cousin. "Not true but thank you. Love you."

"Kisses." Florrie blows a kiss and is gone.

Hugh is out the door right behind her. "Back in thirty."

* * *

I am alone, just me and the pets. I tape a piece of paper over the camera on my laptop. Perhaps I'm becoming paranoid. Maybe I'm getting smarter. Either way, I cannot ignore the reality that the creep factor is growing significantly stronger in the air around me.

In my column and my books, I've given multitudes of women advice, telling them never to ignore the tiny voice inside them. It's always sending us signals, loud and clear, but usually, we tune those messages out. That inner compass is a fountain of wisdom that exists to guide us and to protect us when need be.

With nearly all of life's big regrets, we can usually look back in our personal history book and see that, actually, we did know what to do or not do, but we ignored the signs. Usually, when we mess up, it's because we are driven by fear. I need to take my own advice for a change.

I need to seriously consider leaving this little town and moving back to the city. It would be better for everyone, for Florrie, for the aunts, for Hugh, and for me. It would be safer for everyone, too. Maybe I can pick up this dream of living by the lake a few years down the road from now.

My leaving town would even be better for Lil' Dick. He could try to disentangle himself from Iris and her fundamentalist church friends. He wouldn't have to be cramming the Scriptures, and pretending he's found the Lord, and hanging out in a town he doesn't belong in and isn't welcome in.

Ixnay the last part. Sometimes I have to remind myself that Lil' Dick is not someone I have to concern myself with anymore. He constantly tries to push his way back into my life, but he's not a part of my life any longer, and I don't have to allow him entry into my thoughts. Note to self: I am in control of who I do, and do not, devote my time to thinking about.

I know I need to listen to my own advice, but I cannot hear the little voice inside me right now. It's being drowned out by all the noise in my mind from the mass of moving parts and broken puzzle pieces: missing women and frightening husbands and fanatic Christians and departed best friends and beloved children living too far away. I need to find some peace.

Tires crunching on the driveway mean that the sounds of Hugh and Ryan's loud voices and grinding saws will soon flood my brain, too. No peace for me here this morning that's for sure.

One thing I do know, my best bet for bliss is in that gorgeous Great Lake stretching out on the endless horizon before me.

Spook is drunk on the sunlight that streams onto the deck of the screened-in porch where he lies motionless. The warmth has sent his body temperature soaring and illuminates his shiny, black fur. I ruffle his belly, but he refuses to acknowledge my presence or to allow himself to be disturbed.

Zen cat—I could learn from him. Zoe and I amble out the back door to head down to the beach.

Instantly, the breeze begins its healing massage of my head, the sand a relaxing kneading for my feet. Walkers can go for a good two hours along Sunset Beach before hitting an impasse that can't be traversed. But if they're up for a long swim around a rocky peninsula, they can hike even farther.

Zoe and I walk for three-quarters of an hour before changing direction to head back to the cottage. We both wade out into the water periodically to cool off. I miss my four kids desperately. I haven't spoken with them in three days, which is highly unusual for us. The absence hasn't gone unnoticed by my daughter, who has sent me numerous texts including the words: abandonment, neglect, and where the hell are you?

By the time the dog and I approach our home stretch of beach, my demeanor is much improved. I feel centered and clear-headed. The noise in my mind has quieted down, and I can hear myself think again. I can hear that voice inside me that I can always count on to tell me the truth if I'm willing to listen hard.

I ask myself the questions, what should I do? Should I leave this town and get the hell away from these deranged people who are intent on stealing my peace from me? Should I shove off in order to protect my loved ones and spare them the shitstorm that is my life right now? Should I, too, run away and hide for a while, the way the illusive Lillian seems to have done? Or should I stick it out, fight back, claim my territory, and defend my dreams?

I promise to trust and follow whatever guidance my inner wisdom offers up. Just please goddess, give it to me straight.

Waiting. Tuning in. Opening up. Listening. And then it comes to me loud and clear. I hear the answer to my question ride in on the waves. The words my inner voice shouts at me now are, "Fuck fear!"

Okay then, I've received my instructions, screw 'em. I'm not going anywhere. Decision made.

I'm scared and excited at the same time. I can do this. The Universe has got my back. Faith in myself is all I need. And more coffee. That would help, too.

Chapter Twenty-Four

Whe we arrive back at our cottage, the dog and I stroll from the beach across the sandy grass and climb the mossy wooden steps toward the sweet old structure that is my cozy new home. I stop to admire the quaint little building. Her weathered cedar shakes glisten like the tresses of a silver-haired crone, still stunning and spry beneath the creases of time. I marvel at how deceptive appearances can be. This well-worn dame has withstood the lashings of a hundred years of rough and destructive winter storms, but she's still standing, and so am I. It's going to take a lot more than Lillian's asshole of a husband to knock me off my foundation.

All of a sudden, Zoe charges off at full tilt, barking. She could be after a squirrel. She doesn't bark at Hugh and Ryan anymore. She's already used to them being on the property. I hurry after her, calling, but as usual, she ignores her softie of a master. I don't want her going onto the road, so I run after her, hollering her name. I round the corner at the front of the cottage and almost run headlong into three extremely somber-looking people who, terrified of the dog, have pressed their buttoned-up bodies flat against the side of the house.

I halt before we crash into each other and manage to grab Zoe by her collar and pull the dog back from the trio of parishioners, whom I recognize from their visit here the other day. Before any of us can get a word out, Hugh has climbed down off a tall ladder leaning against the bunkie and is jogging toward us, looking pissed.

"I told you busybodies to stay off my jobsite. What do you think you're doing here again bothering my client?"

The woman answers, still out of breath from the scare of the dog, but despite that, she manages to muster up a tone of voice that is both accusatory and surly. "Your client? Is that what you call her?"

I can do surly too, "Watch it, lady, or I'll let go of my guard dog's collar."

Zoe barks and snaps at the old hag, and she shrieks and leaps backward. The dog must be able to sense her innate nastiness. Onward Christian soldiers.

One of the two men attempts to intervene and diffuse the situation. He's visibly nervous of the dog, Hugh, and me—the witch—as well, I am sure. All three of us are snarling at them.

The man's voice is shaky. "Uh, we're here on behalf of Living Wellspring Church. The elders asked us to hand-deliver this letter and offer our sincerest apology for any harm or grievances that the congregation may have caused Ms. Malone in any business conducted by us personally or publicly. Please accept our deepest apologies."

The man stretches out his hand to offer a sealed envelope, but he doesn't dare take a step any closer to the dog and me.

I take the letter from his hand, rip open the envelope, and skim over it. Obviously, my lawyer wasted no time in threatening legal action against these meddlers and their church council for slander. He'll probably be even quicker at sending me his bill.

I don't have to take any time at all to formulate a response. The words flow from my lips like poison from a dart frog, "Please pass along my response to your church elders, council members, and entire rabid congregation, especially Miss Iris Froot Loop McTavish, and your newest member, Mr. Dickwad Valentino: I most emphatically do not accept your apology, and you can all roast in whatever hell it is you're afraid of ending up in, but which, I assure you, is exactly where your gossiping ways will land you. Now get off my property and stay off." Wow, that felt good.

Hugh looks pleasantly surprised at my eloquent response to the skittish church delegation. "What she said. Now get out of here before I throw you out." He points a long, strong arm in the direction of their vehicle. I forgot I am not supposed to look at his arms anymore.

The three church mice scurry back to their soccer mom van just as fast as their bible-thumping, judgmental little feet can carry them, then they disappear down the road in a cloud of dust. Or maybe that's brimstone.

Hugh regards me with obvious admiration. "Booya. I knew you were a firecracker, but you really know how to give it good."

"Yes, I do. So you'd better watch yourself, mister, if you know what's good for you." I smile.

"No worries there. I have every intention of staying on the right side of you, Gina." Hugh laughs and goes back to work on the bunkie.

There are a few ways to take what Hugh just said, and I accept them all. Not overthinking things is my mandate for the rest of the day. Zoe and I go inside the cottage. I feed the pets, choose green tea over coffee, then sit down to read the whole of the letter.

The church meddlers have attached their letter of apology to the letter they received from my lawyer to which communication, they responded. My lawyer's kickass warning would have left most people quaking in their wellies, never mind a clueless, local church council consisting of a bevy of, if not totally brainless then certainly completely wisdomless, sheep, who didn't have enough smarts or sense between them to figure out that listening to a known town looney toon, namely Iris, and her newfound, equally unbalanced sidekick, Lil' Dick, would land them in a witch's cauldron of hot water.

I mean come on, people. You have two jilted, obsessive, ex-spouses who show up at a church council meeting with tall tales of spells and hexes and poppets made against them by their high functioning, successful, and clearly mentally healthy exes who have obviously moved on with their lives and don't want anything to do with their former partners.

Would any thinking person call a public meeting and discuss how to get the rejected exes their long-gone former spouses back, and attempt to enlist the superpowers of the big guy in the sky to do it for them? The last time a church group pulled this kind of a coup was Salem, 1693, and look how that turned out for everybody.

I put the letter away in a file folder and optimistically assume that Dick and Iris will have slithered back under their respective rocks to lick the wounds of their most recent humiliations for a while. One can always hope.

I send messages to my offspring and manage over the course of an hour and a half to get all of them on the line for good, long catch-up chats. We switch to FaceTime for a bit so I can see their gorgeous mugs and they can see Zoe and Spook and the lake. We make plans for the next time we will be together in person. They'll all be home for Christmas, and then in the spring, I promise them I'll return to Europe, and this time, we'll all meet in Edinburgh for vegetarian haggis, and Scottish shortbread, and Highland's whiskey.

My babies—the best things on the entire planet. Their voices are my happy balm. After speaking with them, I'm recharged and perfectly content, knowing they're healthy and thriving and far away from the stresses and potential dangers swirling around their mother. Nothing matters more.

Time to catch up on my work, now, which is way overdue. I'll try to get as much accomplished as possible before the sun sets, and Florrie shows up to ply me with alcohol and fill me with her fantabulous food.

I check my inbox. Finally, a response from Lillian's friend.

Dear Ex-Whisperer,

I'm sorry to tell you I no longer believe that our friend Lillian has left her husband and fled to a shelter. I talked to some of her neighbors, who told me they saw Lillian's husband drag her out of their home last week. They said she was crying and that he was pulling her roughly down the sidewalk and forced her into his car. She didn't have a suitcase. No one has seen her since. No one has seen her husband, either. It looks like he left town. The neighbors said they often heard loud fighting coming from their house and know that the husband used to beat Lillian and even threatened to kill her. I think our friend Lillian is gone for good. The police should be notified.

Sincerely,
   Friend of a friend

Not the news I was hoping for. I feel sick to my stomach. And still, no details provided on where Lillian lives or any personal information that would help locate her. Why the hell not? Is it really because this woman doesn't want to get involved? She could be helpful anonymously. People suck.

I reply:

Dear Friend of a Friend,

Thank you for replying to me. I have been in contact with the police, but they can't do much because we don't know Lillian's name or address, and no missing person report has been filed. I asked you previously if you could please send me any information you have that might help us find her, and that is what we desperately need to help Lillian. The neighbors you speak of must live awfully close to her to have heard their arguing. You yourself know who the neighbors are since you have been speaking with them. Can you please give me this neighbor's address and name? You don't have to get involved beyond that. Please help. Lillian's life may depend on it.

Thank you,

The Ex-Whisperer

I forward the email to Floyd and Lloyd then telephone them immediately. A receptionist puts me straight through to Floyd.

I'm aware that my voice is less friendly than usual. "You got the letter I forwarded? Surely this is enough for you to investigate Lillian's disappearance now, Floyd. The woman is in danger."

"I'm not arguing that as a possibility." Floyd is clearly concerned but not very confident. "It might be enough to warrant an investigation if we had the name of someone we could interview. There is nothing in the email from Lillian's friend for us to follow up on."

"What about the body shop where the bumper was repaired?"

"The guy paid cash for a rush job. Harve didn't take any of his information down."

I suppose Floyd's job is to keep the lid on things whenever possible. "My people have got their ears to the ground for any signs of this guy. We haven't seen the car around at all, so I'm hoping he's skedaddled. When was the last time you heard from him?"

"Nothing since you found my laptop in the dumpster in front of the aunts' restaurant."

"Okay, that's good news, then. We want him to disappear."

"I want him to be caught and charged."

Floyd's voice reeks with reassurance. "I hear ya. We're pretty certain he's committed B and E and petty theft, but like I told you, so far we don't have any evidence to prove either, so chances are we wouldn't be able to make those charges stick in court."

I can't contain my disdain. "I guess Lillian's husband is smarter than all of us."

"He's slipperier for sure. Our best bet right now is to wait a bit to see if this woman replies to your email with a name or address for Lillian. If she does, we'll be on it lickity split. If not, then I could send this to the RCMP and see if their IT people can trace the email back to anywhere that would help us out. That is a heck of a long shot, and it also takes weeks on average. They're not going to treat this as a priority when we have no other evidence and there hasn't even been a missing person report filed. I know this is upsetting, Gina. Let's hope you hear back from the woman, and she gives us something to run with."

"Thanks for your help, Floyd." I only half mean it, and I hope he can tell.

* * *

For the next few hours, I catch up on work. I hear the trucks pull out of the yard when Hugh finishes for the day. By the time I look up from my computer screen, it has grown dark inside the cottage. My butt hurts from sitting so long. I switch on lights outside and in, let the dog out for a quick piddle, then lock the doors.

It's not long before Florrie and Snowflake come by. My amazing cousin has brought a delicious dinner from her bakery again, and I am starving.

Right after her, Hugh shows up, showered, and bearing a couple of bottles of really nice wine although he does seem extremely anxious.

I enjoyed the solitude that settled on parts of the day. I was able to catch up on a lot of life admin stuff, but I'm happy to have company now as the hour grows later. And my company is eager to be updated on the status of my stalker and his missing wife.

I show them the email from Lillian's friend, whom I have not heard back from and am beginning to think I may never hear from again. Floyd was right. People like to stick their noses into places where they smell action but aren't interested in follow-through if it requires accountability. I simply cannot relate. If someone needs your help, you help, end of story.

I also fill Hugh and Florrie in on Floyd's logical but unenlightening rhetoric. Basically, his advice was to sit around and do nothing. I suck at that. But Hugh sucks at it even harder.

Throughout all of the chatter, the three of us have been chowing down on Florrie's black bean veggie burgers with zucchini and corn and sweet potato fries with tangy lime dip, but now Hugh is pacing back and forth in the room, obviously overdosing on adrenaline. "I know what we have to do. I hope you two are ready to hear this."

Florrie's eyes widen. "Can I register my No vote before I even listen to your proposal?"

Hugh shakes his head. "That's not permitted under the rules of engagement. The police don't seem to be picking up the gauntlet based on the latest words Floyd had for Gina. I have an overwhelming feeling that it's do-or-die now for Lillian's husband. And that means he is going to take drastic measures to get what he wants before he gives up the ghost in his wife's disappearing act."

Neither Florrie nor I can speak. We may not even be breathing.

"I've been turning every possible scenario over in my head, and I think this is our best bet. Maybe our only one—we're going to set a psycho trap."

I hate that I know the answer, but I ask the question anyway, "What's the bait?"

Hugh stops pacing. "It has to be Snowflake."

Chapter Twenty-Five

Florrie interjects again, "I object. Is objecting permitted?"

Hugh sighs. "Go ahead."

Florrie, "I don't want to catch a psycho, and I don't want to risk the pup."

Hugh continues, "We're not going to try to apprehend the guy, and Snowflake won't get hurt. We just want to lure him in close enough so we can get a good look at him, maybe even get his license plate so the police can catch him. At the very least, this sicko will hightail it out of town once we can identify him, and that's the goal."

I am dreading hearing Hugh's idea, but our options seem virtually nonexistent. "I'm tending to agree with Hugh after my phone conversation with Floyd. Lillian's friend's email is extremely alarming but also a dead end. We already knew her husband was dangerous, but now we basically have confirmation that he's a full-fledged violent offender."

Florrie surrenders reluctantly. "Okay shoot. Let's hear your plan."

Hugh resumes his pacing. The dogs are following him back and forth across the room with their eyes because he's twirling a sweet potato fry between his fingers. "Our guy is watching both of you because what he's really watching is his wife's dog. He's waiting for Lillian to return to retrieve her little Snowflake."

Florrie interjects, "Unless Gina's theory is correct, that this guy actually killed his wife and this scary stalking stuff is all just a big show."

Then I interject, "After what Lillian's friend said about the abuse the neighbors witnessed, it's looking more and more like the guy did kill his

188

wife."

Hugh is trying hard to get his idea across despite our interruptions. "The reality is none of that matters anymore. I mean it matters, but there is nothing the three of us can do about it one way or the other. This guy's goal, when it comes to us at least, is the same one whether he killed his wife or not. If he didn't kill her and Lillian ran away from him and dumped Snowflake here for Gina to take care of, then he's watching you both waiting for his wife to show up to collect her dog so he can grab her when she makes an appearance."

He has my attention. "And if he did kill his wife?"

Hugh continues, "If he's pulling all this stalking bull to fool everyone into believing he's a concerned husband who'll do anything to get his wife back, then at some point, he'll close the curtain on his show. That would probably happen after enough people, and especially the authorities, have taken notice of him acting like he's going wild with grief over the loss of his wife. Once he thinks enough people have bought his story, it'll be mission accomplished for him, and he can finally split for good."

Florrie is disgusted. "How to get away with murder."

I get it. "All his worries will be over because no one, including the authorities, will go looking for a woman who has gone into hiding to escape her abusive and controlling husband."

Florrie recaps, "So if he killed Lillian, then he'll disappear on his own as the finale of his performance."

Hugh nods. "Right."

It is making sense to me. "What we want to do is speed up his exit."

Hugh leans over the table. "Exactly. As soon as we can identify him, this guy is gone one way or the other. We just need to lure the big fish out of the deep waters."

Florrie's voice is laden with dread. "Does your idea involve us swimming alongside this shark?"

Hugh shakes his head. "Not you two. Just me."

"And Snowflake." Florrie protests, pulls the dog up onto her lap. "No way are we putting an animal in jeopardy."

Hugh still tries to sell us on his sting. "Gina is going to arrange a meeting with Lillian to give Snowflake back to her. Our guy has to know about it, so he shows up."

That shouldn't be difficult. "I can put some phony posts up on my site as long as Lillian's husband thinks they're legit."

Hugh shakes his finger at me. "But I'll be the one handing Snowflake over to Lillian."

Florrie is trying to follow along. "But there is no Lillian."

Hugh continues, "Right. We just want this guy to show up so we can get a look at him and hopefully his vehicle. After a few minutes of waiting around, I figure Lillian's not going to show. I put Snowflake in my truck, and I leave. But you two are hidden, watching from a safe distance, and you're going to be on the lookout for and take photos of whatever vehicle drives up."

Florrie is fretful. "What if he tries to grab Snowflake?"

"If he wanted to get a hold of Snowflake, he probably already would have tried snatching him from one of you. If he does come for the dog, I'll put Snowflake on the ground. You two call him and grab him and book it out of there, and I'll let my tire iron do the talking."

The plan sounds scary but doable. "We need to do this somewhere secluded where there aren't many people around so we can make sure we spot him. Do we arrange for the meeting to take place here?"

Hugh shakes his head. "No, that's too dangerous."

My next thought feels a lot better. "How about the lighthouse?

Florrie perks up. She is getting on board. "All summer long that's ground zero for watching the sunset, but with the tourists mostly gone now, there will only be a few stragglers."

This all seems manageable. "They'll leave as soon as it's dark. We could set the meeting for ten o'clock to make sure it's quiet there."

Hugh likes it. "Sounds like a plan. Maybe the guy won't even show up, but it's worth a shot."

Florrie responds by jumping up and grabbing three glasses and the bottles of whiskey and Baileys off the kitchen counter.

"Liquid courage, anyone?" She pours.

* * *

An hour later, the three of us are as brave as any drunken sailor. Hugh, Florrie, and I are huddled around my laptop at the kitchen table.

I look up from my computer and squint at the unfriendly, pitch-black squares that are the cottage windows at this hour. "He could be outside watching us now."

Hugh lifts his glass. "I'm hoping so. That's what we want."

I'm posting to my website. "We have to make it sound like Lillian and I are speaking in innuendos but not make it so subtle that her husband doesn't understand what we're communicating."

Hugh, "Exactly."

I get up to draw the curtains closed. "Question. If he did kill his wife, and he reads my posts and sees that Lillian is writing to me, he's going to know we are full of it and that we're trying to pull a fast one. What's he going to do then?"

Hugh, "I think he's still going to book it out of town. Maybe even faster in that case. Things will have gotten too dicey even for him if it comes to that. He'll want to put distance between us."

I sit back down, start typing away. "Okay, here goes. You guys tell me if this sounds too subtle or too sledgehammer obvious."

Florrie takes a deep breath. "Give it to us, girl."

"I'm writing it as a comment under one of the letters on my site because it's not the sort of thing I would normally post and respond to, and Lillian's husband might notice that if he's been following me closely. Hopefully, he's reading everything I put up right now."

There is a little excitement in Hugh's voice, uncommon for him. "He's definitely reading if he didn't kill his wife and he's still hoping she'll contact you and show up to collect Snowflake, so that works for us."

I read the comments aloud.

Hey Lillian,

The gift you dropped off to me last week is lovely but a little too small,

191

and to be honest, white isn't my color. Am I able to return it to you?

Affectionately yours,
  The Ex-Whisperer

Dear Ex-Whisperer,
  I'm happy to accept the return. I can meet you tomorrow night for pick up.

Lillian

Hugh, "Sounds good to me, but I don't read this sort of stuff too much, so I'm probably not the best gauge."

Florrie, "I do, and I think it sounds fine. A little cagey, but I think it'll do the trick. Lillian's husband probably isn't in the habit of reading this sort of thing either, until the past week at least. Go ahead and post it."

I read out my reply.

Dear Lillian,
  Tomorrow night at ten o'clock at the Lighthouse is great. I'll have the small white one ready for you to collect.
  See you then.

Affectionately yours,
  The Ex-Whisperer

I post all three comments. "Done. Let the games begin."

"I need a little more courage." Florrie tops up our drink glasses.

Hugh throws his whiskey back in one shot. "Let's hope he bites."

Florrie lifts her glass. "After tomorrow, my sister-in-law over in Sauble Beach is going to keep Snowflake for me for a bit until we're sure the coast is clear, and this creep is long gone. Then that little munchkin is coming back to his forever home with me."

"You're going to keep Snowflake permanently?" Hugh is surprised.

Florrie bends down to ruffle her dog's fluffy ears. "Of course. We are a bonded pair now. I love this little guy."

"That was fast." A private message comes in from Lillian's friend. I show it to the other two.

Dear Ex-Whisperer,

I just read some comments on your website from Lillian. It sounds like you're meeting up with her. Does this mean that she is okay? Would love to know if she is safe. Can you let me know?

Friend of a friend

I'm feeling unsettled by this woman. Something's not right. "Does that seem weird, or is it me?"

Florrie shrugs. "Not weird that she's following you and reading all the comments. I mean she kind of feels like she's a part of the mystery right now. At least, she's tried to insinuate herself into it."

Actually, what I feel is ticked off. "It's kind of cheeky that she has refused to answer my requests for info about Lillian, but she thinks I would give her this info now."

Hugh, "People are weird. I wouldn't waste too much time on it. We've got enough balls in the air to juggle right now."

* * *

The following day, the two dogs and I spend quiet time at the cottage. Hugh and Ryan work diligently on the bunkie, and it's coming along beautifully. Hugh calls me outside to go over various issues like how wide I want the steps at the back to be and whether I want the overhang on the rafter tails to be longer than the original design. We act as normal as can be, try to keep our tension—both the sexual and anxious kinds—under wraps.

We pretend that tonight is just another evening rather than the covert

193

affair we have planned.

The day drags by slowly for me. It seems as if I check the time on the clock more than I do anything else.

Florrie texts me often, mostly just strings of emoji, so I know she doesn't know what to say or do with herself, either.

Hugh waves goodbye from the yard, heads home as soon as he's finished working for the day at five.

As darkness falls, I only keep one light on in the cottage while I wait for Florrie to pick me up in the car she borrowed from her brother. Lillian's husband would know what we drive so we don't want him to see our vehicles anywhere near the lighthouse.

Between the strangeness in the air and my frazzled nerves, the pets can feel something is way off, and they are out of sorts, too, barking at most everything they imagine they hear.

Intermittently, my imagination gets the best of me too, and I get up to peer out the window in case Lillian's husband is outside, watching my home.

Paranoia is creeping in and every little noise makes me jump. I move the fireplace poker to lean it against the wall near the front door in case I need it to defend myself. I take a small but sharp knife from the kitchen drawer and put it in the pocket of my jeans. This a first—I've never armed myself with a knife before. I've watched too many *Criminal Minds* episodes, and they're coming back to haunt me now.

I sit still in the darkest corner of the cottage and listen for any sound that breaks the silence. In truth, it's never actually silent at the lake. The more you listen, the louder it gets. The waves lap gently and rhythmically against the sandy shore. The high-water breaks against the natural rock jetty over and over and over again. The whip-poor-wills sing in tireless chorus. The crickets chirp without resting.

I don't notice a strange noise occurring outside; rather, I notice that the continuous nighttime noises I've been tuned in to are suddenly suspended. There's a pause in the birds' songs, an interruption in the insects' chatter. An eerie quiet settles over the lake and the bush.

Something is out there that wasn't there before and doesn't belong there.

Both dogs begin to growl. The cat scrambles to hide underneath the bed.

I kneel down on the floorboards and peek out a window to stare into the blackness along the road. It's a new moon tonight. She can throw no light to assist us in our clandestine endeavor.

I know I am looking at a thick forest because I know that the trees are there, but I can't see the trunks and branches themselves for the darkness shrouds them completely. Someone is out there. And whoever it is, the dogs don't think them friendly.

Something moves near the road. I'm sure of it. A flash of pink flesh. A wrist protruding from the sleeve of a jacket, perhaps, or the base of a bared neck. It's not something, but someone. It's him. It has to be.

Headlights approach in the distance, driving southward on the road. It's nine o'clock exactly. I step away from the window. The dogs continue their low and steady growling. I press my hand against the pocket of my jeans and trace the outline of the knife concealed there. A white car I don't recognize turns onto my property, pulls up close to the cottage.

I've turned my phone on silent, but I see the screen light up when a text comes in.

It's from Florrie: *It's me in the white car. But there's somebody in the bush.*

Chapter Twenty-Six

I text Florrie back: *I'm coming out now.*

I scoop Snowflake up into my arms and open my front door to step outside. Zoe protests aggressively at being left behind in the house, and I have to use my legs to push her back inside, close the door against her.

My heart is pounding against my rib cage. In five quick strides, I'm at the car. I leap into the passenger seat and lock the door in one quick motion.

Florrie is as white as a ghost. "I saw somebody moving behind those trees." She points across the road.

"Did you notice a vehicle parked anywhere nearby?"

She shakes her head.

Inside the cottage, Zoe has seen the strange car on the property and me outside, and she is barking as frantically as I've ever heard her.

I peer into the moonless forest, strain my eyes—can't make out anything, but I can feel someone there. A chill runs down my spine. "It must be him."

Adrenaline is obviously coursing through Florrie's veins as well. Her hands quiver on the steering wheel even though she grips it tight. "I could only see the outline, but the figure looked kind of small—I thought maybe it was a woman."

Snowflake buries his little face in my lap. "Let's get out of here."

Florrie turns the car around to drive back into town. Quickly.

The bewitching smell of rain is brewing in the atmosphere. The air is charged and intoxicating. You can never tell what a storm will bring. Sometimes it bestows a welcome cleansing and cooling. Sometimes it ushers in a much-needed surge of electric excitement. But there are those times, like tonight, when the Heavens threaten to release a deluge of dread and danger.

* * *

All the shops are closed on High Street. Even the couple of restaurants that serve dinner are only lit in the back kitchens where the cooks still work cleaning up. The stately vintage lamplights cast pale circles on the sidewalk like eerie apparitions marching towards the water. We drive to the bottom of the street where the town's landmark towering flagpole, the tallest on the Great Lakes, flies the red and white Maple Leaf. The flag thrashes wildly in the gusts that have suddenly whipped up. The beating of the banner and the crashing of the waves drowns out all other sounds. The forbidding lake looks a cold gray in the dark. Waves pound relentlessly against the stone pier at the foot of the historic lighthouse—the sentry, perpetually on duty keeping watch over all the town.

An angry squall is rolling in. A handful of people out for their evening strolls pick up their pace, hurrying home before the skies open up to soak them.

Florrie and I drive slowly down High Street toward the lake, looking into each parked vehicle for signs of our lurker. All of them are empty. At the bottom, where the street circles in front of the lighthouse, we follow the loop around to head back inland toward the shops. At the top of the street, in the hardware store lot, a truck flashes its lights twice, and we pull in behind it.

I hand Snowflake over to Hugh. "We just drove down to the flagpole and back up. There's no one sitting in any of the parked cars. But there was someone in the forest around my place tonight before we left."

Hugh tucks the dog under his arm. "It was probably our guy. It's only nine-thirty. He likely wouldn't show up here yet. Remember, you two wait five minutes before you drive down after me. And make sure you stay hidden behind the bushes at the side of the lighthouse. Do not come out for any reason except to grab Snowflake if I put him on the ground. And keep your eyes peeled for anything out of the ordinary."

Florrie's voice is drenched in worry. "Be brave, little man."

Hugh chuckles. "I'll try."

Florrie smiles. "I'm talking to the dog."

Hugh winks, then climbs back in his truck with Snowflake and drives off toward the water.

Florrie and I watch the clock and follow in Hugh's tracks exactly five minutes later. We do the loop at the bottom of High Street again, checking out the vehicles that line it—all still empty. We pull up at the rear of the half-dozen parked cars, kill the engine, climb out as quietly as we can. Executing our best attempt at silent and swift, Florrie and I stumble along the sidewalk and slip behind the wall of bushes that stand next to the lighthouse, precisely as planned. We wait. Fifteen minutes tick painstakingly by.

At ten o'clock on the dot, Hugh slides out of his truck carrying Snowflake. He crosses to the old wooden door of the weather-beaten lighthouse and stands in the half-shadow thrown by a broken marine light.

A red car approaches slowly. It parks right behind Florrie's but keeps its engine running. Hugh glances over at it.

Florrie's whispers are loud, but luckily the smashing waves and snapping flag are louder. "Could he be driving a red car now?"

I squint but can't see the person inside it. "I don't know." I use the camera on my phone to zoom in on the driver. "Not him. It's a woman."

I text the same message to Hugh. He looks at his phone, reading it a moment later. He never once looks in our direction.

Florrie, still whispering too loud, "Probably a rendezvous for a torrid affair. The guy whose wife doesn't understand him will be pulling up shortly."

Hugh checks his watch and the perimeter of the area regularly. So far nothing unusual.

The wind surges in strength. Mini tornadoes of sand spiral up off the beach and swirl across the road, making it even harder to distinguish shapes in the dark and more difficult to hear anything above the howling.

Another fifteen minutes crawl along. It's a quarter after ten. Perhaps no one is going to show up tonight. I'm trying to figure out whether I am relieved or disappointed.

Hugh texts me: *It's 10:15. I'm going to head out. Hopefully, our guy is watching. Keep a lookout for a few minutes after I leave in case you spot him. Try to get his license plate if you can.*

The headlights of another car roll toward us. It moves slowly, and Hugh stays put for the moment, keeps his eyes on it. It drives to the lighthouse at the bottom of the loop then follows it around to go back up High Street.

Florrie, ace detective. "There was a couple inside that one. Probably another pair of cheaters looking for a place to make out, their plans thwarted by Hugh. He's cramping everybody's style tonight. And I'm getting a cramp in my leg. We should leave now. The guy's not coming, thank God."

I shush her. "There are two people coming toward us on the sidewalk." Two square black figures blur into the darkness of the night. I text Hugh to let him know.

Florrie crouches down to get a better look at the oncomers from beneath the bushes. "They're kind of short. Nooooo!" She stifles a scream. Barely.

I jump. "What's wrong? Keep quiet!"

A way too loud whisper from Florrie, "There are two massive rats! Coming right at us." Florrie leaps behind me to use my body as a human shield.

I muffle a scream too. "Damn it! I hate rats!"

"Look at their teeth—they're huge! Eeeeek." Florrie grabs my shoulders, stifles her shriek into my back now.

She's right. Two fat brown rodents are scurrying in our direction, saliva spewing from their curled lips. All I can think of is the movie, *Willard*. I am silent screeching into my closed fist, high knee running on the spot. I don't know where we should bolt to. Rats are fast.

When the vermin skitter into the lamplight, I can see that the creatures are on leashes. It dawns on me—I recognize these rodents.

Jesus Mary and Joseph! It's Peppita and Peppeto. The black squares lumbering along the sidewalk behind them are the aunts. What the hell?

Before I can react, the intense white light of automobile high beams from a fast-moving, approaching vehicle flood over us. The aunts spin around to look at the speeding car.

Zia Angela yells out, "Pazzo!" *Crazy.*

"Rallenta! Rallenta!" *Slow down.* Zia Rosa waves her fist in the air threateningly.

The small dark car screeches to a stop in the middle of the road, just in front of the lighthouse, and a man jumps out of it. He barrels toward Hugh, who has seen him coming and has braced himself in a wide stance, Snowflake still in his arms.

Mere seconds later, the man with the shaved head, arms covered in snake and skull tattoos, throws a wild mistimed punch that fails to connect. Hugh turns his shoulder into it to protect Snowflake, then he drops the little dog onto the ground—our cue to grab the pup. Hugh straightens up with a fast right hook that meets the jaw of Lillian's husband with a crack loud enough to be heard above the crashing waves and wailing wind. The man's head snaps back, but in a flash, he recovers, and his arms throw windmill punches all over Hugh's body.

The aunts are screaming in Italian at the men and at the dogs. Peppita and Peppeto go totally berserk, trying to get at Snowflake, who frantically books it toward the beach to escape the chaos. Florrie chases after Snowflake, yelling out to him. I jump out from behind the bushes to stop the aunts from going any closer to the men.

Naturally, the aunts are so startled by my sudden appearance they shriek in unison—their reflexes react simultaneously, and they start swinging their mammoth handbags through the air, bringing them down on the top of my head. *Boom. Bam.* Now I scream out—that bloody hurts—I'm seeing stars. Even as a kid, I figured their purses had to be filled with bricks. I don't know how they manage to lug those cases around. Maybe they designed them specially for self-defence purposes—true battle-ax bags.

I raise my arms over my face to shield myself from the heft of the lethal luggage. "Stop Zias! It's me, Gina!"

Rosa pulls her arm back mid-air. "Gina? Whatsamatter for you?" She spares me the wrath of her weighted purse but smacks me upside the head with a scolding hand instead, which in comparison, does not hurt at all.

Angela crosses herself. "Madonna! You scared us to death!"

Zia Rosa is shaking her finger in my face. I see three for everyone on her hand.

Zia Rosa boxes my ear again for emphasis. "What are you doing out here? It's dangerous. Look at these *pazzi* people!"

The three of us look in the direction of the lighthouse where Hugh and Lillian's husband are now wrestling on the ground. I try to focus my vision. The two men are fighting, fists flying wildly and connecting with faces and rib cages. Crunches and cracks.

Florrie runs up to them, Snowflake in her arms. She starts kicking at Lillian's husband, but who knows where her heavy-booted strikes are landing. Peppita and Peppeto see Snowflake and yank hard enough to pull their leashes out of the hands of the shocked aunts. In an eye blink, the rabid Chihuahuas are in the middle of the ruckus. A few wayward kicks and erratic punches send the little dogs reeling. I never knew humans were capable of producing sounds as loud as the aunts do in that moment.

Instantly, the old battle-axes are ringside at the fight, swinging their cement block valises at the flailing bodies bucking in the dirt—and making contact every time. If it wasn't for Mother Nature's deafening cacophony tonight, I'm sure half the town would have heard the commotion and called the cops on us by now. I stumble in the direction of the riot to try to pull the aunts out of the fray, and I am met with the impact of a flurry of fists and feet and purses in all regions of my body. I manage to push the aunts back from the brawl, and in turn, the aunts succeed in reining in their frenzied Chihuahuas.

In that moment, Snowflake squirms out of Florrie's grasp, manages to leap out of her arms, and runs onto the street. Behind Lillian's husband's car, a ghostly figure kneels. A pale, blond-haired woman in a white coat. Snowflake runs to the woman, leaps into her arms. Florrie chases after the dog, but the woman hurries back to jump inside her parked red car with Snowflake buried beneath her woolly coat. Before Florrie can reach her, the woman pulls a quick U-turn and squeals away down the road. Yelling out to Snowflake, Florrie chases the vehicle until it turns down a side street and disappears into the night.

I manage to pull my phone out of the pocket of my jeans. My useless little knife falls out onto the ground. I brought a knife to a handbag fight. I snap a shot of the license plate on Lillian's husband's car, then I crouch beside the flailing men and start shooting and ducking, hoping some of the photos will be of Lillian's husband. It's difficult to pick him out in the roiling mess of thrashing limbs. I can't be sure who's who. The men are just a mass of mud and brightly colored bodily fluids smeared across their faces and over their torn clothing.

I holler a rant, "I've got your photo, you scumbag, and I'm sending it to the cops right now. They're on their way. I've got your license plate, too. You'd better get the hell out of here before they arrest your ass."

In response, Lillian's husband releases his part of the wrestling grip that he and Hugh are entangled in. This lapse allows Hugh to land another uppercut—but now, Lillian's husband is fighting to stand up and get away from him. Once Hugh realizes his opponent is no longer battling back, he stops struggling, too. Lillian's husband scrambles to his feet and staggers to his little black car, falters climbing into it, then starts the engine and roars off down the road in the same direction as the woman in the red vehicle.

Gale force winds whip around us with wrath, and suddenly, the thunder clouds above break open in a fury. We are all soaked to the bones in less than a minute. Hugh struggles to climb to his feet, extends a bloody hand to help pull me to my own. I stumble along, herding the aunts and their dogs toward Florrie's brother's car, and pile them into the back seat, ignoring their unending stream of questions and complaints in both English and Italian.

Florrie meets me at the car, having returned from her marathon run empty-handed, out of breath, and full of tears. "That woman stole Snowflake. I couldn't catch up to her." She takes in my battered face—cries louder. "Oh my god, you look like a prizefighter—who lost."

All I can manage to get out is, "I'll meet you at the aunts.'"

Hugh limps to his truck, and I hobble alongside to clamber in next to him.

Chapter Twenty-Seven

nside Happily Napoli, the five of us sit with towels over our wet shoulders. The aunts hand me a second one to rub my hair dry. Everything hurts. They have the kettle on and already have a large plate of cheeses and bread on the table which no one is yet able to touch.

The skin on my face is tight and sticky. I slowly raise a hand to touch my cheek. It's bumpy, streaked with something raised and cakey. Dried blood over cuts, I assume. Zia Rosa tells me there is only one bad gash, and she cleans it up quickly. The antiseptic stings.

Zia warns me, "You gonna be sore in the mattina. There lots of bruises underneath. Come here for risotto tomorrow. It's easy to chew."

Zia Angela has a bowl of warm water and a cloth that she uses to tend to Hugh's cut and battered face. He is already turning black and blue. His nose has doubled in size, and his cheeks are marked with rivers of red. He's in a lot worse shape than me.

Florrie and I stare at Hugh's injuries openly and rudely.

He attempts a smile, but it's comically crooked. "You should see the other guy."

It's a valiant effort to cheer us up, but no one can muster a laugh. Florrie is despondent, her face tear-stained, and all of us are in shock.

Zia Angela rubs Hugh's eyelid with the cloth, and he winces at her touch.

Zia Rosa hands me a bag of frozen peas to hold against the baseball-sized lump protruding from the back of my head—the result of a blow I'm sure she inflicted on me herself with her lethal luggage.

Peppita and Peppeto growl and snap incessantly, playing tug of war with one of the wet towels. Truly annoying.

I push Send on my phone, let Hugh and Florrie know, "I forwarded the photos of Lillian's husband and his license plate to Floyd and Lloyd."

Hugh flinches when Zia dabs peroxide on his open cuts. He turns to me. "Gina, I think you should get checked out at the ER. You could have a concussion."

"I could have, thanks to the cement blocks the aunts carry around disguised as handbags. But I don't. You might have one, though. You also look like you need some stitches."

Hugh shakes his head. "I don't."

Florrie is serious. No jokes from her tonight. "Hugh, you could have broken ribs."

Hugh, still negative, "You know what a doctor does for broken ribs and concussions? Nothing. Squat. They send you home and tell you to rest and not to go downhill skiing for a couple of months. I promise not to take up any extreme sports."

I scoff at all of us. "An entire room full of stubborn asses." There are no objections to my statement, no offence taken at the truth spoken.

Zia Rosa pours chamomile tea. Everyone has what they need for the moment, and the mud and blood has been mostly cleaned away, so the aunts move to the next phase. They stand in front of me, hands on their hips, glaring angrily.

Zia Angela, "*Mio Dio*. What were you doing hiding in the bushes?"

Zia Rosa, "In the *notte*?" *Night.*

Forming words pains my face. I can taste the salt from the blood inside my mouth. "What were you two doing down at the lighthouse by yourselves at ten o'clock at night?"

Zia Angela looks at me as if I'm stupid. "It's the new moon in September." I raise my hands up. Gimme a clue.

Zia Rosa rolls her eyes, exasperated with my ignorance. "You can only pick the echinacea at the *Settembre* new moon. You gotta take the coneflower tea for the winter colds or you going be having the flu till spring. We go to the butterfly garden at the beach to pick the echinacea flowers tonight."

Zia Angela is alarmed. "What we gonna do now? We didn't get the flowers."

Rosa shrugs. "We're gonna have to get it tomorrow."

Of course, Angela's voice rises. "It's no gonna be good tomorrow. The new moon she's tonight."

Naturally, Rosa's voice rises even louder. "Whattaya gonna do? It's pouring the cats and dogs out there."

Their loudness is like a sledgehammer on my skull, and since Hugh is also wincing at their every word, I figure it must be just as painful for him.

Florrie's voice is so quiet that it gets all our attention, and we turn to listen to her. "How are we going to get Snowflake back? That woman kidnapped him."

I smile at her. That hurts, too. "She probably thought she was rescuing him from truly horrible people. Snowflake was terrified, and we looked like a bunch of maniacs brawling on the street."

Florrie attempts a touch of levity. "Small dogfighting ring."

The vicious little Chihuahuas snarl at each other over the torn towel on the floor. The aunts give them cookies. Rewarding bad behavior—their training method is coming back to bite them in the ass, literally.

Florrie sighs. "You're right. I would have done the same thing. Maybe if I put an ad in the newspaper and put signs up explaining that we're actually responsible dog owners, she might return him to me?"

I'm not hopeful. "Probably not if she recognizes you as the madwoman who chased her car through the streets for a quarter-mile."

Florrie is perplexed. "I was surprised. Snowflake ran right into her arms. Do you think it could have been Lillian?"

I pause to consider her theory. "Anything is possible, but Snowflake was terrified and desperate to escape the chaos. I think he would have run into anyone's arms to get away from the mayhem. If it was Lillian, she must have read my messages online to know about the meeting tonight. Same as her husband did. It's possible, but a long shot."

"If it was her, she probably didn't want her deranged husband to get a hold of Snowflake." Florrie sounds forlorn but resigned. "I guess I'll go with that theory—it makes me feel a little better. I'm sure going to miss the little guy, but maybe he's back with his real mom now."

Hugh's first aid is complete at last. "One thing's for sure. That was some lethal force action. Our suspicions about the guy being a full-on psychopath were correct."

I take a sip of tea, try not to let the heat sting my split bottom lip. "A psychopath but not a murderer. Even if that woman wasn't Lillian, the fact that her husband tried to grab Snowflake basically proves that he didn't kill her. He would only want the dog if he could use it to coerce Lillian into going back to him."

Hugh agrees, "Whether that was Lillian or not, I think it's safe to assume she's long gone by now, and so is her husband. I expect they are both a couple of hundred miles from here. Doubt we'll ever hear from either of them again."

The aunts focus their scolding on Hugh now.

Zia Rosa looks him up and down suspiciously. "So why you beating up Gina's friend?"

Hugh's not sure how to answer. He turns to me for help.

I leap in to try to save him. "He's not my friend, Zia. I don't even know that man."

Zia Rosa shakes her head as if I am getting more *stupida* by the minute. "He's your friend who was in our restaurant with the computer. I told you about him."

I shake my head. "He's not a good guy, Zia. Trust me."

Zia Angela leaps to the conclusion they're hoping for. She turns back to Hugh. "Is it because you're jealous? You don't gotta be jealous. He's a married man."

Hugh is suffering all kinds of discomfort. We all are. The lights in Happily Napoli flicker off and on. The storm is getting stronger. The aunts gasp, scuttle about procuring candles and a pack of matches.

I gingerly rise out of my chair, babying my back. "It's late. *Le signore*, you two need to get to bed before the power goes out. We're going to go home now." I shake my finger at both aunts. "And no going out in the dark moon to pick flowers."

Double air kisses all around—hurts too much to touch anyone. Hugh and Florrie thank the aunts for the tea and snacks and first aid. My generous zias sling a bag over my good shoulder filled with the uneaten cheese and bread they served, of course, and we make our exit.

The rain is torrential, the wind ferocious. The three of us push against the fierceness and fight to pull the vehicle doors open. We jump in, and the storm violently slams them shut after us. Limbs could have been lost. Hugh follows Florrie and me back to my cottage, windshield wipers at full speed. It takes twice as long to get there, and I spend the drive worrying about Zoe and Spook. They will be scared all alone in this wicked storm.

* * *

When we finally arrive at the cottage, it is in total darkness. I know I left the outside lights on, but the power is likely out. Florrie shrieks when she runs splashing through the inches deep puddles and pushes against the torrential rain to make her way to the front door. It's difficult to hear her voice above the deafening cracks of thunder and the raging winds. The three of us are instantly soaked to the bones once again. It takes me and Hugh a minute to catch up. We lean hard into the punishing gale, arm in arm, and press against the tempest, moving as fast as our battered bodies will allow. The storm steals the last shred of my strength.

I unlock the cottage door as quickly as possible and flip on the light switch, but there is no juice. The dog and cat run to meet us in the dark, and Zoe is barking as if she has gone mad.

I bend down to pet them. "Oh, poor babies."

Florrie uses her phone flashlight to search for candles and matches in the kitchen drawers and gets the torches lit. The cabin is bright and cozy in less than two minutes, and I feel so grateful to be safely tucked inside its refuge even though my wet clothes cling uncomfortably to my cold and bruised skin. I pull towels out of the cupboard for each of us to dry off, while Hugh hunts for the whiskey and Baileys and is already pouring.

I want to get changed into warm sweatpants, but a frenzied Zoe can't wait to get outside. "I'm taking the dog out to piddle."

Hugh limps across the room, grabs her leash from the hook at the door. "I'll take her out."

Can't say I'm not incredibly appreciative of the offer. "Thank you."

I have never seen Zoe pull on her leash so hard. She almost takes an unsteady Hugh off his feet as she drags him down the slippery steps of the cottage.

I close the door behind them, wait by it for the pair of them to return. "Zoe is acting super weird."

Florrie lights the candles on the kitchen table. "It's a scary storm, and she was alone in the dark. She'll settle."

A few moments later, I open the door for Hugh, which creates a wind vortex that blows out all the candles in the room. Florrie shrieks. The cat flees under the bed. Hugh struggles against the storm and has to use all the energy he's got left to pull the dog inside the house and slam the door after her.

"Zoe, what is wrong with you?" I take the leash off her.

Hugh pulls his sweatshirt off over his head and wrings the sopping hoodie out over the kitchen sink. "I don't know. She was trying to pull me down to the lake. Wouldn't stop barking."

"I guess she's that freaked out from the storm." I attempt to calm Zoe with a gentle massage.

Florrie relights the candles. I avert my eyes to keep from staring at the sinewy muscles rippling across Hugh's naked back.

I hand Hugh a double shot of whiskey. "Your boxing days are over, champ." His sculpted chest is painted with purple blotches where powerful fists impacted his torso.

Hugh lifts the glass. "Happy to hang up the gloves." He throws the whiskey back, winces. He is in a lot of pain for sure and clearly looking for a way to dull the aching.

I delicately lower myself into a chair, try to get the dog to sit next to me, but she won't stop whining, pacing in circles, scratching at the door. Then she starts barking and refuses to stop for anything. The sharp pitch is reverbing against my cranium. Same for Hugh, I'm sure.

I am at a loss. "She's never acted like this before."

Florrie visibly shudders. "She's acting like there's someone outside."

The three of us exchange frightened glances.

Zoe won't let up with the barking.

"I'll go back out with her." Hugh leans heavily on the table to pull himself to standing.

Florrie wrings her hands. "I don't think any of us should go out there. I think we should call Floyd. It could be Lillian's husband. He's bound to be pissed and looking to finish the fight. Neither of you have any feistiness left in you, and I'm sure not going to take that maniac on."

Hugh shakes his head. "I'm certain that Lillian's husband has taken a powder. He knows we have his photo and his license plate. Zoe is just unnerved by the storm. And she's picking up on our jumpy energy to boot. I'll be right back. I promise." Hugh puts Zoe on the leash again and hobbles toward the door. He turns back before he leaves and picks up the fireplace poker still resting against the wall. How reassuring. Zoe pulls him outside with all her might, and they disappear into the blackness.

Florrie and I nervously watch out the window on the lake side, but it's too dark and miserable to see much of anything. As soon as Hugh and Zoe go around to the back of the cottage toward the lake, the two of them vanish in the murk. The dog is still barking frantically, but the sound is barely audible over the raging wind and crashing whitecaps.

A shiver runs down my spine—a disturbing sensation that is becoming far too familiar. "Something's out there. I can feel it."

Florrie's whole body is trembling. "It's not safe for Hugh or the dog to be outside."

Too much time passes. At least four minutes.

I wobble across the floor to the door. "I'm going to go check on them. Call the police if I'm not back in two minutes."

"No! You can't go out there, Gina." Florrie grabs my arm to hold me back.

Just then, the door thrusts open. A blast of wind and torrent of rain surges through the opening into the cabin, sending Florrie and me reeling backward. Hugh pushes inside, Zoe willingly following him this time. He shoves the door shut behind him and locks it. When he turns back to face us, he pulls a drenched, blackened rag out from under his arm. We stare at the bedraggled bundle, dumbstruck. The rag wriggles.

Florrie, "What in tarnation?"

The rag whimpers.

I am astonished. "Snowflake?"

Chapter Twenty-Eight

Hugh holds a weary, straggly Snowflake up so we can get a better look at the pint-sized pup. "He was tied to the same tree in the yard as before. Poor little guy has been out in this brutal storm for a long time. He's pretty scared. And cold."

Florrie throws her arms around Hugh's neck. "Thank you, thank you, thank you, thank you!"

Hugh grimaces. Even hugs hurt. "Don't thank me. It was all Zoe. That's what she's been trying to tell us, why she wouldn't settle."

Florrie hugs a soggy Zoe long and hard and then grabs the sodden and filthy little Snowflake and cries along with the tiny trooper.

I digest this latest shock. "So, it was Lillian at the lighthouse tonight, then."

Hugh nods. "Now we know for certain that she's definitely alive."

As if in response, the lights in the cottage flicker then blaze back on, blinding the lot of us.

I shield my eyes with my hand but flinch—it smarts to touch my bruised face. "And it was Lillian who tied Snowflake to the tree in my yard. Both times. She must feel so desperate. She's on the run from her abusive husband and can't take her pet with her. Poor thing."

Florrie sniffles in sympathy. "I'm glad that Lillian got to say goodbye to her little guy at least."

Snowflake enjoys a leisurely bubble bath in the bathroom sink, and by the time Florrie has finished fussing over him, he looks as good as new. Florrie joins Hugh and me at the kitchen table and keeps the pooped pooch on her lap so she can hand feed him bits of cheese and bread.

Zoe is the real hero of the day, and she has been rewarded with multitudes of cookies and many belly rubs from all of us.

I marvel at the dog's instincts and intelligence. "Zoe knew Snowflake was out there in the storm, and she just would not give up until we listened to her."

We sip on our drinks, and focus on the pets, and work hard at avoiding the things we should be discussing. The entire night seems surreal. Hell, the entire past few weeks seem surreal.

None of us are saying much. It's late, and we're all tired. Hugh is sore, and I am sore, and we should definitely be calling it a night. But the heaviest thing weighing on me right now is overwhelming guilt. I am feeling sorry for myself and for everyone who is unlucky enough to have anything to do with me. The Advil and the Baileys aren't helping matters.

I have to lay the guilt out on the table. "This entire mess is my fault. I will never know how to sufficiently apologize for getting both of you mixed up in all this horrible, life-threatening mess. I'm so, so sorry for everything that's happened."

Florrie rallies to adapt an overly chipper voice for two o'clock in the morning. "I'm not sorry. For the most part, it's been exciting, and I love my time with you. And I wouldn't have Snowflake if you hadn't come back to town and gotten me mixed up in all this horrible, life-threatening mess. So, it's all been worth it." Florrie winks at me.

Hugh's voice is sober and serious. "Gina, I'm the one who needs to apologize for everything that happened tonight. This whole thing was my idea, and it turned into a complete catastrophe."

I interrupt him. "You didn't plan to have my eccentric aunts and their pet rats crash the party with their new moon herbal remedy hunting."

Hugh shakes his head. "It doesn't matter. I'm sorry about everything that's gone on these past couple of weeks. So much of it is my fault. All the crap with Iris and the dangerous turn with Lillian's husband tonight. You're all beat up because of me."

Florrie leads the cheer. "Hugh, if you didn't come up with your idea to lure Lillian's husband into the open so we could identify him, he would still be skulking around in the woods terrorizing Gina. It all worked out." She qualifies her argument. "If he's really gone now, that is."

"You're not the reason I got mixed up in this train wreck with Lillian and her husband." I feel bad for Hugh. He should not be taking this on. "This is my stuff, and I have brought this mayhem down on you guys and the aunts and Floyd and Lloyd and the entire town, really. I'm the reason Dick is in Sunset Beach now, and wherever he goes, trouble follows. I need to give some serious thought to my future here."

Alarm registers across Florrie's face. "Don't go there, Gina. Everyone loves having you home."

Hugh sounds a little nervous, too. He combats his emotions as he always does, with facts and logic. "Your ex-husband is a conman, and my ex is bonkers. We can't control those two. The fact that our whacko exes found each other and teamed up isn't our fault."

Florrie's lips curl in disgust. "The fact that Dickiris feed off each other, two rotting peas in a pod, infecting one another with their obsessiveness, isn't your fault, either."

A bit more Baileys and I am borderline morose. "The Universe has been sending me some loud messages. Me trying to go home again hasn't been working out so great so far. For anybody. I'm looking for peace, but all I've found here and brought here is turmoil. And turmoil is the last thing I want and the opposite of what I need. I promised myself this was my year to let go of things that I don't want or need—things from my past that no longer serve me, things that make me feel bad. Maybe this little town is one of those things."

Florrie intervenes, snatches up the bottle of Baileys and my bottle of Advil from the table, and puts them on a high shelf. Keep out of reach of children. I try not to laugh because it's too damn painful.

"You can't leave town." Florrie's eyes look desperate.

I smile at her. "It's late. We should get some sleep." I'm a master at avoidance mechanisms.

The others are too tired to argue with me. Florrie and I hit the sack. Hugh crashes on the couch.

* * *

When I wake in the morning, I lie in bed unable to move. This must be what it feels like to be hit by a bus. Cripes, even my hair hurts. My eyelids feel thick and heavy—it's an effort to open them. At least fifteen minutes pass by the time I'm able to pull myself fully upright onto the edge of the bed and tug on a pair of leggings and a loose T-shirt. During that struggle, my mind is flooded with thoughts that pain almost as much as my bruised flesh. Left brain—moving home was a mistake. I am not meant to be here. It's time for me to leave, for my own and everyone else's sake. Right brain—I promised myself I'd never lose my home again or give up any of my dreams because of a man. I should stay in this place despite the overwhelming evidence to the contrary and suffer and make everyone around me suffer because I am a stubborn idiot.

I need to escape me.

The wonderful smell of brewed coffee is a massive motivator that draws me toward it. The elixir I desire, the drug I require. Slowly, painfully I make my way into the kitchen.

Florrie pops a couple of slices of toast into the toaster. For me, of course.

"Don't do anything for me. I'm fine. I can take care of myself."

"Yeah, I can see that. You look great for a hundred-year-old broad, ready for your close-up?"

"I also doubt I can chew anything without screaming." Zoe makes her way toward me, tail wagging only half-heartedly. She is also clearly exhausted from the stress of the horrendous night.

Florrie pours me a cup of coffee, sets it down on the table, carries on making the toast anyway, Snowflake tucked under her arm the whole while.

I'm grateful that I didn't have to walk the extra two feet to reach the coffee pot. I carefully lower my body down onto the seat of the kitchen chair. It seems a long way away from my standing position.

A plate of buttered toast is served up for me next. Florrie is concerned about the animals. "The pets are all traumatized."

Zoe settles on the floor next to me, and I reach down to pet her as best I can. Spook cuddles up against his dog sister to give and receive comfort.

"Me too." I need more coffee. Florrie can sense this and is already pouring. Bless her.

The saws and hammers begin their morning symphony. I am amazed. "It's barely eight o'clock. Why is Hugh working today? He's got to be in incredibly rough shape if I feel as bad as I do—he took a whole lot more on the chin than me. He should be taking the day off."

"You know Hugh. He's a worker, and he's also got a man to keep going." Florrie sits down at the table with a coffee for herself.

I let the steam from my coffee mug warm my face. "I need to get a ton of work done today, too. I'm so behind." More guilt.

Florrie pushes the breakfast plate toward me. "You're not up to doing anything. Eat your toast, invalid. Doctor's orders."

My fabulous cousin and I stare at each other for a long moment and share a lot of information without speaking a word.

"You're going to leave town, aren't you?"

I nod. Florrie looks so sad that it breaks my heart.

I reach across the table to hold her hand. "It's in everyone's best interests. And don't worry, you and I will make sure to see each other often. We won't let so much time pass by again."

A single tear rolls down Florrie's cheek. "It just doesn't feel like you gave the situation enough time, Gina. You didn't get to experience normal life around here."

"That's the problem. I don't think things will ever get back to normal here as long as I'm around." I know I'm delivering a final blow, and I hate to do it, but . . . "Gal, I'm going to give myself a few days to get mobile, and then I'm going to close up shop and head back to the city. I guess there's some truth after all to the old saying that you can never go home again."

Florrie's eyes tear up full-bore now. Mine, too. We hug it out for a while, and then she leaves with Snowflake to go to the bakery.

I watch her drive away and then call outside to Hugh. He's carrying lumber from his pickup to the bunkie and has a load of two-by-fours balanced on his shoulder. When he sees me wave him over, he sets the wood down, meets me at the door of the cottage.

I usher him inside, close the door behind us so his man Ryan won't overhear.

Hugh smiles, his mouth even more crooked and swollen than it was last night. "How bad does it feel today?"

"A hundred out of ten."

"That's pretty bad." He cocks his head, takes me in.

"You?" I know I sound awkward, cold even.

"Nothing a few weeks in bed wouldn't help." His eyes read mine—I think he's trying to guess what I'm about to tell him.

I really can't bear to look at Hugh's battered face, so I keep my eyes on the cup of cooling coffee in my hands. "I've made a decision. I'm not going to stay here. Maybe I'll give this town another try in a few years, but for now, I know it's not the right time and place for me. I'm sorry for this and for everything else that's gone down. I'm not going to have you continue with the work on the cottage. Let me know what I owe you for the work you've done on the bunkie to date and for any loss of work, you will have incurred by our understanding that this project would go on for a few months' time."

Hugh is obviously shocked by my words, but in truth, it's a look of crushing disappointment that registers most visibly across his face. I hope I'm not intentionally hurting him, but then again, who the hell knows what I'm doing anymore? I'm not sure that I do. My life has felt like a magnitude 8.0 earthquake for months. Correction—years. And earthquakes harm all sorts of random casualties unlucky enough to find themselves in the vicinity when these natural disasters crack open and swallow their victims whole. That's me, I guess—a natural disaster.

Hugh's voice is rife with a desperateness I've never heard from him before. "I don't want things to end like this between us, Gina. I know things never actually got started, but I was really hoping that they would when the timing was right. And even if that's not what you want and we don't have a future together, I don't want to not finish the work on your cottage."

Still can't look him in the eye. It's getting even harder to now. "It's clearly not in either of our best interests to get in any deeper personally or professionally."

"What are you going to do?" Hugh sounds sorrowful.

"I'm going back to the city for a bit, and then I think I'm going to drive out west with the pets. Spend some time living on the coast. I'm going to take six months or so and write another book. My publisher's been after me to do it, and it's time." Me the earthquake now sends out seismic aftershocks.

Hugh holds his hands against the sides of his head. " I have really messed up here. I was supposed to help make your dreams come true, and I've helped destroy them, instead. Some builder I am. Some frickin' friend."

"You didn't do anything wrong. I've just changed my mind about some things. For numerous reasons."

Without another word, Hugh walks out of the cottage.

Chapter Twenty-Nine

A while later, banging outside reaches my ears. I look out the window at Ryan loading the truck with the construction equipment, pulling up stakes at this camp. There is no sign of Hugh or his truck.

My cell phone rings. It's Lloyd.

"Hear you're looking like a UFC fighter. How ya feeling, slugger?"

"How the frig can you know this already? I didn't send you pictures of me."

"It's Sunset Beach. Everybody knows everything. That's the best thing and the worst thing about living in this little Peyton Place."

"I guess you're right, there."

"My sources tell me that the small dark car we've been on the lookout for was at the lighthouse last night, and the driver, who we assume is the husband of your advice column reader, whom you believe to be missing, or possibly deceased, assaulted you. Do I have the facts straight so far?"

"Sounds like you know more than I do. You got the license plate of the black car and the blurry badly-lit photos of the guy that I sent you last night?"

"I did. He won't be too hard to find. We'll definitely be picking him up and laying assault charges."

That's dicey. "I really don't want to press charges, Lloyd, and Hugh doesn't either. The truth is, we kind of tricked Lillian's husband into meeting us. We were just hoping we'd get a look at him, and he'd know that we could identify him and that might be enough to encourage him to stop stalking me and leave town. We sure didn't expect the guy to go gonzo trying to snatch his wife's dog."

"Why would he want his wife's dog so badly?"

A long pause ensues, and then I stammer—my head is too sore for fast thinking. Lloyd knows he's been right all along and that I've been wrong. I've been trying to force Floyd and Lloyd to investigate a victimless crime. And the hits just keep on coming.

Lloyd zeros in. "You think he was trying to get the dog, so he'd have the leverage to get his wife to either go back to him or at least meet up with him?"

More stammering from me.

Lloyd feeds me the lines slowly, "So now we think Lillian is alive, correct?"

Impressively, I am able to make words now. "I'm pretty sure Lillian is alive, yes."

Lloyd is patient. "So, there's no need for me to have this guy picked up, then."

I object. "I still believe his wife is in danger. And he is going to hunt her down until he finds her. Can't you bring him in and scare him, at least?" Weak argument.

Lloyd's voice is gentle. He speaks to me like the fragile patient that I am at the moment. "I'd like to have a little talk with this guy to make sure he never bothers you again at the very least. Leave it with me."

"Okay, thanks, Lloyd. Chances are he's crossing the border into Detroit by now."

Lloyd chuckles. "You'd be surprised how many people are too stupid to get out while the getting's good. Give those assault charges some thought, and we can talk about it after I have seen whether our guy has any priors. I'm going to run his plate, find out who he is. Then we'll know the name and address of your missing friend, at least, and we can see what we can find out on her whereabouts. I'll keep you posted. Good work, Columbo."

* * *

People say day two of an injury is always twice as bad, and I can attest to the fact that is utter rubbish. It's fifty times worse. My face is throbbing, my

219

headache next level. My physiotherapy today will be attempting to type on the keyboard of my laptop.

I open my private email to find another letter from Lillian's library friend.

Dear Ex-Whisperer,

I'm certain now that Lillian is dead. Lillian and her husband both went back to their home late last night. But a few hours later, a neighbor saw Lillian's husband putting a large bundle in the trunk of his car—and he was covered in blood. Lillian is gone, but they didn't see her leave the house. By the way, Lillian's husband's name is Kyle Kowalski. He's from Picton.

Friend of a friend

I'm totally perplexed and pissed off by Lillian's friend, and by her neighbour—how would anyone not have called the police to report what they saw? A woman's life is in grave danger. Or worse, she's already been murdered. I immediately forward the email exchange to Lloyd.

Dear Friend,

You need to tell the police what you know and give them the names of these neighbors you're speaking to. I understand that you don't want to get involved, but what you are talking about is profoundly serious, and you could be charged for obstructing justice by withholding this evidence. I am forwarding your email to the police, and they might find you through the IP address of your computer, so you should just contact them voluntarily. I am not involving myself any further in this matter. Do not contact me again.

The Ex-Whisperer

My head is pounding, and it feels far too swollen to make room for any additional complicated thoughts. I know all of this is way beyond my scope now, and I need to leave it to the experts to find Lillian's husband and bring him to justice if they're able.

I proceed to empty my brain. I spend the next two hours mindlessly surfing the net, and I suspend all thought processes completely. Facebook is fantastic for numbing one's mind, and I need mind numbing today. I creep the walls of people I have never met, see pictures of their grandchildren whom I do not know, and it's oddly satisfying. For a time.

Every few minutes, I am snapped out of my Facebook stupor by the Nancy Drew part of my brain that refuses to let sleeping dogs lie. My old nemesis Guilt also rears its ugly head, and after a while, I cave to the pressure. I text both Florrie and Hugh and ask them to come over as soon as they can.

Florrie replies by text. It starts out with a dozen crying face emojis then she writes: *Am on my way over with our dinner. Be there in twenty.*

And she is.

* * *

Florrie sets a delectable box of Honey Lavender cupcakes on the table and puts the kettle on for tea. She is still sad about me leaving town, and I do not have a clue what I'm feeling on the subject. In an effort to dull our aching hearts, we eat far too many sweets with a nice aromatic oolong, but it doesn't help. We are going to miss each other like crazy.

Half an hour later, there is a knock at my door. Hugh calls out to let us know it's him. Florrie jumps up to usher him inside.

Hugh is frosty. "What's up?"

Self-protection. I get it. Hugh doesn't know what the hell I might hit him with next. Cyclone Gina. More reason for me to be on my way ASAP.

Hugh refuses a cup of tea, sits stiffly and silently at the table, prepared to listen to what I have to tell them. I read the message from Lillian's friend aloud. They are both shocked, of course.

There is a long moment of silence, and I'm guessing the three of us are likely thinking the same thoughts.

I state them aloud, "It's our fault that Lillian is dead. We lured her near her husband, and as a result, he was able to get to Lillian, and he killed her—because of us."

Florrie's stunned expression tells me that she was not thinking the same thoughts as me.

"We're to blame for Lillian's death?" Florrie is gobsmacked.

Hugh is unmoved. "We don't know for sure that she is dead. That so-called friend of Lillian's is not exactly reliable. If she was so certain there had been a murder, why didn't she call the police?"

I find that pill hard to swallow, myself. "Same reason the neighbors didn't call the police when they thought Lillian was being abused—because people suck."

"Hugh's right. Maybe Lillian's not dead." Florrie is optimistic as ever. "There's no evidence, and the police haven't found her body, or else Floyd and Lloyd would have been on the blower to us by now."

"You guys are missing the point." I'm getting frustrated by their reluctance to join me on my colossal guilt trip. So, what if it's not currently supported by facts? When did Guilt, or for that matter, his twin sister Worry, ever care about facts? "But what if Lillian is dead? We caused that."

Logical Hugh refuses to come along for the remorse ride. "No, we did not cause that. We didn't lure Lillian anywhere. We had no idea she was hanging around town watching you."

Florrie is fidgety. Her eyes dart about nervously. "And watching her husband. And Snowflake. Maybe that was Lillian hiding in your woods last night. It looked like it might have been a woman. Maybe she's still out there. Or maybe her ghost is out there now." Florrie is on the verge of working herself up into a frenzy. It's all just too much for her. For anyone.

Except for Hugh. He rolls his eyes. "Let's not go there." He's dug his heels in at the opposite end of the spectrum.

I would like to be able to calm Florrie down, but I'm nowhere in the vicinity of calm. "You're right. I'm sure it was Lillian in my woods last night. That's what I'm saying. She read my messages online and showed up at the lighthouse where her hostile husband was because of us."

Now, even Mr. Cucumber has lost his cool. "If Lillian is dead, we didn't kill her. But let's wait and see if anyone is dead before we start confessing to murder."

And Florrie is officially over the edge. "Even if we didn't kill Lillian, we could still be considered accessories to the crime. We could do time for that."

Hugh can't take any more. He stands. "If you two want to have a few drinks, I'm down. Otherwise, I'm going to head home and drink alone."

* * *

A couple of hours later, you could not find any nervous tension in the room if your life depended on it. We have successfully drowned our demons for the time being. All three of us are happily drunk. I am aware that it's a recurring theme in the past two weeks, and I fully intend to put an end to it once my battered body has come out the other side from my UFC match and I no longer need to drink through a straw.

Florrie has cranked up the volume on her Spotify Motown playlist and has pulled Hugh onto the kitchen floor to join her in her incredibly unique "It's Raining Men" dance routine. I must admit, they're a very cute pair, even if Hugh looks a lot like Frankenstein Monster Mashing, with his scarred face and lopsided limp. I am trying extremely hard not to laugh, but only because of the pain in my jaw.

There's a loud knocking at my door. Zoe goes wild, barking ferociously. The dancing stops. The terror sets in. We exchange piercing stares between us, all of us thinking exactly the same thing.

Oh. My. God. Is it Lillian's husband? Or Lillian's ghost?

"Open up. I know you're in there, Gina Malone. Come on, hurry up, it's raining men out here." It's Lloyd.

I let out the long breath I've been holding. Florrie nearly collapses with relief. Hugh reacts in kind, unlocks the door, and swings it wide open.

It is Floyd *and* Lloyd. The Co-Police Chiefs for the Town of Sunset Beach are gracing my doorstep. I'd have absolutely no idea who was who if not for the name badges, they wear.

When the rotund twins take in the sight of my face along with the spectacle of Hugh's, they exclaim simultaneously with the exact same inflection in their voices, "Jiminy Cricket, you two had the stuffing knocked out of you." How did they do that?

Hugh and I answer in perfect unison, "You should see the other guy." How did we do that?

Everyone laughs.

Florrie pulls chairs out. "Sit down, gentlemen. I'll put the kettle on."

And they do. And she does.

Lloyd plonks down onto his seat. "We're glad to see you're all three here so we can fill you in all at once. Saves us some time. Excellent work on your part getting that license plate, Gina. That made our jobs a whole heck of a lot easier. Why don't you take it from here, Floyd?"

Floyd, "Sure thing, Lloyd." Floyd reads aloud to us from his notes, "So, our perp's name is Kyle Kowalski, thirty-eight years old of Picton, Ontario. Electrician. Unemployed presently after quitting his job two weeks ago, one day after his wife disappeared, according to witnesses. Married to Lillian Kowalski, thirty-five years old, unemployed. She hasn't been seen by neighbors for nearly two weeks."

Florrie interjects, "But a neighbor saw them arrive at their home last night. That email Gina got from Lillian's friend."

I protest, "And they saw the husband Kyle, covered in blood, stuffing a body-sized bag in the trunk of his car."

Head shaking from Floyd. "Not any of the neighbors that have been interviewed so far."

Floyd flips to a new page in his little black book. "Picton Police sent uniforms canvasing door to door in the Kowalski's neighborhood, heard pretty much the same story from everyone. The couple have lived at their address for around ten years, kept to themselves for the most part. Had a cute little white dog named Snowflake."

Lloyd chimes in, "The next-door neighbors say they often heard loud arguments, mostly Kyle's raised voice. And like Floyd said, as far as the report Gina received from Lillian's unnamed friend, no one is admitting to having seen anything the night of the disappearance or last night. That's not unusual. That's often where good Samaritans draw the line when it comes to getting involved in a case."

The brothers hand off to each other with expert timing. Back to Floyd. "Some of the neighbors did see Lillian with bruises to the face periodically, and police were called to the home on five occasions over the past three years. Kyle's got priors. He's been charged with domestic assault as well as four counts of assault causing bodily harm in various barroom brawls. One neighbor reported to the uniforms that Lillian told her about a month ago that she was afraid Kyle might kill her."

I'm appalled. "Did that neighbor do anything to help Lillian?"

Lloyd shrugs. "Said she told Lillian to report it to the cops. All the neighbors seemed to be afraid of Kyle. This punk is a real piece of work."

Hugh, Florrie, and I are all suddenly sober.

Florrie is wide-eyed. "This guy who's been watching us sounds even scarier than I imagined. Thank God Snowflake doesn't have to live with him anymore." Maybe not all of us are totally sober.

Lloyd reprimands us. "Yup, you three were messing around with an extremely dangerous prior offender. Not the smartest shenanigans you lot have ever gotten up to."

Hugh is clearly agitated. He stands and starts to pace. "Has this Kyle Kowalski been picked up yet?"

Floyd, "Not yet, but there are warrants out for him and his vehicle. As long as he's still driving the same car, we should have him in custody in pretty short order."

If its possible, Florrie's eyes have grown even wider. "So, he's still out there on the loose?"

Lloyd pats Florrie's shoulder to put her at ease. "For now. Not to worry too much. We have patrol cars checking up on all three of your homes regularly until Kyle Kowalski is apprehended. You'll see the uniforms coming around throughout the night. There's a chance this guy will come back here to finish what he started with you."

Chapter Thirty

Floyd is pointing a stern finger at me. "Probably best if you all stay together for the time being." He turns to Hugh. "You can keep an eye on these two, stay here with them tonight, can't you?"

As always, Hugh is stoic. "Of course."

I object, "I'm perfectly fine here on my own."

Floyd and Lloyd both eye my swollen eye.

Floyd, "Not according to that shiner, you're not. Plus, it doesn't look like you'd be able to make a quick getaway if you needed to."

Lloyd leans in close to me. "Take a tip from me, missy. Accept the help while it's being offered. It's the wise thing to do."

Floyd and Lloyd push away from the table.

Floyd carries their drained teacups over to the sink. "That's it, then. I think you people are up to speed. We'll call when we get anything else."

"Thanks for the tea. You kids can get back to your dancing, now." Lloyd chuckles. "Don't throw your backs out." He winks and smiles.

Hugh sees the officers out the door, locks it after them.

We all sit silently, looking at each other for a long while. It's a lot to take in.

Florrie perks up first. "Guess it's another PJ party for us. Who wants popcorn?"

* * *

Several hours later, Florrie and I are asleep in our beds and Hugh on the couch. The dogs bark every hour or two at every little noise outside, and every time they do so, Hugh gets up to look out the windows to see whether there's anything, anyone out there.

He lets us know each time that it's only a patrol car making its rounds, checking on us, pulling up in front of my cottage, and stopping for a few minutes every time it passes by. This should make us feel better, but instead, it seems to put us even more on edge.

When, sometime in the middle of the night, the pounding starts on the door of the cottage and the dogs go berserk, all three of us leap out of our beds and run into the living room in terror.

The officer at the door is identifying himself, but we can't hear him right away for the deafening barking of the dogs. When we do realize it's a cop, Hugh unlocks the door, lets him inside.

The constable is apologetic, but the urgency in his voice is easily detected. "Sorry to wake you. The chief has asked the three of you to come to the station house immediately."

Florrie is alarmed. "Oh my God. Has someone been hurt?"

"No, no one's been hurt. It's pertaining to the ongoing investigation the chief was discussing with you earlier."

Hugh is pulling on his boots. "Did they pick up Kyle Kowalski, then, or find his car?"

The young cop takes his job very seriously. "I'm afraid I can't comment, sir."

I pull a hoodie on over my pajamas. "Okay, so we'll drive into town now, then."

The cop holds the door open for us, wants us to follow him. "I'm to drive you all into the station, ma'am. Now."

* * *

Both Floyd and Lloyd are waiting for us at the station house when we arrive, looking uncharacteristically serious. No time for friendly small talk tonight. The three of us are ushered into an interview room.

We sit silently, waiting to hear the reason we have been dragged out of our beds in the middle of the night. We all know it can't be good.

I venture forward with what is to me the worst possible scenario. If it's a negative to this question, then everything else will be not quite so bad. "Did you find Lillian's body?"

Florrie gasps audibly, covers her mouth with both her hands as if she's afraid she might scream if she hears a yes answer.

Floyd shakes his head gravely. "No. No body."

I'm so relieved. "Oh, thank God for that, at least."

Lloyd takes over. "But we did find Kyle Kowalski. He was about to cross over into Quebec and then was likely planning to head into the USA at the Vermont border. He was driving the small black car in question, registered in his name. The vehicle had repair work done to the back bumper in the last couple of weeks."

Hugh blows out a breath. "Well, at least you've definitely got the guy who's been stalking Gina. That's good to know."

Floyd nods in agreement. "We're confident we have the individual we've been searching for in custody at this time."

I'm not getting the answers to the big questions fast enough. "The message Lillian's friend sent me said she saw her husband stuffing something into his trunk two nights ago." I'm afraid to hear the answer, but I have to ask, "Did you find anything in the trunk of Kyle's car?"

Floyd is nodding again, stone-faced. "We did. We found traces of blood inside the trunk. Also, numerous articles of women's clothing, bloodstained. As well as a man's T-shirt, also bloodstained. We'd like you to look at some photos of Kyle Kowalski and see if you recognize him from anywhere."

I thought hearing that Lillian's body had been found would be the worst news possible, but this doesn't feel much better. "He did kill Lillian after all."

Florrie lets out a tiny shriek. "Oh my God."

Hugh is visibly shaken. "Holy crap."

Floyd and Lloyd are tight-lipped. They begin sliding a series of photos along the table so we can inspect them.

First up are pictures of various men, and we're asked if we recognize any of them. Florrie points to one and says she thinks it was possibly the man she saw fighting with Hugh on the ground at the lighthouse, but it was so dark, and there was so much motion and commotion she can't say with absolute surety. Hugh picks out the same man with about the same degree of confidence. I agree with them. One man looks very much like the man I photographed during the fight.

Next, they show us photographs of various articles of women's clothing. All of them are covered in dark wine-like stains, which they tell us is blood. We don't recognize any of the clothing pieces until we see a picture of a white woolly coat heavily soaked in dark red blood.

Florrie barely whispers, "The woman who snatched Snowflake was wearing a white wool coat like that one."

Floyd hands Florrie a photo from a driver's license. The pale, blonde woman looks like a ghost. "That's her. Lillian."

Finally, they show us a photo of a man's red T-shirt, also bloodstained. The shirt has the letters IDGAF printed across the chest. We all stop and stare at each other, mouths open.

"And? Do any of you recognize this T-shirt from anywhere?"

We all nod.

Floyd picks up his little black notebook. "Where did you see it?"

Florrie answers, "We didn't see it, but my cleaner, Sarah, did and she told me about it."

Lloyd is writing everything down in pencil. "When was this?"

Florrie's voice is stilted, spacey. "Last week. Sarah called me when I was at Gina's house to tell me that a man had come into the bakery after hours asking if anyone had seen his lost dog. He showed her a photo of Snowflake, Lillian's dog but my dog now. When I asked Sarah what the man looked like, she said he was wearing a red T-shirt that had IDGAF on it."

Floyd turns to his brother. "I guess we'll bring young Sarah in, then. She should be able to identify Kyle Kowalski."

Lloyd nods, picks up the phone to make the call. They're not about to waste any time.

Floyd and Lloyd get to their feet. We three sit dumbfounded.

Lloyd is in a hurry. "Thanks for your help. Officer Brown will drive you back to Gina's place now, and we'll be in touch if we have anything further to discuss with you. Which is very likely."

Floyd smiles. "Thanks for coming in, folks. Hope you can get back to sleep."

"Not in a million years." Florrie scoffs.

We are ushered out of the interview room and pile into the cruiser.

Young Officer Brown drives us home and doesn't leave until he's satisfied that we're locked inside the cottage safe and sound for what's left of the night.

* * *

Days pass, and we hear nothing from Floyd or Lloyd or anything else regarding the investigation or the arrest of Kyle Kowalski. There has been nothing in the papers pertaining to his arrest or the death or disappearance of Lillian Kowalski. All three of us have searched them online but found next to nothing.

I receive no further emails or letters addressed to The Ex-Whisperer that have anything to do with Lillian. It's been radio silence from her anonymous library friend.

Things should be settling down and getting back to normal in our lives, and I believe that they are for Florrie and Hugh. For me, things are in upheaval again, or more accurately, still.

I'm packing up to move back to the city and moving is always chaotic and stressful. Small-town life in adulthood is a failed experiment for me. But at least I gave it a shot, and I don't regret that.

Florrie and the aunts are extremely unhappy that I've decided not to stay in Sunset Beach. I just cannot seem to settle in comfortably, I suppose. I'm not sure why that is, exactly. For a while, I tried blaming Hugh, and Iris, and her new friend Lil' Dick, and poor Lillian, and her horrible husband, Kyle Kowalski, but I'm past all that now.

I've spent a great many hours walking this beautiful beach with my beautiful dog, and I've taken full responsibility for my own happiness and unhappiness. Of course, over a month ago when I sold my home and left my neighborhood of twenty years, I knew I was embarking on a whole new chapter in my life and that it would be difficult and scary and exciting all at the same time.

I knew it would take time to adjust and didn't know what to expect exactly, but I'm constantly being surprised by what each day brings me. I may not know precisely what I want at this point in my life, but one thing I know for sure—I'm looking for things that make me feel good. In fact, there's nothing more important to me than feeling good. By definition, that means that I'm healthy and happy and all my loved ones are, too, because that's the only way I can feel good.

Next week, I turn fifty years old. The half-century mark. Wow, still trying to process that concept. It's definitely time for me to do me, and I'm aware the only obstacle in my path now is myself. I had better not start getting in my own way now that I've finally cleared everyone else out of it.

The other morning, Hugh approached me once again to say that he very much wanted to finish the work on my cottage, but my mind hasn't changed with regards to that, or to him. He's a great guy, but clearly, it is just not meant to be between us. As far as the cottage renovations go, they can wait until if and when I ever make my way back here.

After a few more days pass by, the newspapers finally carry a couple of articles about Kyle and Lillian. Eventually, the story makes the national news. Advocates for domestic abuse victims take up the gauntlet and use Lillian's case as yet another example of the weak and often nonexistent support systems available to women in situations similar to Lillian's.

Forensics was able to find traces of Lillian's blood in her home, likely from prior abuse, that matched the blood found in the trunk of Kyle's car. Her DNA was corroborated through information provided by her family physician and dentist.

Several of her neighbors agreed to cooperate and provide official statements to the police about Lillian's comments in the past regarding her fears that Kyle might try to kill her and about the violent arguments they had overheard going on in the Kowalski house. But no one ever came forth to say they saw a bloody Kyle stuffing a body-sized bag into the trunk of his car the night Lillian disappeared, the way her friend described in the last message she sent me.

The previous domestic abuse charges were going to weigh heavily against Kyle in court.

The police were also entering the emails Lillian sent to me as evidence in the case. The IP address from Lillian's library friend turned out to be untraceable, and I never heard from that woman again. With all the news coverage of the case, I am sure she'd be aware that at least Lillian's memory was receiving some measure of justice now even though the system had failed Lillian in her life as it does millions of women who are victims of abuse just like her.

The police detectives I talk to all believe that, despite Lillian's body not being found, the case against Kyle Kowalski will most definitely be made. Even though the entirety of the evidence against him is circumstantial, there is a lot of it, and it's very convincing.

The Kowalski trial is extremely high profile because of the heavy connection to the major social issue of domestic violence. It's also an election year, so a number of politicians are driving the issue home. I'm glad about that.

The Crown Attorney informed me that this proceeding is a career-maker for him. He said it's challenging from a legal strategy standpoint because it's a murder trial without a body, but there's all that damning circumstantial evidence to run with.

Despite the difficulties, the cocky, ladder-climbing Crown Attorney told me that this case is a cakewalk, open and shut. I'm happy to hear it. Lillian deserves to receive justice even if it's too little too late for her. Hopefully, other women can benefit from the heightened awareness her case brings to this important issue.

* * *

Only three days left at Sunset Beach. On my last day, I'm having dinner at the aunts' place to bid them *arrivederci*. I'm going to try my best not to let so much time pass before I see the old gals again. None of us are getting any younger, and of course, this fact is in my face even more than usual since I turn the big five-oh in a couple more days.

Today, I'm taking care of all the last-minute life admin stuff that complicates every move for everyone. I go into the main post office to arrange to have my mail forwarded.

Gail has been the Post Mistress here since I was a little girl. She looked eighty years old then, and she still looks eighty years old today. I guess that's one way to avoid ageing. If you look super old when you're young, people never think you get any older. I wonder whether it's too late for me to try to pull that one off.

Since I happen to be in the Post Office, Gail hands me my mail, rather than having the letter carrier deliver it. I inspect the lines on her face closely as she takes her sweet time checking to make sure that it is, in fact, my name on each piece of federal property that she is handing over to me. I suspect she's just nosey and is interested to see who might be writing to me.

Gail smiles broadly. "How about that? A postcard from Nicaragua. You've got friends in faraway places. Your aunts are always telling everyone how popular and famous you are. I guess they're right."

I smile back and thank Gail, carry my pile of mail away. While I cross the street on the way to my car, I wonder who I know who would be vacationing in Nicaragua. More than that, I wonder who I know who still sends postcards to people. Are postcards even a thing anymore?

I climb into the driver's seat of my jeep and shuffle through the mail. Bills and junk mostly. And the postcard. Yup, it's from Nicaragua. A picturesque photo of a white sandy beach dotted with blue umbrellas that stretch into a disappearing horizon. Really, this generic photo could have the names of a thousand different beaches printed across the face of it in a vintage script and nobody would know the difference. I flip the card over to read the back. The post date is one week earlier.

Dear Ex-Whisperer,

Thank you for taking care of Snowflake for me.

I am stunned.

The card is from Lillian.

Lillian isn't dead.

Lillian's husband didn't kill her.

Lillian has run away to Nicaragua.

But before she left, Lillian framed her husband for her murder.

Chapter Thirty-One

Florrie and Hugh sit across from me at the kitchen table in my little cottage. They stare silently at the postcard from Lillian, turning it over and constantly passing it back and forth between each other as if something more might appear that will offer up some sense in the matter.

Florrie's voice is shaking. "This is unbelievable. Lillian must have put her own bloodied clothes in the trunk of Kyle's car."

Hugh, who is squinting and rubbing his eyes, continues to inspect the postcard. "And put her blood on Kyle's clothes, too. She must have been in town watching Kyle and watching us the whole time to be able to pull this off. It was very well planned and executed."

I've already thought all these same implications through. "I know. Lillian's 'library friend' who wrote to me with all the incriminating messages, including telling me the story about the body being stuffed into the trunk of Kyle's car, was Lillian herself. And she led Kyle up here to my cottage. To me."

Hugh looks at me gravely. "She risked your safety to ensure her own."

Florrie is totally distraught. "She went to a whole lot of trouble to get away from this guy. He must be way worse than we know. I guess the only way Lillian could ever feel safe was if her horrible husband was in jail. Or dead. It might have been simpler for her to kill him. I feel sorry for her. But now I feel sorry for that devil, too. Is that weird?"

I shake my head. "No, I'm feeling conflicted, myself. Lillian would be the prime suspect if her abusive husband had been murdered. But he would be the prime suspect in her disappearance. This scenario was much safer for her."

"Lillian is one smart cookie." Hugh meets my gaze. "Except for sending the postcard. She tripped herself up there."

Florrie is sympathetic to Snowflake's other mommy. "One mistake for the love of your sweet pet. I get that. And Lillian trusts Gina. She wouldn't think that Gina would give her up after all that's gone on."

I'm at a complete loss. "What am I supposed to do?"

Hugh is matter-of-fact. "You have to take the postcard to the police. No question. A man is on trial for a murder that he didn't commit. For a murder that no one committed. There is no murder case."

Florrie isn't so certain. "Well, Kyle Kowalski is a very bad man."

Hugh is getting riled up, which isn't Hugh. But Hugh hasn't been himself over the past while. "They can put Kyle Kowalski in jail for being a very bad man especially if he's hurt his wife in the past, but they can't put him in jail for the murder of his wife. She hasn't been murdered. You can't let that happen, Gina."

I reach for a wine bottle, fill three glasses, try to remain calm. "I understand that, but if I hand this postcard over to the police, I get a very bad man off of his possible life imprisonment sentence, but in exchange, I hand his wife a death sentence. Kyle is a man who was charged with physically abusing his wife when they lived together, and when she left him, he hunted her down and was willing to go to any lengths to find her, which includes all the horrible, scary stunts he pulled on the three of us."

I down my wine, pour myself another, which I am aware is probably a very bad idea. "If Kyle gets out of jail now, knowing that Lillian framed him for her murder, knowing she's in Nicaragua, how pissed do you think he's going to be, then? Lillian thought he was going to kill her just for leaving him. She's a dead woman walking if I give the cops this postcard."

Hugh attempts to reason with me. "I hear what you're saying. It's obviously your decision to make. Neither of us can help you with that. You're the one that has to live with yourself, Gina, whatever you decide. Now that Florrie and I are aware of this evidence, I'm wondering if we're bound to tell the police what we know?"

"I guess you can talk to a lawyer about that. In the meantime, I am going to ask you not to do anything until I figure out what I'm going to do first. I need to think this through."

Hugh and Florrie nod silently.

* * *

I am torn as I have never been torn in my life. I don't want to be anybody's judge, but I've been thrust onto the bench in this matter.

After two sleepless nights and tortured days, I make an appointment with the Crown Attorney handling the case. It's not for me to decide the fates of Lillian or Kyle Kowalski. It's for a proper judge and a jury of their peers to do so.

I hand the postcard over to the arrogant Crown Attorney. He is shocked, of course, who wouldn't be, but more than anything else, he seems visibly disappointed. His career-making case against Kyle Kowalski just went up in smoke.

He tells me that he will not be assigned Lillian's case due to conflict of interest. That's if they can even find her and extradite her to Canada, and if Kyle doesn't find her first and kill her for real this time.

The man-boy Crown Attorney sounds like a petulant child. I want to remind him that this really isn't about him, that he is not the main player here. His life is not one of the two hanging in the balance, and the importance of his legal career is not on par with human life and freedom. I don't actually say any of these things to him. It's obvious that this raging narcissist wouldn't understand a single word.

* * *

It's my last night in Sunset Beach for a long time to come. I don't know when I'll be back, but I don't think I'll be in a hurry to return.

I love this part of the world, but obviously, it's not for me. Not for now, anyway. And my being here sure hasn't done the townsfolk any favors.

Especially Hugh and Florrie. The Universe could not have sent signs and signals any louder or clearer. I need to take some time to heal—to wait until all these memories have faded from my mind. The bad and the good ones. I need to forget Lillian who tricked me and her husband who stalked me. And I need to forget Hugh and stop thinking about what we almost shared. I drive to the aunts' restaurant to have a last dinner with the quirky Calabrese ladies. I will miss them dearly.

I park on the street near Happily Napoli, and my eye catches a silver car stopped farther up the road. Dickiris. And they have a freaking telephoto lens on a camera peeking out a side window, pointed in my direction.

How the hell did they even know I would be here at this time? I guess the aunts spread the word, as they do. I pose for a shot in the middle of the street with my middle finger raised high. And I'm reminded of one very good reason why I'm choosing not to stay in this too tiny town.

I yell at them, "Knock yourselves out, Dickiris! "

Inside the restaurant, as always, it smells like a slice of heaven. When I step through the doorway, I stop short for a second. It's ridiculously dark, and I take a moment to let my eyes adjust, but they don't. What the frig is going on? Has the power gone out? Where are the customers? Where are my aunts? I'm about to call out to them when—

Surprise! So many voices. So much volume.

Holy crap, I almost die of cardiac arrest right on the spot.

The lights turn up. I'm momentarily blinded by the brightness and deafened by the screaming. My God the screaming. There's a huge banner with Happy 50th emblazoned across it. Florrie charges toward me, the aunts right on her heels. The three of them fight over my cheeks.

My vision begins to return. The room is filled with balloons and streamers and the faces of people I love dearly. Twenty of my cousins, uncles and aunts, my old childhood gal pal Cordelia, Floyd and Lloyd, and so many other lovely old friends and neighbors from my little hometown, that on good days, maybe isn't too tiny after all. And then the biggest, best birthday surprise of my whole life...

The crowd parts, and four angels step forward.

All my babies have flown in from Europe for this monumental event. They run toward me and throw their arms around me, bowling me over, and I'm sure that life could never be sweeter than this very moment whether I live for a thousand years more. And I cry like a total blubbering idiot because I'm that ridiculously happy.

When the shock of all this goodness begins to calm, someone else steps to the fore.

It's Hugh. And he's wearing a kilt. Oh. My. God. And he bows and kisses my hand, and then he straightens and plants a long, longing one on my mouth. And I can't stop smiling. And everyone's cheering and clapping.

But the loudest sound is that of my two boisterous aunts who are screaming as if they just won LottoMax, "He's the Scottish!"

My surprise fiftieth birthday party is the best party of my life. Hello half-century mark, you are stupendous. Life is beautiful and messy, and I am truly, madly, deeply in love with it.

* * *

Maybe you can never go home again because everything in life is always changing, and maybe that's a good thing. Maybe being home is about being at peace with whatever life throws at you, from wherever you are… Maybe I am my home.

Change of plans, once again. And at fabulously flexible fifty, I go with the flow. I'm not heading out of Sunset Beach quite so fast as I had planned. My four amazing babies are in town for a whole week, and they want to spend it at their childhood cottage, playing on the beach and swimming in the lake, roasting marshmallows over a campfire in the sand, and being force-fed delicious Italian food by their doting grand zias in their homey restaurant and being spoiled with sweets from their favorite cousin's cozy bakery. And hanging with their loving mother, of course, who just happens to be the luckiest mom in the whole wide world.

* * *

I check the news headlines regularly, watching closely for developments in the Lillian and Kyle Kowalski case, for word of his release, but there is nothing.

Finally, when I can no longer stand the wait, I phone the cocky Crown Attorney.

"Good afternoon. This is Gina Malone."

"How can I help you, Ms. Malone?" The Crown Attorney is clearly less than thrilled to hear from me.

"I'm wondering what's going on with the Kowalski case. I haven't seen any mention in the news of the postcard his wife sent me from Nicaragua or anything about Kyle Kowalski being released from jail. Are you keeping the details concealed for some legal reason?"

The Crown Attorney sounds even greasier than I remember. "Oh right, the postcard. That's not going to be used as evidence in Kyle Kowalski's murder trial."

I am floored. "What? How can that be possible? It's proof that he didn't kill his wife."

The smarmy lawyer is dismissive. "There was nothing on the postcard to prove it was actually sent by Lillian. In fact, it's far more likely the defendant arranged for this postcard to be sent to clear his name."

I can feel my blood pressure rising. "That's ridiculous. I told you Lillian Kowalski is alive." The brash attorney raises his voice. "Even Kyle Kowalski's defense attorney doesn't want to risk putting the postcard into evidence. He knows his client is guilty of murdering his wife. We all do."

I am pleading now. "You're all wrong."

Just in case he wasn't condescending enough. "How about you let the experts handle it from here and you stick to writing your dating advice column."

I spit out the words, "You slimy bastard."

"So long...Ms. Malonely Hearts."

Acknowledgements

Writing a book is a solitary exercise but I never could have done it alone. I couldn't have created this story without the sympathetic sounding boards offered to me by friends and family even though I am acutely aware it was sometimes done begrudgingly. I accept that and am willing to ignore it because needs must.

To my readers, thank you so much for taking a chance on my firstborn book and for your substantial investment in me through your time, energy, money or any combination of the three. Your choice to pick up my novel and enter its world is a gift to me that I shall treasure forever.

To all the booksellers, librarians, bloggers, thank you for your favor and keenness. Deep gratitude to my enthusiastic Instagram and Facebook community of friends, followers, and bookstagrammers, for championing my novel, for reading, reviewing, recommending, and sharing by posting photos, reels, and news, you made a huge difference. Special thanks to the fellow authors whose work I admire so, for taking the time to read early and provide blurbs for my book baby.

I am honored to have worked alongside kind, brilliant, and inspiring women, whose magical midwifery brought my book into the world... My talented and tireless editors and publishers at Level Best Books, Verena Rose, and Shawn Reilly Simmons, and the amazingly supportive culture they have nurtured amongst their authors. My powerhouse publicist Megan Beatie and her ingenious assistant Stephanie Elliot, who overcame innumerable obstacles to make good shit happen. The gifted and masterly Indie Editor Maggie Morris, who saw everything I missed and made me work harder to make the book better. To the extraordinarily creative and skilled social media dynamo Kaitlyn Wosik. Each of you fabulous females helped shape the fate of this book and my path as a writer.

Deepest gratitude to my parents Eric and Merle George, and grandparents Edward and Kathleen George, and Leon and Florence Orser, whose sky-high visions of me and what I would accomplish in this life tricked me into believing I could make all my dreams come true. You were right after all. To my many fab and fun cousins and my dear Uncle Hugh, Uncle Bruce, and my two Aunt Shirleys, the trove of loving memories I carry from my times with you enrich me beyond measure. To my sweet, long-lost sister Carla Hall, who searched for and found me after a lifetime apart. To a couple of horribly toxic people in my life (every family has a few—you know who you are), I carry the scars of the near-fatal wounds you inflicted but they remind me that I survived you and thrived. Thanks for the tough teachings—don't let the door hit you on the way out.

Special thanks to my smart, funny, magical, and deeply caring gal pals, old and new. Irene Yaychuk-Arabei, Lori Merritt, Debbie Parker, Jill Johnson, Mary Chiovitti, Christel Francis, Denise Furlano, Diane Kozak, Cyndie McOuat, Michelle Mayhew Barnes, Heather Meneses, Debbie Sabourin, Tina De Medeiros, and best guy pals, Edward Bastos, Don Parker, and Phil Chiovitti. Thank you for our history, for our future, for your friendship, support, and cheerleading over the years.

Thank you for being there for every wave, my deeply loved ones—for listening to my whacky ideas, my far-fetched dreams, my manic joy, usually chased closely by unfounded fear. I only hold a handful of people in my heart but you are my whole world and I would move Heaven and Earth for all of you. Your belief in me buoys my soul. Your sage advice and fierce loyalty sustain me.

To my Best Friend Forever, Delia Gaskill, thank you for 30 years of daily phone calls and limitless love, laughter, backup, and badassery. I could not have done life without you. Losing you has been my greatest tragedy. Your passion for books and travel and kids and creativity filled my well. I desperately miss our exclusive book club and writing critique group of two. You and your four beautiful boys are my chosen family. Geordon, Rory, Hadyn, and Tanner, you are my children too.

Love and gratitude to my partner Al for his encouragement and support and for giving me the time and space to create that I needed.

To my daughter for being a first reader, building my website, savvy social media assistance, spending countless hours brainstorming titles and tag lines, to my sons for their help with the website and cover design, book trailer, encouragement, inspiration, and so many other things, I thank you. My four beautiful, intelligent, talented, perfect, babies, the most amazing humans I have ever known, Coulton, Roegan, Holden, and Arielle, I will always be your greatest fan. I could not be any prouder of you all. We're a small family but a rock-solid one. I know I'm meant to be a parent and not a best friend to my children, but that's just not what happened. You angels are my best friends and it has been that way since the minute each of you was born. I have learned far more from you all than I could ever have taught you. Coulton, Roegan, Holden, and Arielle, you have brought more laughter, joy, and magic to my life than I ever imagined possible. Thank you for choosing me. I'm the luckiest mom in the world. I love you forever. XXXX

About the Author

Gabrielle St. George (*aka* The Ex-Whisperer) is a Canadian screenwriter and story-editor with credits on over 100 produced television shows, both in the USA and Canada. Her feature film scripts have been optioned in Hollywood. She is a member of the Writer's Guild of Canada, Crime Writers of Canada, Sisters in Crime, Mystery Writers of America, and International Thriller Writers. Ms. St. George writes humorous mysteries and domestic noir about subjects of which she is an expert—mostly failed relationships, hence her debut soft-boiled series, *The Ex-Whisperer Files*, which launches with *How to Murder a Marriage.* She is also the author of the non-fiction GAL GUIDE SERIES: *How to Say So Long to Mr. Wrong, How to Know if He's Having an Affair*, and *How to Survive the Love You Hate to Love.*

Gabrielle lives a wildly magical life on a fairy-tale farm along the Saugeen River and spends weekends at her 1930s cabin on the shores of Lake Huron with her partner (current coupling still alive and kicking) and their extremely disobedient dogs. When she's not writing, painting, gardening, stargazing, moondancing, and daydreaming, she travels the world to visit her four fabulous children who live abroad.

Also by Gabrielle St. George

Fiction: The Ex-Whisperer Files
 HOW TO MURDER A MARRIAGE (The Ex-Whisperer Files, Book 1)
 HOW TO KILL A KINGPIN (The Ex-Whisperer Files, Book 2)
 HOW TO BURY A BILLIONAIRE (The Ex-Whisperer Files, Book 3)

Nonfiction: The Gal Guides
 The Gal Guide to Breaking Up Without Breaking Down:
 HOW TO SAY SO LONG TO MR. WRONG

 The Gal Guide to Cheaters and Liars:
 HOW TO KNOW IF HE'S HAVING AN AFFAIR

 The Gal Guide to Navigating Narcissism:
 HOW TO SURVIVE THE LOVE YOU HATE TO LOVE

SOCIAL MEDIA HANDLES:
 Instagram: @gabrielle.st.george
 Facebook: @gabriellestgeorgeauthor
 Twitter: @GStGeorgeWriter

AUTHOR WEBSITE: www.gabriellestgeorge.com

CPSIA information can be obtained
at www.ICGtesting.com
Printed in the USA
LVHW031640171121
703614LV00002B/249